Lies Of The Land

by

Chris Dolan

Vagabond Voices
Glasgow

© Chris Dolan 2016

First published in May 2016 by
Vagabond Voices Publishing Ltd.,
Glasgow,
Scotland.

ISBN 978-1-908251-68-8

The author's right to be identified as author of this book under the Copyright, Designs and Patents Act 1988 has been asserted.

Printed and bound in Poland

Cover design by Mark Mechan

Typeset by Park Productions

The publisher acknowledges subsidy towards
this publication from Creative Scotland

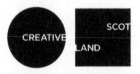

ALBA | CHRUTHACHAIL

For further information on Vagabond Voices, see the website,
www.vagabondvoices.co.uk

For Kate and Mike
And Gard

Lies Of The Land

I

What happened seconds before the Big Bang? Everything shrank into a tiny, vast, space for an eternal nanosecond.

Is that what it's like just before you die? If you know you're about to die. You see it coming, your own personal Big Bang: your heart on the brink of bursting, the final second on the time bomb, the bullet leaving the gun, the nurse holding your hand.

What do you think? You have a single instant, a lifetime, with only your thoughts. God? What was it all about? Who was I supposed to be? What was I expected to do? Maybe we still think we can get out of this, somehow. Is that how it'll be, still desperately wrestling with the world, thrashing about inside, even though there's no time left for your body to do so much as blink?

I wonder about these things. I have to.

That moment of infinite density, unbearable intensity.

They say there was no actual bang. The event – not the first, just first of lots of firsts – was silent. Like a hush in the middle of the endless night. The darkest hour.

Whatever the agent of Death is – the clogged artery, the terrorist's backpack, the gun – it's only the instrument. Death plays it. Nobody is truly at fault. Not the fanatic, not the cigarette, the assassin. Death existed before life, and every single thing since that ridiculous Bang is born of it. Everything that has ever happened has led to you lying there on the floor, in your bed, falling, falling. Death knows what to do: when the lever must be thrown, the curtain dropped. The trigger pulled. No point in blaming yourself, or the doctor, or the hand trembling before your eyes holding the gun.

You're too late. The blaming's already been done.

This. Has. Got. To. Stop.

A piledriver inside her cranium, mouth like a landfill, just enough energy to prise open an eye. Which was when it got worse. Much worse... Who the hell's the guy snoring in bed beside her? This is a new low, even for you Maddy.

She didn't dare move. Much as she'd like the snoring to stop – not loud but a kind of deep, disturbing pitch that might incite dogs to attack – and to figure out exactly what had happened here, she really, really, didn't want to wake him. What did Dan once tell her? You'd rather gnaw your own arm off than wake the bugger up.

A quick self-frisk under the bedclothes: maybe wasn't so bad. She was fully dressed. Slowly it came back to her. Usual after-work drink in the Vicky. She'd tried to extricate herself at closing time. Hadn't tried hard enough. Fuzzy images of some bar she didn't recognise but clearly had a late licence. And, oh yes, her *pièce de résistance* – inviting everybody back to her place. Opened the last couple of bottles of Louis' Italian wine. Put the party mix on her iPod and danced around like a flaming eejit. Like she was still twenty-one.

But how she and the walrus here had ended up together in bed ... that remained a blank. Was there some pathetic attempt at amorous union? He seemed to be dressed, from the armpits up anyway. She wasn't ready to check beneath the surface. Wriggling a bit, it didn't *feel* as if anything had happened. But had there been intentionality? What would her defence in court be? Temporary insanity. And in Confession? If you were too hammered to get your pants off, the thought was still there. Is that venial or mortal?

Have to mend your ways, Maddy. You've turned forty for Chrissakes. And what about Louis? Him being three thousand miles away across the Atlantic wasn't an excuse. That he hadn't been in touch in over a week maybe is? And to be fair, ignore the snores and this guy was actually quite presentable. In fact, more than presentable. She hadn't lost her touch. Early thirties? Groomed, or had been. Face of an angel with a five o'clock shadow, just the way she likes 'em...

Stop! Get out of here. Do some work. Maddy Shannon's form of penance. Three Hail Marys and four hours of case compiling. Where can you buy a hair shirt in this day and age?

Whoever-he-was didn't budge as she slipped out of bed, just a momentary hiatus in the rhythm of his grunting. She smoothed herself down, found her shoes, closed the door quietly behind her. Made a cafetière of extra strong coffee, ignoring the bomb site of the living room. At least there were no more bodies sprawled on sofas or chairs. Please God don't let there be anyone crashed out in her office, the back bedroom.

Nope. All clear. She turned on her laptop, set down the coffee, went to the loo, threw water on her face, swallowed a couple of co-codamols and returned to start her punishment.

For Maddy Shannon, Procurator Fiscal, work was more than a method of alleviating guilt. It helped ward off the gloom. Scrutinising the folly and pain of others took her mind off her own defects and transgressions. The February morning outside her window was limping into a grey half-life, like it couldn't think of an excuse for a sicky. If she could prosecute the day itself, a dismal reflection of her inner self, she would. Share the pain.

Her Majesty's Advocate versus Garner. The heart sank. Mr Ewan Drummond had been playing a medal tie with Giffnock Golf Club's captain Mr Richard Garner. On the seventeenth tee, in full view of the clubhouse where Garner's friend and the club's president, Jack Menzies, was drinking, Drummond suffered concussion as a result of being struck on the head by a three-iron. Mr Drummond claimed that not only was the blow deliberate but that neither Garner nor Menzies came to his aid. Mr Garner refutes this saying it was an accident and that an ambulance had been called. A barmaid on duty in the clubhouse agreed that Menzies had in fact seen the incident and had "pissed himself laughing". It was only when Drummond came round and stumbled to the clubhouse that Menzies finally phoned the ambulance – some twenty minutes later.

Jeez. Were there any ciggies left from last night? No. Be strong Maddy, stay put, work on.

Ewan Drummond believed that both Garner and Menzies "had it in for him". They had accused him previously of wearing the wrong clothes for the game, and for using nonconforming golf clubs. God, she had to get these twats. Moreover, Drummond was winning the round when he was struck.

First thing Monday morning she had the pretrial debate to attend. Garner's lawyers had questioned whether in fact this ought to be a civil suit against Giffnock Golf Club. Citing some obscure case, they were really trying to throw doubt on Ms Shannon's decision to take this to the High Court of the Justiciary. Maddy had shrugged: an indictment had been served on Garner and everyone had been happy to proceed. She'd love to go for broke. She hated golf; golfers more.

It was hardly multiple murder or international corruption – oh what had happened to those young prosecutor's dreams, hunting down and locking up evil geniuses, keeping the entire nation safe? Now she was reduced to protecting the populace from dull men in stupid jerseys. But a wrong had been done and Maddy wasn't one for letting that go.

The therapy worked. The little local difficulty of waking up next to a stranger had been replaced by her old internal wrangling. A lifelong compulsion to retreat within, think through a problem, consider every angle. Keep the gloom at bay. It drove people around her crazy. She'd turn off, forget where she was and, sometimes, the arguments going round and round in her head drove her to act impulsively. Made her do things she later regretted.

There was a knock on the door, and her mystery bedfellow put his head sheepishly round. "Eh. Hullo. Name's Doug. Pleased to meet you."

"I'm sure we've met before somewhere, sir." She got up and stretched her hand out. "Maddy Shannon."

"Oh I know who *you* are."

"You do?"

"Doesn't everyone?"

"You want a coffee, Doug?"

"I believe my condition is properly called veisalgia. Brought on by misadventure incited by the consumption of certain chemical compounds. Caffeine is merely a panacea. What I really have to do is go home. Immediately. And die."

"Your patter must have been better last night. You don't, by any chance, remember exactly how you and I …?"

"Be assured, dear lady, it is not how it looks."

"You're a lawyer."

"You remember."

"No. Just the shite you talk." This kind of banter, like late nights, surrounding herself with people, dancing under the influence, they were all just ways of soldiering through a day. "Tell me straight. I can take it. I think."

"There were one or two others here. Sam Anderson?"

"Would that be a Sam of the female or male variety?"

"A lady Sam. We all danced a bit. Talked a bit and, if memory serves, you did some good old shite-talking yourself, with respect. Before doing a disappearing act. Sam and her husband Stuart ordered a taxi home. I was supposed to join them but felt I should be civil and inform you. Whereupon I made three mistakes. First listening to you tell me yet again how Italy is a much more fun place to get drunk in. Then, out of weariness, sitting on your bed.

Then lying down, at which point Stuarty and Sam presumably gave up waiting. Sorry, there was a fourth mistake – at some point during the night I must have got under the bedclothes."

"Well I hope I made up for being boring by providing you with a comfortable sleep."

"Oh I never said you were boring. Far from it. And, had my veisalgia not kicked in I would have tried to be more gallant."

He took a step towards her, but Maddy put her hand up, in a way, she thought, that must make her look like a lollipop lady. "You have to go home and die, remember?"

"Ah yes. Sorry."

"Samantha Anderson? ... Please don't tell me you're from JCG Miller? Christ, talk about sleeping with the enemy."

"How can you say such a thing? We defence lawyers have nothing but the utmost respect for the Crown Office and Procurator Fiscal Service."

Doug – she felt it too late to ask his surname – shuffled out into the hall and searched for his jacket. His mobile pinged and Maddy smiled as he tried to don his jacket and retrieve his phone from his trouser pocket at the same time. Louis' Montepulciano did terrible things to your motor control. Or maybe it was the cocktails before that. Or the Mexican lager before that. Doug read the text and she'd never seen a man sober up so quickly. He furrowed his brow, narrowed his eyes, reading the text over several times.

"Can't believe it."

"What?"

"You just mentioned his name a moment ago."

"Who?"

"Julian Miller. My boss."

"What about him?"

"He's dead."

"Oh my God. I didn't know he was ill."

"He wasn't. Says here he was murdered."

Detective Inspector Alan Coulter eyed the cars in the Merchant's Tower underground car park. Miller's car had been identified and was cordoned off. A few cars along sat a vintage Rolls-Royce Silver Shadow. He walked away from Miller's Audi A3 – he's seen plenty of them, typical lawyer's car, but a vintage Rolls Silver Shadow. That was swanky. Then he made his way up to JCG Miller's office suite.

The place was like Sauchiehall Street on a Monday morning, hoaching, everyone going about their business: SOCOs, forensics, photographers, keeping their eyes down, only speaking in low voices if they had to. It wasn't respect for the dead, it was being called out early on a Saturday to go through the rigmarole of work. A woolly suit directed him towards Julian Miller's office.

Once people had cleared a path for him, he saw the victim. Sitting at his desk, head slumped. If it wasn't for the puddle of blood on the desk and the modern-art splatterings of more blood and brains on the wall behind him you'd think the man had dozed off.

"Good morning," Coulter said to those in the room. He wasn't being flippant. This is their job, important to keep things civil.

"Mr Julian Miller," Bruce Adams, crime scene manager, informed him. "I imagine you've met before."

They had. Coulter could remember at least three cases where dangerous nutters had walked thanks to Miller's talents. And that was just off the top of his head. Perhaps not the best phrase, given his old sparring partner's head was burst open like a blood orange.

But that was years ago. Julian Miller had swapped criminal law for corporate around the turn of the millennium. Less courtroom swashbuckling and newspaper headlines, more moolah. Enough, Coulter would have thought, to drive better than an Audi A3. Maybe the Rolls was Miller's as well.

"Point blank," Adams was saying. "Must've been sitting at his desk when someone walks in – walks right up to him – and shoots. Forensics will confirm, but my guess is the gun was held about six inches from his head."

"Who found him?"

"The caretaker. Looks after all the offices in the building. Which is mainly JCG Miller. They have the ground and first floors. The top one is empty at the moment."

"And here's the gun." Recently promoted Detective Sergeant Amy Dalgarno, suited and booted, held it up already bagged.

"You found the gun?" Coulter peered at it, surprised. "A Glock. What is it, a compact?"

"G19," Adams said, before Amy had a chance.

"Bit gangland, isn't it? Where was it?"

"Constable found it in a bin in the car park below."

"We sure it's the gun that killed him?"

"Not for certain. Not yet," Adams said, "but if I were a betting man."

"Why would a killer leave his shooter behind?"

"Some kind of calling card?" Amy asked.

"Sergeant, please, no. Bad enough it's Saturday morning when I should be having a lie-in. Calling cards suggest there's more to come."

When they turned away from him Alan Coulter nodded a farewell to Julian Miller. Thoughts competing in his head. Live by the sword … unkind, and probably unjust, Miller just did his job well. Coulter had dealt with the murder of acquaintances before but they were usually among the short, brutal, lives of a harsh city's poor and desperate. The victims of chaotic home lives, rash crimes, generations of neglect. The debris of an unjust world. They weren't normally Audi drivers in designer suits living, as Coulter remembered, in elegant Killearn, highly respected and even more highly paid. Despite all that, Miller's body was just like all the rest – blank, finished, silent. The end of life always seemed to Coulter a kind of cosmic let-down. An anticlimax. It was what led to it that troubled him. Were Miller's final moments, minutes, hours drawn-out torture? Or was it the surprise of his life? *Guess who!*

Maddy managed to fight off the urge to go to the crime scene. She had plenty of reasons to. COPFS had a right to be there and she was the first fiscal in the know. Plus Miller was an old acquaintance and colleague, of sorts. And she was with associates of his quite possibly at the very moment he was being murdered. Actually, those were pretty good reasons *not* to go.

She had a bad name for turning up at crime scenes. Like some sort of ghoul, or frustrated detective. Too keen, like a school prefect: getting into cases too deep from the get-go.

So she went about her usual Saturday morning instead, mobile gripped tight in her hand. Except for the excruciating forty-five minutes of her spinning class. Maddy's weekly memento mori.

There were six other regulars. A couple her own age – in matching yellow and magenta lycra for Chrissakes. Really? In your forties?

And young Tricia, all tidy lines and curly hair, plums for buttocks, long legs. Maddy once told her, naked, in the showers, that she so missed looking and feeling like that. A total lie. Maddalena di Rio Shannon had never looked like that in her puff and had no idea how it must feel.

The young guy at the spinning, fighting the beer belly, always a bit hung-over looking, dripping in sweat – *that's* how Maddy had felt in her twenties. Then there was the older lady – mid sixties? – and the even older gent. They should have been an inspiration, peddling away, resistance screwed down tight, up off the saddle, sprinting, smiling all the way and hardly perspiring. Chuck the fags, cut down on the Pinot Noir, join a walking club and that could be you, Maddy. But every time she came away thinking, We're all dying, in our own peculiar ways, riding stationary bikes, going nowhere fast.

Afterwards, coffee at Mario's Plaice. A greasy spoon attached to a chip shop that mysteriously changed its name about every five years. Always a fishy pun, something to do with the sea, or sole. Maddy's family chippie in Girvan had been called The CodFather at one point, so she could hardly be snooty about it. Glasgow used to have lots of these honest, corny old cafés. It wasn't just that Mario's reminded her of childhood. She liked the screwed-down tables and chairs, the fixedness of the place. The weak coffee, chatting to Sandra the waitress-cum-manageress, the odds-and-sods the caff attracted, not working so hard at being West End.

Having tortured herself physically in the gym, Mario's was where she beat herself up mentally. There used to be a bunch of gym-goers who went for coffee together but Maddy, along with a number of other things, had let that slip. Her social life was too centred around work – Dan and Izzy and Manda. And rookie solicitors, it now seemed, ending up in her bed.

Then there was playing perfect Italian daughter to the Gina Lollobrigida of Maryhill. Or North Kelvinside, as Rosa di Rio – she had dropped the Shannon years ago – preferred to call it. Maddy wondered if bringing her high-maintenance mamma closer to her own home had been such a good idea, or even necessary.

Finally there were far too many evenings alone in her flat working, or emailing and Skyping Louis Casci in New York. She spent a lot of time on emails. Many of them never sent. Too needy. Or boring, going on about work and the sad loss of decent cafés and pubs. Or mucky. She'd learned not to hit "send". Wait till morning. How many times in the cold, wine-free, light of day had she thanked the heavens she hadn't hit that button. If she'd got one of those emails from *him* she'd have reported him to the police. If only for offences against prose.

Her phone rang at last ("Happiness", the Blue Nile. She'd been going though a nostalgia kick for her favourite old Glasgow band).

"DI Coulter, good of you to call. What've you got for me?"

"I gather you already know most of what I know," Coulter sounded like he was calling from a busy corridor. "In fact you knew before me. How do you do that?"

"Networking, Alan."

"So you'll know that Julian Miller was shot dead by a pistol around 6 a.m. this morning."

"Six o'clock? Busy firm, JCG Miller."

"And on a Saturday too. Apparently they're in demand these days. Partners working all day Saturday, the rest of them Saturday mornings."

"Make hay while the sun shines."

"Found by a caretaker, seated at his desk in JCG Miller's offices. How well did you know him, Maddy?"

"No better than you. Only came across him once professionally, I think. The Petrus case. Five years ago? He won that round."

"You were socialising with his employees last night, I hear."

"Yeah, I heard that too. Samantha Anderson, and her husband, Stuart, came round for a nightcap. Sam is JCG's conveyancing woman."

"She seem okay?"

"Full of the joys." Of what Maddy could remember, that seemed to be the case.

"Unless she left after six this morning, it wasn't her who told you about Miller."

"Am I being interrogated here? There was another member of JCG with them. Douglas received a text around 8.30. Well, he told *me* around 8.30. When I took a coffee in to him. In the spare room. He couldn't get a taxi and—"

"No need to justify your lifestyle to me. You know I'm endlessly jealous. Douglas. That'd be…" she heard Coulter flick through a document. Hoped he'd find the name quickly: she had forgotten already. "Mason."

"That's the fellow."

"I'm going to see him, and everyone else at the firm now. Want me to give him your regards?"

"Why not. He didn't get them last night, if that's what you're fishing for. Anything else interesting so far?"

"Are you officially assigned to this case?"

"I've already emailed Binnie. So unless the bastard tries to bypass me again... How do you know it was a pistol? You found it?"

"If it turns out to be the weapon used, yes. The killer made very little attempt to hide it. In a rubbish bin in Miller's offices' car park, yards away from his car."

"Made no attempt, or he didn't know you're supposed to. Maybe it was a she. *Crime passionnel*. Perhaps he or she followed him by car to the office?"

"Now I'd never have thought of that."

"Anything in the car? Damaged at all?"

"Nope. James Blunt album in the CD player."

"Maybe it was suicide."

Zack Goldie, the caretaker, was a fully qualified doctor but never did his foundation years. "I like this kind of life better," he told Coulter. A twenty-six-year-old with the wearied disappointment of an octogenarian.

"I'd have thought you'd be overqualified for a jannie's post?"

Zack laughed, his black thick curly hair quivering. "I checked that with the agency. They guy said, 'Medical degree, son? We've got lads in here with a string of O-levels as long as your arm.'"

"I suppose finding someone with his head shot open must be less traumatic for a medically trained man like yourself?"

"Not really," Zack Goldie's pupils shrank to pinheads as if he was seeing the blood and brains again. "That's why I never completed."

"What made you go into Mr Miller's office?"

"He's often already in when I start. I like him to see me so he knows I amn't late. Usually just pass by, say hello, ask if anything's needing done."

"You normally work Saturdays too, Zack?"

"Always. Relief caretaker does Mondays and Tuesdays."

"Did you know that Mr Miller would be in today?"

"Nearly all of them have been in Saturdays for the last few weeks. But Miller and Crichton have been here every Saturday since I've worked here."

"And how long is that?"

"Eight months."

"You were the only person in the building this morning, apart from Mr Miller?"

"Yes."

"Was the main door open?"

"He always left it open. Mr Crichton or one of the other staff would normally be in just after him."

"And you didn't see anyone else in the building?"

"No. Everything was normal, until…"

"What do you think, Zack? Miller was dead before you arrived?"

"I s'pose."

Coulter got up to go. "You ever come across anything like this before?"

"What? A dead man sitting at his desk at dawn, blood all over the shop? No, sir, I have to say I haven't."

Coulter believed him.

Back upstairs, Miller's office cordoned off now, Coulter looked around the rest of the suite. Merchant's Tower is a pretty good address, with the price tag to go with it. Big airy open space with desks and offices off, all in muted colours, rugs not carpets, the desks a deep rich red – oak maybe?

Bill Crichton arrived and stood at the main doorway like a man who had lost his keys. He just stared, as if trying to work out which of these many strangers might know where they are. A constable brought him over to Coulter.

"Is this the time you normally arrive, Mr Crichton?"

Crichton gaped at him for a moment – slight build, balding, late forties, conservatively dressed, he gave Coulter the idea that he was somehow smaller than he should be. That, despite the success and the wealth, life had compressed him – then absent-mindedly checked his watch. "Yes. But that's not why I'm here. The police phoned."

"I'm sorry, sir." Coulter moved back into the open plan where DS Dalgarno was finishing a call. Crichton followed him vacantly.

"How many work here, Mr Crichton?"

"Eh? Oh. We're the two partners, Bill and I."

"What's the 'JG' in the title? C for Crichton I assume, and J. Miller, the deceased."

"No, the 'J' is for Jardine. Julian worked for the firm Jardine and Graham. They made him a partner about ten years ago and added his name. Phil and Ronnie retired when I came in five years ago. Jules made me a partner immediately." Coulter decided that Bill Crichton was genuinely upset. "Don't know how it's going to be from now on."

"You were telling us about the staff." DS Dalgarno changed the subject back.

"Yeah. The two of us. We have a team of four lawyers, two researchers, two trainees. Six admin, support staff, two of them part-time. Do you want to meet them all now?"

"In a moment. Could we go through to your office, sir?"

"Of course. This way."

"Is Douglas Mason around?"

"Actually, no. We spoke on the phone. He's very upset."

Crichton's office, like the man himself, was smaller than Coulter expected. He'd only had a glimpse so far through open doors to the other offices, they all seemed at least as big as this.

"Did your partner always come into work so early, Mr Crichton? Six a.m.?"

"Usually we're both in a good hour or so before the others. But I didn't think Jules would be in so early today."

"Why not?"

"We had a late meal out last night."

"Just the two of you?" Dalgarno asked.

"No. With clients. Fulton Construction. Their MD, Tom Hughes."

"Any special reason for this dinner?"

"Nothing specific."

"Which restaurant, sir?"

"Nick's. In the West End."

"What time did Mr Miller leave?"

"Late. I didn't really look at the time." Bill Crichton looked distracted, taking off his jacket and dropping it on his desk rather than hanging it on the coat stand at his elbow.

"And you left with him?"

"Yes."

A middle-aged woman opened the door without knocking, agitated. "Mr Crichton? What's happened?"

"It's … Julian, Debbie."

"Oh no."

Maddy had intended to spend a bit of time on the Garner case, but found herself looking back through files and emails for Julian Miller and his company. She couldn't get the picture of Julian Miller, dead in his office chair, out of her head. She could picture the scene well enough. She'd seen too many recently dead people. None quite so dismal and sinister as two boys in Kelvingrove a couple of years back – infancy and innocence so quickly mutilated, annihilated. Miller was a successful man in his prime and his death, in comparison, clean. Those teenagers – "neds" Bruce Adams had called them – had had to cling desperately to the sliver of slippery life they'd been granted. Miller had all the advantages and all the equipment needed to climb confidently to life's summit.

There is, Maddy believed, a point in crying over spilt blood. Chaos had exploded in that chic little office in the Merchant City, and order needs to be restored. If it isn't, the darkness she too often feels inside will spill out into the real world.

Her search didn't reveal much and she knew it wouldn't. Bill Crichton, in reports, transcripts, newspaper articles, the odd direct email, came across as serious, maybe a bit severe. But Maddy had met him in person often enough to think he was just shy, quite a pleasant bloke. Julian Miller was flashier, wittier, Gucci and Ralph Lauren suits, the more ambitious of the duo. They reminded her of something she once read Paul McCartney say about himself and John Lennon. John was hard on the outside, with a soft centre. McCartney confessed to be the other way around.

There had been lots of communication between Miller and Crichton, and others in their team, and the fiscal's office. JCG Miller were a decent enough bunch to work with – even if they had won more than their fair share of cases against the Crown.

It occurred to her that she should get in touch with Sam Anderson. She owed her an apology – inviting a near-stranger and her husband back to her house then, if Doug Mason was right, dancing under the influence of alcohol. Then going to bed without as much as a goodnight. It'd be interesting to see what Sam made of her boss's murder. It took a while to find a number – no home contact, but a mobile found on the end of Anderson's work emails. She tried the number twice. No joy. Perhaps Sam didn't use that number at weekends.

Halfway through reading a report on a criminal negligence claim that Maddy had played no part in, an email from Louis came through.

"Just a quickie." (If only.) "Any possibility of you coming over here for Easter?"

"Not unless you want my mum, three aunties, two uncles and a skein of cousins too."

A moment before the reply, then: "skein?"

"You Americans can't speak proper." Then she wondered if skein was a Scots word. "Anyway, it's your turn to come over here."

Their correspondence, messaging or Skype, was always light-hearted. Banter was a way of neutralising the distance between them. Not just the miles but the feeling she had that they were on different planets. And the universe was accelerating wasn't it? Planets moving slowly apart, stars dying. On email she could be talking to anyone; on screen it was like Louis was on TV, a fictional character. Sometimes she felt lonelier, when they were united electronically. The sheer distance, the tininess of them both. Insignificant, on either side of the black Atlantic.

"Well, guy I know is offering me tickets for opera or something in Central Park."

"Or something?"

"Classical. I think. You like classical don't you?"

"Do I?"

"Listen, Maddy, I'm doing this on the run. Got to be out the office pronto. Meeting with Parks and Recreation. Play safe, etc."

"Thus the freebie? Corruption! Louisgate. I can see it now."

Smiley face.

"Can you make it over here? I'll get tickets for the Krankies."

"I'm not even going to ask. Okay, I'll see what I can do. Skype tomorrow?"

What was wrong with tonight she thought but didn't type. Hot date? Sex club? Worse, ex-wife?

There was no way of either of them knowing what the

other got up to. She knew only too well that that was true of couples married for twenty years, living in the same house.

"Sure."

"Miss ya."

Before she could sign off, her mobile rang. Unknown number, but she knew it'd be Doug Fraser, or Mason or whatever. "Hello?"

"Doug Mason. Remember me?"

"I may have had a glass of wine too many but my short-term memory's not that bust. John." At the same time she typed: "Me too. A *domani, tesoro*."

What did she have to worry about? One man invites her over to New York while another, younger one, is hot on trail.

Put another way, Louis calls in dutifully; Mason's a common or garden pussy hound.

Douglas Mason didn't have much to tell. Coulter and Dalgarno had hung around the office all morning – they were still there when Doug got in at lunchtime. Taking statements from everyone. Now they'd gone to speak to Marion, Miller's wife.

"But she knows already presumably," Maddy asked. Doug wasn't sure. It was possible she didn't. Radio Scotland had only said a body had been found, city centre. They hadn't specified where or identified the victim.

The partners had been out last night wining and dining a cash cow businessman. Presumably Marion had noticed Julian hadn't come home. But that's all Doug knew. He was more intent on trying to fix up a meeting with Maddy. On various grounds – talk about the murder, thank her for last night, show himself in a better light. Maddy made up a few engagements for herself, but left him – and herself – with a glint of hope.

She'd hoped Coulter would call, between the office visit and the "death knock" – what cops and hacks call telling kith and kin the bad news. Why should he? This wasn't

her case yet. Might never be. Binnie – her boss, *the* fiscal –
would have his excuse: she was already involved. Too close
to the victim. But, with Miller being in the game, that was
true of every fiscal and advocate in the land. Even if she did
get it, there was nothing she could do for weeks to come,
until police reports began to come in and she could start
preparing a case. Then again, ever since *she* – not Glasgow's
Finest – had cracked the case of those two murdered boys,
DI Coulter had taken to confiding in her. Even asking her
advice, in a roundabout way.

Back then everyone had told her – especially Maxwell
Binnie – that she had overstepped her authority, gotten too
involved in the case. Dan made a habit of saying she should
make a career change. Join the polis. Maddy worried that
all her colleagues now thought she was in the wrong job.

The murder of Julian Miller wasn't affecting her the way
those two boys had. It was tragic, and violent and, as with
all murders, a gap had opened in the universe. One that
would never quite close, even if somebody were caught
and convicted. But she couldn't deny it, it intrigued her.
Worried her. It was close to home. Too close. She had compiled a good number of cases involving murder – nearly
twenty years in the job, it was unavoidable – and prosecuted some of the killers in court. But this was the first
time that someone she actually knew had been killed. In
her city. While she was in bed – oh dear God – with one of
his employees.

Killearn is a rich sleeper town a few miles north of Glasgow,
wearing the surrounding hills like a fur coat.

It would have been a pleasant drive there if it weren't
for its purpose. Every now and then, when the guilt gets to
him, or the fear of imminent death, or worse, a stroke, this
is the route Coulter takes on his road bike. From Milngavie
on, the houses become ever bigger and more exclusive.
There's a sharp uphill behind the reservoir that gets the

blood pumping. Then out past Strathblane to Dumgoyne Hill.

"My favourite hill in the whole of Scotland," he told DS Dalgarno as they passed the whisky distillery at its foot. "Not that high, but the views are incredible."

"Yeah, I've done it."

"Tougher climb than you'd imagine, eh?"

"Good workout, though. Gary and I try and do it, up and down, in under an hour."

Coulter let that slide. Last time he'd climbed it it took him nearly half the day. But it wasn't just the ascent, the days out, that made him love Dumgoyne. It was the fact you could see it from almost anywhere north of the river in Glasgow. At meetings he'd stare out at it, over the city's broken skyline. On rainy days commuting, or shopping with Martha, or dealing with Glasgow's even more broken people, you could look up and there it was, still and quiet and ancient. Dumgoyne was Alan Coulter's prayer, his dreaming spire.

They found Miller's house easily. Imposing, even among these stout buildings, in creamy stone set back from the roads, some of them turreted, with pillars and porches. The Millers' front garden was like something out of a TV pro-gramme: water feature, shrubs and plants of every hue even now in late February. Someone was green-fingered or, more likely, they hired a gardener.

When she opened the door Marion Miller was impec-cably dressed, as if she was going out for the afternoon, low-cut top, a single diamond pendant, expensive-looking pashmina, heels. Alan reached for his ID.

"Don't bother. I know who you are. I've been expecting you. Come in," she said, smiling broadly. As they entered, Amy Dalgarno whispered, "She's coping well."

They followed her into a sitting room, the kind of room that Coulter couldn't believe people actually lived in. Like one of those rooms you might see in a tour of a National

Trust property. It wasn't so much the dimensions as the perfect orderliness of it. And so much stuff. His own living room was a quarter the size and had the compulsory telly, chairs, couch, coffee table. People must spend not only a lot more money than he had, but a lot more time, finding and placing ... stuff. Dresser, ottoman, bookshelves, lampstands, piano, pictures, ornaments. Stuff he didn't have names for. And yet the place felt empty.

Marion Miller sat herself neatly down, perched on the edge of a massive armchair, crossed her legs and placed her hands, palms down, on her knees, still smiling sweetly. "I phoned his office this morning. Yes, before you ask, I did wonder what had happened to him."

"You don't seem too upset, Mrs Miller."

She'd be around the same age as her husband – fifty-two when he had died, they had already established – tall, aware of her own attractiveness. She hardly looked at all at DS Dalgarno.

"You were expecting a weeping widow."

"That tends to be the normal reaction."

"I've been a widow for years. To Jules's work, golf, and making his life look like he was living the dream. I suppose he was. Just it was *his* dream, not mine."

"I'd have thought, given the manner of his death..." Coulter was bewildered.

"Live by the sword, die by the sword." The very thought that had occurred to him. But he was a near-stranger to the deceased and he had dismissed the line as shallow.

"What do you mean, Mrs Miller?" Dalgarno asked, innocently. Mrs Miller glanced at her then settled her gaze back on Coulter.

"Well, look at this place. I know, you must be thinking: he works, she spends. Not so. Everything inside and outside the house was carefully chosen by Julian. All to create the right impression. Even the house itself, in the middle of bloody nowhere. Albeit an expensive bloody nowhere. You don't get to afford all this without rubbing a few people up the wrong way."

"Including yourself, Mrs Miller?" DS Dalgarno, it seemed, hadn't taken to the woman.

"Let's just say Jules and I had worked out a … modus operandi."

"You sound as if you almost expected it," Coulter said.

"No, I did not. I won't pretend to have been saddened by the news. But surprised, yes."

"I take it you can't account for your husband's movements last night?"

"He wasn't in the habit of asking my permission to stay out late, no."

"I'm afraid you'll have to identify your husband's body, Mrs Miller." Dalgarno added, "It won't be pleasant, ma'am. He was shot through the head."

Marion Miller paused for a moment then, for the first time looking Amy in the eye, almost whispered, "I'll manage."

Taking their leave, Coulter wondered if it was all an act. He had seen many strange reactions to death. He wasn't the only one who didn't understand it or know what to do in its presence. Shrink from it, deny it, laugh at it. Create a shell around yourself so that Death can't get to you.

Nick's was one of the places Maddy avoided in the West End. She feared she might run into someone she had prosecuted. There were always four-by-fours outside and every time she passed it seemed that middle-aged men in camel coats, Costa del Crime tans and polished bald patches were going in or out. She knew it was inverted snobbery but Nick's was new West End, stick-thin peroxide blondes in spray-on denims, heels, Fendi and Vuitton bags, big watches on both her and her beau. What really made her laugh was, alongside the SUVs, were Ferraris and Porsches that were obviously hired. Obvious because the men hung around beside them, leaning on them or making calls with the tops down, desperate to be seen before they had to hand them back next week, or maybe even tomorrow.

She'd tried to persuade Alan to meet somewhere else, but he'd insisted, for some reason, on Nick's. Annoyingly, she arrived before he did. She considered leaving and walking round the block – she'd taken the pack with a few cigarettes left in it from Friday night – but it was getting snell outside. Anyway it was fascinating inside. Perhaps she'd been hard on the place. Certainly full of aspirationals but they all seemed jovial enough. She had to admit it, she was a bit jealous of these women. Maddy could never be bothered with putting on much make-up. Wasn't organised enough to have the time for it. But if she could click her fingers and have her hair as coiffured and shiny, her eyes as sparkly, skin as sun-kissed, she probably would. Though she'd never admit it to anyone.

Alan came in looking even more out of place than she did. Crumpled coat, trousers gathered at the ankles, and wet too, so it must have started raining. He looked like a door-to-door salesman who'd just had a particularly unsuccessful winter's day. Yet he still looked classier than anyone else in the joint. Greying elegantly, hair a week past needing a cut, posture of a mature, professional man – and eyes bright as a boy's. She watched him as he got them both drinks at the bar. Maddy had given up waiting to be served but a young barman took Alan's order immediately. She couldn't hear what he'd said, but the young man smiled broadly at him. Five kids, an ailing wife, and thirty years chasing lowlifes, Alan Coulter still had charisma. Something trustworthy and unexpectedly optimistic about him.

"Why here of all places?" she asked when he brought over his half of lager and her spritzer.

"Work."

"This is where Miller and Crichton were last night with their clients?"

"Correct. You hungry? Food smells good."

"I've heard it's pretty decent. On me."

"We'll see."

"How did it go with Mrs Miller?"

"Very well indeed, as a matter of fact. She was actually pleased to see us."

"What?"

"I don't think she and Julian were getting on terrifically well. It's like she's just got a get-out-of-jail-free card. She's delighted."

Maddy tipped her head back and laughed out loud.

"You have the strangest sense of humour, Ms Shannon."

"Sorry. I like the woman already. Sounds like a one-off."

"I'm not sure she is. I wonder how often, after we leave a family home, having just broken the bad news, widows and widowers dry their tears and feel a sense of relief."

"Well I know my traditional Catholic mamma was over the moon with joy when mad Packie left her. She might even have been happier if he'd fallen under a bus, rather than just fucked off out of her life."

"What age were you?"

"When Dad left? Fifteen."

"And how did you take it?"

"Not as well as Mamma."

They had the early evening meal deal. Mussels for Maddy and beef stew with dumplings for Coulter, followed by risotto and rib-eye steak. Maddy had hoped to find fault but actually the food was good and the service pleasant. Coulter decided he'd leave his car so they could share a bottle of house Merlot. At the table next to them was a well-behaved, smiley family. Perhaps Maddy had misjudged the place.

Coulter called over the young barman he'd ordered the drinks from earlier, and asked if he'd been on the night before.

"No, sorry. Why, is there a problem?"

"Not with the service. Any of the staff here now on last night?"

"Some of the kitchen staff maybe. Unlikely any of the baristas or waiters. We're all students, none of us like working both weekend nights. I'll check."

The restaurant section was on a balcony overlooking the bar. A good place for people-watching. "What d'you reckon," Maddy asked. "It's got the name locally for being a hang-out for wannabes and dodgy businessmen."

"Then it's the same as everywhere else in the country these days. Welcome to Tory UK – just a touch more grasping and frightened than the rest of Blair's Britain."

"Told you. We should have voted Yes."

"Don't start. You really think Scotland would be any less precarious than the UK? There's not a country in Europe where people aren't desperately playing a game that's loaded against them."

It was an old argument between them. Six months after the referendum they were repeating the same mantras.

"It might have been. Might yet be."

"It's not even that you're so optimistic, Maddy. It's all that flag-waving. For a country that, if we ordered another bottle of plonk, you'd be saying you don't even really belong in."

"Nobody belongs anywhere any more."

"Exactly."

"That's a good thing, Alan."

A young waitress approached them, putting an end to the discussion to their mutual relief. "Hi. Matt said you were asking about last night? I was on until seven." She'd be in her mid twenties, overweight and uncomfortable in her uniform of white shirt and black skirt that fitted the other bar girls neatly. Maddy was pleased that she wasn't at all self-conscious or insecure. She spoke with a certain silky assuredness. A student no doubt. Studying what, Maddy wondered. Law? In a couple of years' time she might be up against her in court.

"Did you see a group of men – older men – having dinner before you left?"

"Could be Mr Hughes's party. They were arriving just as I was leaving. He's a regular. Stays late and can be a bit ... overfamiliar? But he tips big."

"How many were here when you left, Miss...?"

"Hollie. There was only one other guy with Hughes when I left. But I checked the book for you. The booking was for three." Organised and thinking ahead, if Maddy did encounter her in a courtroom Hollie would be no pushover. She showed Coulter a till receipt. The inspector raised his eyebrows. "Big bill for such a small party."

"Mr Hughes is the last of the big spenders. Best wines, whiskies. Often goes outside with a fat cigar. He loves showing off."

"You didn't hear, Hollie, if there was any ... aggro, an argument or anything last night?"

"No. Why?"

Maddy looked up at her. "One of Mr Hughes's party had one hell of a head on him this morning."

Saturday night and Maddy was home, more or less sober, and with no surprises to wake up to tomorrow morning. She wasn't entirely sure if this was a good thing or not. In control and living responsibly, or her social life drying up ever more quickly?

She'd watched *La Dolce Vita* again recently – a compunction that hit her every few months. Comparing her own life with Mastroianni and Ekberg dancing hopelessly, beautifully, in the Trevi Fountain. Who needs hope when you have youth, and Rome?

Who would want to kill a solicitor? Plenty of people, probably. And just as many might be sharpening their blades for fiscals. Dan McKillop, her colleague, successfully prosecuted a small Southside businessman for defrauding his own company a couple of years back. The guy's son, private-school educated, was an addict and the money had gone to paying off truly nasty loan sharks and dealers. When

29

the businessman got out of prison he tied a chain to a lamp post then around his neck, got in his car and floored the accelerator. His head was ripped off and smashed through the windscreen. But he had told a friend the evening before that he was going to rip off Dan McKillop's head, not his own. Crazed, embittered, it could have gone either way. Dan never mentioned it but Maddy knew it had terrified the wits out him.

Men and their cars. More recently Maddy had been in Waitrose when someone she had prosecuted made a point of following her up and down every aisle. She got out the shop and he followed her, never saying a word, but keeping his gaze fixed on her. She'd been parked in Huntly Gardens. When she got in her car he was still watching. Whether or not he'd been parked nearby and had followed her home she couldn't be sure. How many people who have a grudge against her know where she lives? This quiet little street she so loves, its elegantly shabby gardens and crumbling stone. The copse of trees outside her living room window full of finches and tits – one day, she'll find out what species they all are. Is it as safe as it looks, as it *feels*? Or is she a sitting duck?

These troublesome thoughts were extinguished by Louis calling her on Skype after all. Folks who see their partners on a daily basis don't notice the changes. They see an old photograph and are amazed at how different mister or missus was not so long back. But hooking up face-to-face on Skype, which could be pretty blurry and jumpy, and in the flesh only once or twice a year, Maddy was only too aware of the changes. Louis' hair a tiny bit thinner, putting on or losing a bit of weight, lines around the eyes. Tonight he looked tired and a little pale. She wondered what he made of her.

"I was supposed to be going round to Sergio's tonight, but little Ana's got some kind of virus." Sergio, Louis' youngest brother; Ana his cute four-year-old niece. She'd met the family a couple of times over there.

"It's a welcome surprise."

"Saturday night? I thought you'd be out."

"No. Going to put on a CD and read an improving book."

"Kama Sutra?"

"Beginner's stuff. You okay? You look done in."

"Thanks. You look wonderful."

"No really, I'm concerned."

"Been a busy week. Quite pleased to have a night in too."

They both relaxed into it, Maddy sitting back, tablet on her knee, Louis crouching over his PC, pouring himself a Scotch. It was the way they managed to pick up seamlessly from where they'd left off, the immediacy of their connection, that reassured Maddy everything was okay. *They* were okay. So long as she didn't think what would come of it. Their work and families thousands of miles apart, little chance of either of them packing up and moving across the Atlantic. They talked again about Maddy enrolling for the Bar exams in New York, fantasising about her practising over there one day, but she knew it wouldn't happen. Not while her mamma was still alone. And anyway the US Bar exams were notoriously difficult. Maybe fifteen or even ten years ago she'd have had the energy for it. She'd seen enough episodes of *The Good Wife* to know that starting a career in American law was a younger woman's game.

She told Louis about Julian Miller.

"There was a lawyer murdered in DC couple of months back," he told her. "Young rising star apparently, and married with kids, I think. Except he was posting online looking for gay sex. Site over here called Craigslist, a gay hook-up outfit."

Maddy didn't tell him that she knew all about Craigslist, and that it wasn't any longer exclusively gay. She'd tried it once herself, a year or two before meeting Louis. There was one guy, he looked very attractive in the picture, describing himself as an academic, an American in Scotland for a conference. They'd arranged a place and time to meet up,

but Maddy got cold feet and didn't show. It was dangerous – which of course was both the up and the downside of
Craigslist's thrill. Was she really going to go to a hotel room
with someone who could turn out to be an axe murderer?
And, professionally, it wasn't such a good idea. She wasn't
ashamed of trying it out, but had always felt a bit guilty for
forsaking the poor man, all horny and rejected. Louis' story,
though, confirmed she had taken the right decision.

"So he agrees on a hotel room with some guy, except he
wasn't a guy, but a young woman intent, she told the court,
to rob him. But a scuffle broke out and she ended up stabbing the legal wunderkind to death."

"Jeez. Wrong place, wrong time."

"The only other thing I can remember was that he was
handcuffed. Whether he put them on himself in anticipa-
tion or she cuffed him, I don't know."

"So Miller's death might be the result of some extramari-
tal jiggery-pokery?"

"Hey, I don't know. I'm just telling you a goodnight story."

"It's possible, though. Mrs Miller was apparently delighted
at his demise."

"Wow. She made that obvious?"

They talked on a bit longer. She told him about her golf
case which he didn't find nearly as silly or as irritating as
she did. Louis liked golf though he seldom found the time
to play. He told her about his workload. A shoot-out in the
Bronx, not his patch but two of the kids were from Queens
and had form. A road rage case, and a series of muggings.
Like Coulter he talked of all these chaotic lives and deaths
with a hint of humour and compassion. A miracle that
none of them, almost everyone she worked with included,
had become cynical or gone mad. She did think, however,
that it might have been nice if her boyfriend (are you still
boyfriend and girlfriend in your forties?) had a different
kind of job. Like maybe a sculptor, or a plumber, or a scientist developing an elixir of youth.

Louis signed off quite animated, she thought, about the prospect of coming over to Glasgow for Easter or before. She was happy not just for herself, but for him. She felt this responsibility, keeping such a long-distance relationship going. Perhaps it would be kinder on both of them to let it wither. Any loneliness *he* might feel, unhappiness, she felt was her fault. Maybe she only kept the thing going to make it up to him somehow. While he was on screen, Doug Mason had tried her phone twice. She smiled. "I'm out and about so I'm in with a shout," she remembered the Paolo Nutini line.

After kissing their screens goodnight, Maddy checked Facebook and got a shock. Mad Packie, Patrick Shannon, her dad, had opened up a page. So far he only had four friends, all men with Irish names. He'd friend-requested her. She decided to sleep on that and decide in the morning.

The press had the story on Sunday morning. "Top Lawyer Slain" etc.

While Maddy took her mum to Sunday Mass, DI Coulter was hard at work, at his desk cursing the press, and whoever had given them details they shouldn't have. There was mention of "dinner out at an expensive WestEnd restaurant" and a suggestion that the police had found the murder weapon. Somebody somewhere was feeding them information. What's new? He threw the papers aside and got down to real work.

A couple of early reports had come through already. The SOCO report confirmed most of what they had surmised yesterday morning. Victim was shot dead at point-blank range with the Glock pistol found near the scene. The sphenoid and temporal bones shattered, cerebral hemisphere obliterated – in other words, Miller's brains were blown out. The pistol itself was interesting. Brand new, never used before, not a reactivated replica. One shot fired, the shot that took the top of Miller's head off. No cartilage residue was found and no fingerprints – a clean enough job, were it not for the fact that the gun itself was simply dumped in the nearest available bin.

There were, however, deposits of soil on the handle. The report hypothesised that the killer was wearing gloves. Dirty ones. Yesterday's fingertip search also found traces of soil in the underground car park, and on the road leading up to it. Analyses of all the examples were being done now.

Disappointingly, DS Dalgarno was off duty and in her place was DS John Russell. Coulter preferred Amy's down-to-earth workaday approach to things. Russell was dogged, fixed in his attitudes and methods. Coulter wondered if the sergeant was too like himself and that's what caused the unspoken strain between them. They were of similar backgrounds, joined the force around the same age, were both married men with kids. Beyond a doubt, Russell felt that Coulter had been unfairly promoted over him, a rankle that wouldn't get any better now that Russell was of an age where he was unlikely to get promoted much further.

"Miller was flash, represented anyone who'd pay his extortionate fees. We looked into who might have a grudge against him?"

Not for the first time Coulter decided he should enrol in a course on management assertiveness – that was the kind of question he should have asked Russell, not the other way about.

"Good idea, John. Maybe you could dig around, see what you come up with? But indirectly. Talk to the staff at JCG Miller. Amy and I already have a relationship of sorts with Bill Crichton and Marion Miller. We'll run with them for the moment." Russell was unhappy with the arrangement. Typically no words, just a nod of the head while he pretended to write something more important on his laptop. Coulter recognised the behaviour – it was how he himself acted with the brass above him.

"Has anyone been to see the guy they had dinner with on Friday night?"

"Tom Hughes. MD of Fulton Construction. He's at a wedding all weekend up north. We've had people round at his office and a couple of his sites. I'm getting word to him now, via the Inverlochy Castle hotel, that I want to see him the minute he gets back."

"We know he's definitely there?"

"Yes, John, we do. Our friends in the north visited him before the ceremony yesterday." Coulter resisted saying, I know how to do my bloody job. "Apparently he was as shocked as anyone, and more upset than Mrs Miller. Before you ask, we have a record of his movements between leaving Nick's restaurant and heading north the following morning. His driver collected him from the hotel, and his wife saw him come in and leave the following morning. We can wait till tomorrow before interviewing him." Coulter picked up a newspaper. "Don't suppose you have any idea who the leak is?"

"Could be anyone. How many were at the scene yesterday morning? Twenty or more officers, photographers, Forensics ... and anyway, who says it came from us? Leak might be the fiscal's."

Coulter girded himself. Any mention of COPFS automatically led to one subject. "They couldn't have had those kinds of details so soon."

"Ms Shannon could," Russell sneered. Here we go, thought Coulter. "Don't let *her* anywhere near the investigation for Chrissakes. I couldn't go through all that again."

"Through what, John? Identifying Jamieson and MacDougall as the Kelvingrove killers before we did?"

Coulter couldn't help himself: Russell said white, he said jet pitch black. He also knew that he was overly defensive when it came to Maddy.

"Yeah well, we might have got to them first if she hadn't been muddying the water everywhere."

"I'm not sure that's true. And anyway, Miss Shannon doesn't have the personal connections with this case."

"No? She knew Miller. And Crichton. Way I heard it she was shagging the arse off one of their boys the night Miller was killed."

"Aren't we supposed to *not* jump to conclusions in this job, Sergeant?"

"What is it with you and Shannon?" Russell tried his best to sound light-hearted, but Coulter knew what he meant. No one had ever said anything directly to him, but he was perfectly aware there were two theories. Either the depute fiscal had a father figure fixation with him, which he encouraged, or *he* fancied her. Which of the two misrepresentations irked him most he couldn't say.

As luck would have it Crawford Robertson was in the building. On a Sunday? The conversation he had with Chief Constable echoed almost exactly the one he'd just had with Russell. Including the warnings about Shannon. Perhaps Russell was right – Coulter's junior was more management material than he would ever be.

Coulter spent the rest of the day setting up the operation, assigning personnel, writing out briefs for each of them, creating an initial timetable for interviews. He set up folders on the computer system and filed all the reports, from Dr Holloway, the forensics team, fingertip search, SOCO, the lot. Officers and researchers were already running searches on all the names so far connected to the murder – Julian and Marion Miller, Bill Crichton, Tom Hughes, all the staff at JCG including Douglas Mason. He noticed that one bright young spark had started a search on Maddalena Shannon.

Once he was sure that all the boxes were ticked, that the traffic boys had been properly notified, door-to-door enquiries under way in nearby Merchant City offices, he got on to the Sundays, giving them all the usual line… Continuing with investigations, nothing of import to report yet, going forward they'll be kept up to date with any developments.

No, at this point in time they did not think there was a danger to the public, but of course citizens should take reasonable care and precautions. He stopped himself from asking the *Daily Mail* in particular, the red top that had the most information they shouldn't have had, who their source was. No point. Where the press could genuinely help was in asking readers who were around the area between 10 p.m. on Friday night and 10 a.m. Saturday morning to report anything that might be of assistance to the inquiry.

Once he was confident that everyone was doing their job – albeit grudgingly in Russell's case – he went round and chatted to those cooped up in the busy HOLMES 2 room (Home Office Large Major Enquiry System – a name of a lousy police comedy show) seeing what progress was being made.

It wasn't that he didn't want to go home to Martha. She had been much better of late. She'd suffered from her nerves and various complaints that had foxed the NHS more or less since the birth of their youngest, fifth, child. Eighteen years ago. But with all the kids away from home at the moment – who knew how long for? What do they call it, "the Ping-Pong Generation"? – he and Martha were living quietly and pleasantly enough. But once a big case like this was up and running he couldn't relax. And if he got restless at home, that could set Martha off on a migraine, or worse.

Maddy had expected, after the Kelvingrove murders, that her mother might take a scunner to the Church. Especially as a favourite young priest of hers, Father Mike Jamieson, had turned out to have a very black soul indeed. But Rosa had a remarkable capacity to edit out anything that didn't fit the world she wanted to live in.

If anything Rosa had flourished since then, and her faith, which Maddy had always thought just part of the Italian mamma act, had deepened. Now in her late sixties she was petite, poker-backed, tastefully dressed. She was a real picture, up in the top pews near the altar, head bowed, rosary braided delicately through her long fingers with their red varnished nails. Although she took churchgoing more seriously than before, Maddy suspected that Rosa made no connection between being devout and being good. If she could please the priest with her devotion while delighting the older males in the congregation *and* be the receptacle of God's love all at the same time, then bravo!

She took Rosa to lunch in Epicures. Not in the dark part upstairs but by the window where she could be seen. Rosa always knew more diners and passers-by than Maddy did. Maddy was quarter of a century younger for heaven's sake, in the prime of life, a career woman – how could Rosa possibly know more people than she did? Admittedly, Hyndland Sunday afternoons were pretty awash with retired ladies and gents who knew each other from Òran Mór lunchtime plays, Glasgow Uni night classes, and dog walking. Rosa didn't have a dog, but that didn't stop her from being an active, and opinionated, member of the club. A couple of weeks ago, passing a woman pleading with her pedigree spaniel pup to stop eating an old piece of bread in a puddle her mum smiled consolingly at the woman and said, without a hint of irony, "At least it's brown bread, dear." There were times, too, when Maddy suspected that her mother spoke to people she had never met before in her life, but charmed them enough for them not to let on. It was a kind of reprimand to her daughter that *she* was the more socially active and polished.

"Oh. There's something I need to talk to you about. You remember Dante?"

"Alighieri? Hell, yes."

"I can tell by your smug little smile that's some kind of clever-clogs lawyer's joke. No, don't explain it to me. Dante Marzullo. He's your cousin, twice removed."

"Mamma, you say that about every Italian in Scotland. Actually, you say it about every Italian."

"Well it's true in a way. But Dante really is, or maybe three times removed. But he's your cousin. And he needs your help. He makes violins, you remember. He gave you one when you were little."

"Oh. Yes. Faintly. He wasn't at all happy when he heard my attempts to play it."

"That's him. He took some bad advice from some *figlio di puttana* and got himself into financial difficulties. Now they're wanting to take his house away from him. Poor Dante!"

"Mum, I work for the fiscal. I can't advise someone on repossessions, if that's what we're talking about."

"You see? You even know the fancy word. That's it. That's what they said they'd do to him. Just have a little talk with him, will you *cara*? Put his mind at rest."

"No, Mum. I can't put his mind at rest. Apart from the fact that I know nothing about the situation, nor am I an expert in the field, putting his mind at rest probably isn't an option. If it's gone as far as repossessing, then I reckon he's done for."

Rosa gave her a look that suggested Maddy herself was throwing poor Dante to the dogs. But thankfully one of her old cronies passed by and she turned her attention to the lady's lovely coat.

Later, Dante forgotten, she asked, again, about Louis and where that was all going. Louis' Italianness – a genuine blessing – was undermined by his Americanness. And his absence. Mamma was always very sweet, any hint of criticism too submerged under wide-eyed concern, little compliments, breezy chit-chat, for Maddy to respond to. But there was always the suggestion that Maddalena hadn't been wise in her choices of men. And this from the lady who had married Mad Packie Shannon.

She decided not to tell her that Dad had joined Facebook and was looking for new friends. That would only spark two obsessions – her ex-husband and the hellish life she had with him, and the dangers of the Internet. Rosa di Rio liked to keep abreast of things, quite prided herself in naming songs and films that were only a decade out of date, but the World Wide Web she was having nothing to do with. Maddy thought it a shame – her mother would make far better use of social media than her father. Or herself.

But the afternoon went well enough. Rosa didn't ask to be taken shopping, or for a lift to see family in Girvan. She was keen to get home early to work on her crochet – her class was the following night and she was behind on her project. So Maddy got home early too, and prepared herself for Drummond versus Giffnock Golf Club's captain and president in court first thing Monday. But she found herself going through emails from JCG Miller & Co. again. Something was nagging at the back of her memory. Nothing in her files or correspondence triggered the memory. Perhaps there wasn't one; the nagging was one of mortality, of a violent death so close to home, but nothing that involved her directly.

She tried Sam Anderson's number again. This time her husband Stuart answered.

"Sorry, Maddy, Sam's sleeping."

"This must be horrible for her."

Maddy tried to summon up Stuart Anderson's face, but it was blurry. She knew she'd met the man before Friday night. Little guy, round as a coconut snowball. Wasn't he in the building trade – a civil engineer or project manager? Something mysterious to Maddy.

"It is, it is."

"Give her my love, will you?"

"When she's feeling better I'll get her to call you. Thanks, by the way, for a lovely night."

"I think I partook of the wine a bit too much."

Stuart laughed. "We all had a few refreshments."

"I was as refreshed as a newt."

"Did Doug make it home all right?"

Maddy thought there was just a hint of lechery in his voice.

For the second night in a row she went to bed at a reasonable hour, perfectly sober, and all her affairs in order. Her life, despite what some folks might think, wasn't so bad. Louis, Rosa, the odd admirer to keep at bay, good colleagues and a satisfying and worthwhile career. And she hadn't had a smoke since Friday night, despite the pack lying on the coffee table, just within reach.

Alan Coulter arrived, as he liked to do, ten minutes early for his meeting with Tom Hughes. The MD of Fulton Construction had billeted himself full-time at his building site in Glasgow's North East. The drive there was not an inspiring one. From Ruchill onwards through Springburn and Sighthill the social problems got worse and worse. Unemployment rose, houses deteriorated, the wreckage caused by alcohol, drugs and violence ever more evident. Coulter could understand Maddy's anger – the Labour Party had been, until the post-referendum rebellion recently, in total control here and for generations. Yet life expectancy was still one of the lowest in the developed world. The sense of hopelessness, of having been forgotten, discarded, felt like an airborne plague. No wonder the police were seldom out of areas like this. He wouldn't admit it to Maddy Shannon but, though he was a firm No voter, he welcomed the change brought about by the mass exodus of votes here and in places like it from Labour. He just felt deeply uneasy about any party that had the word "national" in it.

Driving over the mud of the construction site – there was a large sign, rechristening the area "Belvedere" – those crucial ten minutes early, he saw a burly figure remonstrating with two middle-aged women. Middle-aged might not only be unfair, Coulter reflected, but inaccurate. Here people grew old quickly. Stopping his car a second man in work clothes and hi-vis jacket called to them, "Catch you later, Cathy."

On the dot of nine o'clock Coulter knocked on the door of Hughes's Portakabin office.

"Inspector Coulter? Come in. Terrible business. I still can't believe it."

"I'm sure it was a shock for you sir."

"I must've been the last person to have seen the poor beggar alive."

"Apart from the killer."

"Of course."

"You think it was you who saw Julian Miller last, Mr Hughes, and not Mr Crichton? The three of you were out dining the night before."

"Bill left a bit earlier than us."

"Did he now. What time would that be?"

"About 2 a.m.?"

"And you stayed until when?"

"Probably the back of four before I was on the road."

"Four in the morning? Nick's remained open that long for you?"

"I know the management, and I treat the staff well. It was a lock-in. No laws broken. Take a seat, will you?"

Coulter sat down on a wobbly plastic chair, in a plastic office where there wasn't enough room to swing a cat's claw screwdriver in. They had already run a quick check on Fulton Construction – it turned over millions per annum. Hughes lived as comfortably as Miller, in a 1930s seven-bedroom detached villa in Giffnock that must be worth up to a million itself. Fulton Construction had smart offices in St Vincent Street in the city centre. But Tom Hughes looked perfectly at home in a shaky cabin smaller than your average caravan. No doubt old habits die hard. Hughes, it seemed, had come up the hard way, starting off as an unskilled labourer, eventually forming his own company. Outside the cabin diggers and pneumatic drills growled into morning action.

"You both left Nick's together. Then what?"

"Joe Harkins was waiting outside for me."

"Joe Harkins?"

"Site security guard. Been with me for years. Doubles up as my driver from time to time."

"Was it Mr Harkins who drove you to the Inverlochy hotel on Saturday morning?"

"Aye. He took me home from the restaurant, had a cup of tea while me and the missus got ready to go. We left Glasgow at 6.30ish."

"Not much sleep then sir."

"I don't use it much."

"So you drove off with Mr Harkins. And what did Mr Miller do?"

"We offered him a lift, but he said he fancied the walk."

"Where to? Did he say?"

"To his office, no? He wouldn't walk all the way to Killearn would he?"

"Bit early to go into work."

"Not for Jules. As a matter of fact, by the time he left us and walked to the Merchant City he'd probably be in later than usual."

"And you left him around around 4 a.m.? Julian Miller was murdered around six. Wouldn't take two hours to walk to his office."

"He was probably working. He was at his desk wasn't he?"

"Do you mind if we step outside Mr Hughes? Could do with some fresh air."

Hughes laughed. "My command centre a bit poky for you? Not much better outside – noise and stoor, Inspector," Hughes rubbed his hands in relish, "noise and stoor."

The construction site was huge, Coulter reckoned it must be nigh on a mile square. Around it, in the distance, 1960s housing, falling to bits, some of it already boarded up, gaps like craters where high-rises had been demolished. The site itself was muddy but, so far as Coulter could tell, well organised and well staffed. Drivers were manoeuvring dumpers and excavators, gangers were digging and hammering, a surveyor setting up her theodolite.

"Four hundred one and two-bedroom flats, specially designed for the first-time buyer. A real need for decent housing in this country, Inspector. Shops, a park, all off-road and safe for the kiddies."

Hughes was proud. He reminded Coulter of George Bailey: "Dozens of the prettiest little houses you ever saw." Or perhaps someone else in the movie said that.

"What kind of meeting was it on Friday night, sir? Business or pleasure?"

"Is there a difference? Business, I suppose."

"No wives."

"That's why we call it business," Hughes beamed.

"Were there any … disagreements between you?"

"Not at all. We all got on like a house on fire." It seemed a rather unfortunate simile, Coulter thought. "Always do. I liked Julian Miller a lot. Good at his job and fun to be around."

"The man who drove you home – Harkins? – is he here?"

"Just sent him off half an hour ago. We've another site, smaller than this, Southside."

"Thank you for your time, Mr Hughes. You'll understand if we're back from time to time."

"Anything I can do. Anything at all. You've no idea yet who could have done this?"

"Not yet, sir."

"I read in the papers it was point-blank."

"We'll release all the details as soon as it's appropriate," Coulter said walking away. "By the way. When I was arriving here this morning, you seemed to be having some public relations trouble."

Hughes looked confused for a moment. "Ah. The misses Maguire and Boyd? I've been in this business for nearly half a century Inspector. You don't get to build on this scale without all sorts giving you gyp."

44

"What sort of gyp?"

"Noise. Inconvenience. Mud. Swearing. Eco-fascists. I could go on."

"And what was these women's particular complaint?"

"Ach they were fine," Hughes shook his head sadly, "I told them to put their worries in writing. But it all sounded like a general mixed bag of greetin' and girnin'."

"Let us see that letter when it arrives."

"If you want."

Maddy made her case fervently at the hearing that same Monday morning. "An indictment has been served on Mr Richard Garner, wholly correctly, and it is he, not the unincorporated body of Giffnock Golf Club, who stands accused of a direct attack on Mr Ewan Drummond. As a representative of said club – Mr Garner, as we know, is the captain – in clear dereliction of duty towards the victim causing substantial injury, there may indeed be an argument for a civil suit, but that does not preclude the present solemn case." She read from a written statement by the only impartial witness, Miss Brenda Foley the barmaid, declaring that "it looked like Ricky Garner clouted him on purpose."

The debate was done and dusted in a couple of hours. She'd been worried by the fact that it was none other than Lord Nairne presiding. The criminal fraternity of Scotland must be having a quiet week. But he found in her favour and the debate was concluded.

Ewan Drummond was waiting outside the room when Maddy came out.

"You're not supposed to be here, sir."

"That right?" He was a lanky man with an enormous beard, perhaps the legacy of some Victorian forefather. "Sorry."

"How did you even know to be here?" But Maddy knew the answer to that. Drummond had pestered her, Izzy, Manda, receptionists, maybe even relatives of staff at the

PF's office for all she knew. His determination was as unrelenting as his whiskers. If Maddy had access to a three-iron she'd probably have clobbered him too. "Find a solicitor, Mr Drummond. If we are eventually successful in our case in the High Court it would help you sue in the civil courts."

"It's not money I'm after, it's justice." He walked away, then turned round. "Can you recommend me a solicitor, missus?"

Leaving the building, the February sun faint like a well-poached egg in an albumen sky, she bumped into Forbes Nairne himself. "You conducted yourself very professionally in there, Miss Shannon."

"Thank you My Lord. Although maybe I should've gone for an outright ban on the entire ridiculous game and all its stupid rules and uniforms."

"You say this in the home of golf!" Nairne looked genuinely affronted. "The nation of the Royal and Ancient, manufacturer of highest-quality fairway knitwear? Shame on ye, Ms Shannon." He clapped her lightly on the back, treated her to his best judicial smile and set off regally on his way. He turned after a few paces. "I trust you are pursuing this matter for reasons ither than getting yourself into the big boys' court again, lass?" He laughed heartily and set off again. Nairne had an ego the size of Ben Nevis but Maddy had a soft spot for him. The few times she had been before him it had gone well – there was probably a degree of randy old man about that. Dan McKillop detested Nairne, and their boss Maxwell Binnie was always a bit sniffy. Both of them had fared less well in his courtroom.

And it was straight to Binnie's office Maddy went now. A section case management meeting had started without her. Dan, Izzy Docherty, Manda Morton – the senior Solemn and Summary staff – her place beside them waiting for her. Plus one or two up-and-coming prosecutors Maddy couldn't yet put a name to; a trainee sitting in; Molly Higginson through from the Serious and Organised

Crime Division. And, inevitably, some management geezer with an incomprehensible title involving Supervisory and Corporate Bollocks. She could never remember his name either, never saw him outside meetings such as these. She only knew his car was the swankiest in the car park and he wore flash suits.

"Motiveless attack," Izzy was saying. Her turquoise eyes lent the most brutal and tawdry cases a kind of mystical depth. Maddy never got tired of hearing this ethereal being recounting terrible deeds – she seemed to give both victim and perpetrator redemption merely by citing them. The world might often be ugly, but beauty still existed. "Alcohol fuelled party. Messrs Connolly and O'Hagan punch, kick and drag Miss Kennedy by the hair into the bathroom – all of it filmed on a third, as yet unidentified person's phone camera."

Sexual assault, with intent; Keira Kennedy was still in hospital three weeks after the attack. Izzy was in the early stages of building the case for the prosecution. As each in turn discussed their caseloads that numbing, the necessary numbing, set in like a communal anaesthetic. Without it none of them would get up in the morning. Dan McKillop brought the meeting up to date on his historic crime: "Shameless indecency, indecency with a child, possibly rape – we'll see." An expensive independent preparatory school in the Southside. To date six men, all of them now in their fifties, had come forward to accuse not just one member of staff but claim that there had been a regime of physical and sexual abuse in the early 1970s. "Two of the named assailants are now dead. Another two, including the headmaster, are in their mid seventies. They still deny everything," Dan shook his head in sad disbelief. "We have to date twenty-two witness statements. We're waiting for further defence reports, but I gather they're going for pursuant collusion."

When it came Maddy's turn she briefed the meeting on her most pressing current cases. A fatal accident inquiry.

Aggravated burglary. Production of controlled drugs – Molly Higginson asked to meet her separately afterwards to discuss this in more depth. Some of the evidence and precognitions suggested Maddy's case was connected to a bigger, UK-wide, operation.

Maddy reported on only five of the twenty or so cases she was working on. She left Petrus out – they were all sick of hearing it. But between them all the two-hour meeting was a roll call of human misery and rage, deprivation and greed. And the anaesthetic was kept topped up by palliative legal language: Circumstantial. *De jure.* No basis of plea. Bad character evidence. Solemn proceedings indeed.

After a quick chat with Molly, Maddy went back to see Maxwell Binnie alone.

"It's far too early to decide who takes the Miller case. It'll be weeks before we have anything to work with, and it might not even come to us at all."

"I'm just asking for first dibs, Max." It was only in the last year or so that Maddy had been brave enough to call the fiscal by his first name. Dan had done it for years and the old man hadn't minded. The first time she used it, at a dinner and therefore in a less than formal setting, she thought she'd seen his eyebrow rise a little. Even now the word "Max" felt odd on her tongue.

"Why are you so keen?"

"I've had long protracted commercial negligence cases, domestics, muggings, and now golf violence. I need something to get my teeth into."

The unspoken word between them was "Kelvingrove". The trials against Father Jamieson and John MacDougall had not gone to her. Couldn't have, given her involvement in the prior police investigation. She had no qualms about that but felt she'd been punished ever since, major criminal cases going to Dan, or a hired-in advocate, or even Izzy.

"There is of course a problem in that we all knew Julian Miller."

"I didn't know him nearly as well as you or Dan."

"It would mean you working with Inspector Coulter's team again, and I'm not sure all of Alan's colleagues are as ... respectful as he is of you, or this office."

"That will always be true Max, with respect."

Binnie made a great play of pondering deeply, staring at the wall behind her, as if weighing up the benefits and pitfalls of the entire Scottish legal system before saying, "Very well. Let's put your name down for the moment. We'll see what transpires."

Which, of course, meant nothing.

Detective Sergeant John Russell often felt, if not quite invisible to other people, then faint, or muffled, and that he had to work to make his presence felt. Contrary to popular belief there are no height restrictions in the police, but he was sure that, at five foot seven and a bit, the public thought him small for a sergeant. He pulled himself to his full height for Julian Miller's PA Debbie Hart. Russell went four times minimum to the gym and worked on exercises that bulked him up, as well as bar-hangs and stretches – he knew he couldn't actually get any taller but he might as well get the most out of the inches he had.

"He was very meticulous, Mr Miller," Debbie was saying, looking through files. She was, Russell reckoned, in her mid forties, tall and slim like some of the women he saw down at the gym. He thought she was quite sexy.

"Bit of a slave-driver, was he?"

"A workaholic – and expected everyone else to be one too." Debbie was damp-eyed and her voice was on the edge of breaking. Her distress, he gathered, had more to do with the shock of the killing rather than any affection for her old boss. "I liked working with him. You knew where you were with him. Very clear in his instructions."

"Did Mr Crichton get on well with him?" Debbie continued to sift through files. Russell had asked her to do so but it still irked him that she didn't turn to face him when he asked a question.

"Mr Crichton gets on with everyone." And here there was genuine warmth in her voice.

"What about with the rest of the staff?"

"Perfectly well," her slight frostiness returned.

"And with Douglas Mason?"

"Douglas?"

Russell hadn't met Mason yet, knew next to nothing about him, but he was sure he wasn't going to like him. Because he'd slept with Shannon? If nothing else it showed bad taste. Russell couldn't stomach the woman. Quite apart from getting under police feet and mucking up investigations Shannon was loud, thought herself a big rebel, wore stupid clothes that she thought made her look daring and different but actually just made her look tarty.

"I think Mr Miller had high hopes for Douglas," Debbie was saying. "Mr Crichton too. He's very clever, Douglas." She dropped her voice and eyed him directly for the first time. "There was talk about making him a partner."

She handed over a bundle of about fifteen folders bursting at the seams. "Mr Miller's files for the last month or so. I hope you're not going to take them away?"

"We'll see. If I could find a desk somewhere, I'll have a look through just now."

She took him out to the open-plan space where three younger people were keeping their heads down, working a little too studiously. He clocked that Bill Crichton's door was ajar and suspected the lawyer had been watching and listening to him all the time.

A quick sift through the files told him that Miller had been working on a couple of repossessions, acting on behalf of the mortgage lender. Getting kicked out of your house – that could make a man angry. Enough to kill? A divorce case that looked messy. Miller hadn't worked directly on all these cases; on several of them he had been supervising one

50

of his staff. Douglas Mason seemed to be their family law man. The divorce case was his, also a juvenile delinquency, and a paternity test. Russell wrote down a few names and was pleased with his neat precis of the situations.

"Excuse me," he called over to the woman. She had introduced herself as Debbie Hart and Russell couldn't decide whether to address her formally, Ms Hart, or if just Debbie might give him the upper hand. "Excuse me?"

"Yes, Sergeant?"

"There's no file here for Fulton Construction."

"We've not done any work for them for a while."

"But there was a business meeting on Friday."

"That doesn't mean there was an active lawsuit." It was Hart who was getting uppity with *him*. "Mr Crichton would have the Fulton files anyway. Do you want me to ask him for it?"

Russell waved her away. Coulter had said he'd deal with Crichton, so let him. He was just about to take a photo of a couple of documents with his phone when Douglas Mason came in. He knew it was Mason – self-possessed, trendy suit and hair. He could see why Shannon would salivate over him, but why would *he* bother with a tubby loudmouth ten years older than him?

After a quick word with Hart, Mason came over to him and put out his hand. "Sergeant Russell. This is shocking for all of us here."

"I'm sure it is, Mr...?"

"Doug. Doug Mason."

"Ah. You and one of your colleagues were in town the night of Mr Miller's murder."

"Sam and I. Samantha Anderson. I'll go get her if you like."

"Did you at any point meet up with Mr Miller's party whilst you were out?"

"No. Other side of town. Vicky bar mostly."

"Quite close to here."

"It's our after-work local."

"But I'm given to believe that you ended up in the West End."

"That's right. We went round to a friend's house for a drink."

"This friend being…?"

"Does that matter?"

"Usual procedure, Mr Mason. As I'm sure you already know."

"I live up west myself, and Sam's in Bearsden, so we were going that way anyway."

Mason was trying not to say Shannon's name. Russell was damned if *he* was going to say it first.

"If there's a reason you'd rather not give the name of your friend, sir, the address will do perfectly well for the moment."

"If you insist. I don't know the number, but Lorraine Gardens."

"I'll have that checked out." Russell smirked.

Mason took a couple of steps away and called through an open door on the other side of the central room from Crichton's office. "Sam? You got a moment?"

Samantha Anderson was around fifty years old, bit frumpy Russell thought, and she'd been crying. "I'm sorry, Sergeant, I knew you were here, but I'm not sure I can talk about Jules without tearing up."

"I understand. After you and Mr Mason here were at your friend's, you went straight home?"

"My husband and I got a taxi, yes."

"At what time?"

"It'd be around half past midnight."

Russell saw his moment to strike: "And you, Mr Mason. What time did you leave?"

Mason didn't blink, just smiled amiably. "I was a bit the worse for drink, officer. Bunked over for the night."

While Coulter checked in with CCTV Control Room trying to spot Julian Miller between the hours of four and six on Saturday morning, DS Dalgarno was visiting Mrs Crichton. Clare was plainly more upset by Miller's murder than his own wife had been. Dressed in jeans and T-shirt, pretty despite a dishwater complexion, her hand trembled as she poured water into a pot of rooibos tea.

"Sorry. I don't have caffeine in the house."

"That's great. Try to keep off it myself." Amy lied.

Clare Crichton's hair was tied up loosely in a messy bunch, giving her a kind of kooky look.

"I know you made a statement already, Mrs Crichton—"

"Clare, please. 'Mrs' makes me feel like I'm in hospital or court or something."

"Clare. I hope you won't mind chatting to me about it a bit more?" Clare shook a non-existent fringe out of her eyes. Dalgarno soon realised that this was a personal tic. Something she'd have done as a nervous teen perhaps and now wasn't even aware of it.

"Mr Crichton's business dinners, are they a regular occurrence?"

"As regular as Julian Miller wanted them to be." She spoke very clearly, Dalgarno noticed. Private school? Perhaps a trace of an Inverness accent.

"But they were partners?"

"If you mean, were they equals, absolutely not. Officially Bill is one of the two partners of JCG Miller, but Julian was the power. Shall we sit through next door?"

The Crichtons' style was very different from the Millers'. Amy Dalgarno would have called the house sparse, though she guessed Clare would have called it minimalist. The kitchen, all straight lines and treacherous corners, didn't look, or smell, like it had been cooked in for a while. The hallway was pure white, with a white raffia floor covering, and the sitting room grey – though it had probably said "silver mist" or "turtle dove" on the tin. No photographs anywhere, just one large abstract painting covering almost an entire wall. Dalgarno found her eye being drawn to it all the time she was talking to Clare Crichton. It grew on her. Washed-out yellows and blues, it was soothing, if also a bit melancholy.

"Do you and Mrs Miller sometimes go to the nights out with clients?"

"*I* don't," was all she said, that little flick of the long-gone fringe again, then taking her cup to the window and looking out on a correspondingly minimalist garden. Dalgarno had been impressed by how neat and perfectly mown it was when she had come in. Now she wondered if it was in fact AstroTurf or some such.

"I don't like the late nights. Neither does Bill."

"He was late enough on Friday."

"Usually he slips away a little early if he can. If Julian will let him." Whatever it was that was troubling Mrs Crichton, it wasn't grief for Julian Miller after all.

"He did leave an hour or two earlier than the others I'm told. But you told the officer that you don't know what time he came in at?"

Still looking out the window Crichton said, "I was asleep."

"Thank you for your honesty. You sleep well, Clare?"

"On the contrary." Now she turned to Dalgarno. "My honesty? Would another wife pretend to know when her husband gets in even if she doesn't?"

"That can happen, yes."

"I can't be a very good wife."

Dalgarno smiled; Clare Crichton did not. "Perhaps those wives suspect their husbands of something. I don't. My husband works hard and wouldn't harm a fly. Honesty is the best policy, isn't it Sergeant?"

"Certainly makes our job easier." She sat down and Clare followed, sitting in a straight-backed chair opposite her.

"I didn't mention to your colleague... I have to take something to help me sleep. If it works – it doesn't always,

but it must have on Friday – I'm out for the count. Sorry."
She flicked her imaginary locks again.

"I'm sure it's not important." Amy sat back in her seat,
hoping to engage the woman in a cosy chat about Bill, but
Clare stood up and said, "If there's nothing else?" Amy
couldn't imagine the woman had any pressing engagements, but she did worry that she might break down at any
moment and sob.

Maddy went straight back to her office and requested all
available documents on the murder. Going through DI
Coulter meant she would get more, faster, and without too
much bureaucracy. She mustn't push his goodwill too far.
Even Alan's had its snapping point.

There wasn't much she didn't already know, or had con-
strued from the press coverage. Marion Miller interested
her. The notes on Coulter's death knock stated the occasion plainly: "Mrs Miller did not show signs of distress."
Maddy had met her once, at a dinner. Had barely spoken
to the woman and she'd left little impression, other than
a middle-class wife of a successful lawyer chatting pleasantly enough to those around her. There was some comment she'd made. Maddy couldn't remember what it was,
just that it was a little barbed. Maybe at her husband's
expense.

Dan, Izzy and Manda – in that order, as though according to rank – came in to say hello, see how the golf thing
went, ask her opinion about their own cases. Manda nervous and overwrought; frugal Izzy as pastel and fragile as
a watercolour. Dan on the other hand seemed to swell a
little more with every passing year. But it suited him, the
corpulence, like a galleon with its sails full, speeding him
resolutely through life. You had to look closely, past the
Hugo Boss suit, the restrained campness, the subtle whiff
of Dolce & Gabbana, to glimpse the rough Drumchapel
edges, his squally eyes.

"I've heard tell you're offering your body for the Miller job."

"What, no words of condolence first for our fellow fighter in justice?"

"You're right. I'm sorry. It's a shame. Never knew him well enough to work up a proper animosity. I think you'll do a grand job there. So long as our old boys in blue ever actually manage to find a halfway decent suspect."

"I've only read a fistful of notes and I've already got half a dozen."

"I said halfway decent – I've read bugger all and I've got the full baker's dozen. I mean someone we could actually compile a case against."

Maddy and Dan had joined the PF the same year, risen through the ranks together and were firm friends. That friendship however had been under strain since the Kelvingrove murders. They spoke about it openly – Maddy's feeling that Max Binnie had shown prejudice towards Dan, passing over Maddy when it came to big cases. Especially any that attracted press interest. Binnie had not been pleased that Maddy's name had been splattered all over the news. Until Kelvingrove both had expected that, when Binnie eventually retired, she would become *the* Procurator Fiscal. Now she wasn't so sure, and Binnie's time was fast approaching.

"How's about you and I put our heads together on this one, Dan?"

"No no no. This one's all yours." As he was leaving he said, "And I've a feeling you're going to throw yourself into it. Body first, then the soul. No place for the likes of me."

When he was gone, she sat back in her chair and looked around her office. It occurred to her how little she had personalised the place. Been in this same little cramped space for five years or more and hadn't so much as put a picture on the wall. Just a noticeboard, now defunct, since she'd learned to keep her diaries and notes online. On top of the nearly equally defunct old metal filing cabinet were a few work-related souvenirs. A couple of thank-you and Christmas cards from satisfied customers, an unopened miniature of whisky from some case she couldn't remember now, a cheap medal like she'd seen the jogging ladies get when they'd completed a 10k race, from another forgotten client. Bits and bobs that, in truth, she hadn't got round to throwing out. What was it that prevented her from celebrating what had been a reasonably successful and hard-won career?

She phoned Sam Anderson and agreed to meet at Gandolfi's, it being roughly equidistant from both their offices, and always pleasant.

Coulter had spent the morning staring at multiple screens. Miller had been spotted several times. At Woodlands Road walking towards George's Cross. Same suit he'd been wearing when he was shot and at roughly the right time – 4.35 a.m. Thirty-five minutes from Hyndland Road, that'd be about right if he wasn't in a hurry. He seemed, on screen, to be ambling quite happily, maybe just a little bit unsure of his step after Tom Hughes's brandies. Then crossing George Square at 5.07. At that rate he'd have arrived at Merchant's Tower ten minutes later. What then? Go in, sit down, maybe start some work, until...

"John. Did anyone check? What was Julian Miller working on when he was rudely interrupted? I can't remember any file being open on his desk."

"You wouldn't have seen it, drowned in a pool of blood. But there were papers, forensics are drying them out now."

Their first team meeting of the case. Coulter, Russell and Dalgarno. Not a team in the ongoing sense. There weren't teams these days. Everyone had their own jobs and occasionally they'd find themselves together. Management didn't like teams. They could gang together, develop a sense of loyalty. The brass wanted everyone operating, alone, accountable on an individual basis up the lines of authority. But in a big case like this, something like team spirit revived.

"We've spoken to all the main parties except for Hughes's site manager?"

"Joe Harkins," Russell said. "I'll chase him up again."

"Did anybody notice – we didn't know Bill Crichton had left the dinner party early, until Tom Hughes told us. Interesting he didn't mention it himself, no?"

"He was in shock sir," DS Dalgarno said.

"True. Also, his wife can't vouch for the time he arrived home."

"This lot make police relationships look blissful," Dalgarno said. "Mrs Miller looked like she'd won a watch. And Mrs Crichton's on sleeping pills. She's the very picture of a tense nervous headache."

"And Douglas Mason's banging a procurator fiscal," Russell added.

"Did you have a good sift through the company files?" Coulter changed the subject.

"Every one of them full of pissed-off people. Paternity suit – JCG Miller successful in proving that Daddy's wee boy wasn't Daddy's wee boy after all. In the last couple of months alone two families kicked out of their houses."

Coulter sighed and sat down. "I wonder if they'll give us the manpower to talk to all of that lot."

"I checked with Companies House," Russell continued. "According to JCG Miller's company's articles – it's complicated, something to do with limited liability and favourable provisions but, basically, Mr William T. Crichton stands to inherit the business."

"Does he now? Looks to me like an outfit that turns over a penny or two. He never mentioned that either."

"A lawyer who's economical with the truth? Hold the front page. Also, among the files there was an empty one."

"What, just a plain folder?" Dalgarno asked. "Probably just got mixed up with the others."

"No, it's properly labelled like all the others. Looked to me like it had been full and well used. All frayed and baggy."

"Labelled what?" Coulter asked.

"Just the name 'Abbott', and a reference number. I'll go back and see Debbie Hart."

"What about the murder itself," Dalgarno asked Coulter, "you reckon someone followed him from Nick's to his office?"

"Or was already there, lying in wait. I think we should have a longer chat with Bill Crichton. Maybe he's got over the shock now."

Gandolfo was the Pope's out-of-town residence, she knew that just from being brought up a Catholic. Café Gandolfi had a certain holiness to it too. It was the first of the "new Glasgow" fancy eateries. New being from 1990, the Year of Culture, or perhaps from '88, the year of the Garden Festival. The city suddenly getting a makeover, like a manky and brattish wean being soaped and scrubbed and told to act proper, there are visitors coming. New Glasgow actually only comprises a couple of square miles in the West End and half a mile or so here in the Merchant City. Plus a few buildings in the town centre given a facelift. The rest of the city was locked out and told to shut its face. In Maddy's experience life in the outskirts, the schemes, had got worse, not better, in the last quarter of a century.

They were shown to a table, made from wood, like all the others, that looked like it had been washed up a hundred years ago on some tropical beach. All rounded, sculpted by the elements, so that you couldn't stop caressing it, warm to the touch.

"How are things at the office?" Maddy asked Sam when they had ordered.

"Strange. Nobody knows what to say, so we say nothing. Get on with our work like nothing had happened."

"There'll be changes, eventually, presumably."

"S'pose. I can't see Bill running the firm by himself for any length of time. Jules was the business brain. Bill never liked that side of things."

"Think he'll headhunt for someone?"

"Maybe. If Jules hadn't died I'd have expected Doug to be made a partner. But he's a bit inexperienced to replace Julian."

Maddy found herself saying: "Nothing happened." She regretted it immediately. "With Doug I mean." Maybe Sam hadn't considered where Doug had slept. By raising the subject was Maddy admitting guilt? And why the hell should she care anyway? "I was a bit out of it. Even if I hadn't been... Especially if I hadn't been."

"Poor boy's a bit lovelorn if you ask me. Then again, I'm not sure how much anyone's behaviour there has to do with the murder, or something else."

"It's not about me, Sam. I told you, nothing happened. Nobody tried to make anything happen."

"He says he keeps phoning you but you won't take his calls."

"He's tried twice. And sent two text messages, one of which I answered. I've got a partner."

"You have?" For the first time Sam Anderson's eyes brightened. Nothing like gossip to alleviate the trauma of murder.

"It's not a secret. Louis. He's American."

"Meaning he's *in* America?"

"He's a policeman in New York."

Sam nodded sagely, her short bob quivering for a second after her head had stopped moving. Not a real partner then. Real partners don't live three thousand miles away.

Their food arrived. Maddy had, as always in Gandolfi, scallops and black pudding. A combination made in heaven, candy-sweet scallop like a day at the seaside, the sausage more adult, fleshy. Whoever first put the two together should be given a Nobel Prize. It also made her feel patriotic – something she struggled to do generally, despite her vocal support for the Yes vote. Sam got rocket and roasted pear salad which made Maddy feel guilty. Then again she'd been good ordering fizzy water – after Sam had ordered it first.

"I hear Jules's murder is going to be your case?"

"Jesus, news travels fast. Not necessarily. We'll see what happens. By the way, I still haven't said sorry for Friday night."

Sam smiled. "Stuart said you were embarrassed. I don't know why. We had a lovely time. You were on good form."

"Was I?"

"Very nice wine. Now I remember, you did say something about it being given to you by a boyfriend. For some reason I thought you'd said *ex*-boyfriend."

"I did not. I wasn't that pissed. Apart from anything else I wouldn't have said 'boyfriend'. Makes us sound like fifth-year schoolkids."

"What do you call him, then?"

"Paramour? Inamorato? Can't call him 'partner', he's too far away. Manfriend. Bae?"

"Bae?"

"You need to keep up with the hit parade, Sam. I shouldn't have gone to bed before you'd left."

"It wasn't a problem."

"You got home okay?"

"Truth be told I was a bit the worse for wear myself. Went straight upstairs and was dead to the world. Oh, what a terrible phrase. That night of all nights. Stuart, though, you seemed to have got him going. He stayed up late. Doing God knows what, playing old records maybe – you must've put him in the mood. All I remember was him getting into bed in the morning when we'd normally be getting up."

She worked all afternoon, task after task, repeating in writing what she'd said to Ewan Drummond in the morning, typing up notes on the debate, winding up proceedings so far, methodically, mechanically like the metronome she'd been supposed to use for violin practice in Girvan. Finally raising her head at 4.45 she called it a day.

A group of women met on Mondays at 5.30 for a run. It was something that, every week, Maddy promised herself she would do. She'd done it twice in as many years. This morning, like so many others she'd packed her trainers and kit – usually just to humph them back home again. But she had no excuse today. So she made her way to the baths club. She didn't travel much by subway these days, either walking, or taking a bus, occasionally her car, to and from work. She found the experience disappointing. There used to be that smell, didn't there? Health and Safety or some other dullard must have decided it didn't suit the New Glasgow. Also, they'd changed the look of the stations. They used to be pokey and dark, passengers huddled together, a hint of danger and mystery. Now they were all plastic and swathes of grey. Everywhere in the world was beginning to look like everywhere else – standardised, eezy-kleen, soulless.

Getting changed she worried if she'd be able to run at all. A couple of weeks ago she'd been walking up University Avenue when she saw her bus approaching. She broke out into a run – only to discover it was slower than her walk. So she broke out into a walk again. She worried even more about her rusty social skills. She knew most of the women who would be going out, but not well. She wasn't sure she could make conversation any more without being surrounded by workmates and with a glass of wine in her hand.

As it turned out social skills were hardly required as, after a few yards, she could barely breathe let alone speak. But she managed to keep up, albeit with the slowest group, all of whom had ten years on her. Happily the run wasn't long. At the end of February it's dark before six. The route was mainly through Kelvingrove and the Botanics. For thirty minutes she jogged along quite happily once her breath had evened out. They passed near the spot where she had seen the discarded bodies of two sad kids but she averted her eyes and fought against the internal darkness. It was getting darker in the external world too – the fading light over the River Kelvin was smoky, harking back to a pre-rebranded city. The trees of the Botanics, thinning and softening in the evening air, suggested the still older days of Burns – *through its mazes let us rove, bonnie lassie O.*

Their run was elongated by a few minutes when, reaching the back gate of the Botanic Gardens, they found that some jobsworth, or a parkie who wanted a pint before tea, had locked it, or hadn't bothered opening it in the first place. They had to double back, climb a steeper hill than Maddy had ever run before, up a narrow path towards another gate. Even with the two or three stragglers around her she wasn't sure running here was such a good idea. With dark closing in on them, who knew what lay behind those bristly, glowering bushes.

There was, at the very top, a public bench. Quite possibly a pleasant place to sit in the morning sun, less so in the gloom. So all the runners did a double take as they passed and saw there was indeed a couple sitting there now. They couldn't have chosen a more secluded place for their tryst – reasonable enough had they been teenagers out for a fumble before dinner. They certainly wouldn't have expected a dozen middle-aged women in ill-fitting Lycra to file right past them.

The smooching couple were equally middle-aged – there's no hiding the shape and posture of fifty-somethings. And a guilty posture at that, heads hung low, their backs turned suddenly towards each other.

It took Maddy a minute to put names to them. She knew she recognised them and, just as she realised, Marion Miller looked sharply away. Bill Crichton glanced up. It took him a minute to make the connection too, but when he did he shrank back. Too late. Shannon, Depute Procurator Fiscal, had clocked them, and he knew it.

John Russell had given Alan Coulter a lift home. He and Martha had downsized a year ago and he still wasn't quite used to being a Southsider yet. He liked it, preferred it to the affectations of Kelvindale. He went once to a play at Òran Mór (by mistake – it was a "live" soap opera in the bar, ambushing innocent drinkers) and remembered a line from it: "The Southside – just like the West End but without the wankers." There was indeed something more homely, less effortful, about his new home in Cathcart.

"It reminds me of France," he told Russell.

"France?" the sergeant looked at him as if he were mad.

"When we were over visiting Kiera – that's my second oldest—"

"I know who your family are. You never stop talking about them."

"She was in this village. In the Midi. The French don't care about anybody else. They live the way they want to and let you do the same. It feels a bit cold at first, but I got to like it. It's the same here, nobody gives a shit who you are or what you do, so long as you put your rubbish in the right bins."

Coulter often found himself over-talking when he was with DS Russell. John wasn't an easy man to be with. It was like a career-long interview, with Russell as the canny cop saying little and waiting for Coulter to make a mistake. But he didn't dislike the man. They were too alike.

Talking about Kiera he became aware he was going back to a house without kids. So much of his and Martha's lives had been about the kids. Now, he wasn't sure what he was *for* any more. He'd been a dad, the breadwinner, there hadn't been room for existential angst. When Martha had been unwell he had reasons, duties – look after her, keep the family informed, sometimes just keep out her way. Now she was doing fine, thank God, going out, getting involved, finding a sense of purpose, just as he was losing his.

He and Russell talked over the Miller case, thinking through scenarios rather than hard facts. Dodgy dealings in the workplace? Clients with a grudge? Matrimonial disharmony? Crazed killer on the loose? And why leave your murder weapon behind? Apart from anything else, they're pricey things guns. Maybe the culprit wants to be caught, or maybe he's playing some game. Maybe he's just an idiot. Or *she*, as Maddy had said.

No further forward, Coulter opened the door to bid his final goodnight, when Russell's phone rang. Someone from the HOLMES room. Russell spoke in his sergeant's voice – which for some reason was louder and lower-pitched. "Oh aye?" And "When?" "How much for?" He angled his body slightly away from his boss as if it was none of Coulter's business. Even when he finally hung up he waited a beat before letting him in on it.

"The Millers are insured."

"Aren't we all?"

"For six million quid. Each."

Coulter whistled. But maybe that was normal for rich lawyers. "Who took out the policy?"

"Joint. They both did. Mrs Miller's going to be a very rich lady."

As he walked up the path to his door, Coulter wondered if people actually still murdered for an insurance payout? There must be couples, maybe in this street, who sit watching *MasterChef* together secretly plotting ingenious ways to eradicate each other. But would they ever do it? They'd get caught. It was too obvious. Wasn't it?

She really must try and keep away from Kelvingrove and the Botanics. Shit keeps happening to her there. She sat with both her mobile and her landline on her lap. Just phone Coulter, tell him what she'd seen. But she knew there would be a call, any moment now, and she'd like to hear what he had to say first.

She was wrong, it wasn't a call. It was a knock on her door.

Bill Crichton shuffled into her living room like a wean who'd been caught stealing an apple.

"You know what I'm going to ask?"

"Don't tell the polis? Sorry, Bill, no can do. You know that. How did you get my address by the way?"

"I called Sam Anderson."

"Was that wise? What did you tell her?"

"That I was organising thank-you cards to be sent round all those who've been kind since Julian's murder. I hid your name in amongst a few others."

"I wouldn't buy that for a minute."

"Don't think she did either."

Without taking his coat off, Crichton sank into, rather than sat on, a chair. She noticed there were grass stains on the hem. He looked pretty soggy all together.

"I'm not so worried about Coulter. It's that whatsisname, the sergeant, Rumford."

"Russell."

"You know what the police are like. They want a result. They'll jump on anything. They'll make a big deal of Marion and me. Nothing will come of it in the end but they'll lose weeks barking up the wrong tree."

"Ah, so you're concerned about public finances."

"To a point, yes. But also the hell it'll cause me and Marion, and all for nothing."

She sat across from him. "This isn't the way I'd handle this situation."

"No? What would you do?"

"'It was nightfall, the persons Ms Shannon saw were yards away. A clear case of mistaken identity. Me and Marion Miller? Don't be silly.'"

"Maybe you're a better liar than I am."

"Am I?"

"I'm not stupid, Maddy." Calling her by her first name, it sounded wrong, given the circumstances. But what else would he call her, Ms Shannon? Maddalena? Either felt just as bad. "I may still take that course of action – always deny – if you don't hear me out."

"Too late for that methinks. After phoning Sam? And what precautions did you take coming here? I've got pretty nosy neighbours."

"Let's hope it doesn't come to that."

"Want my advice? As my Nonno used to say, the truth will oot."

"Maddy, you know Clare."

"Mrs Crichton? No I don't. I've seen her with you once or twice. You struck me as a very happy couple."

"Thanks for that. And by the way, we were. Maybe still could be. What you saw tonight is less than it seems. I'm not going to lie to you—"

"—But you want *me* to lie for *you*?"

"I want you to employ a little judgement. Yes, Marion and I have had the odd clandestine meeting. Maybe once or twice there was some contact. Julian was a hard man to work for, harder to be married to. That's not to say I didn't like him. He was my friend and good to me."

"Great to have pals, eh?"

"And despite her cavalier attitude Marion, though it's fair to say she was no longer in love with him, wished him no harm. We had already agreed to stop meeting up when ... this happened."

"Isn't it always the way."

"If you could just cut it with the sarky remarks."

"Begging your pardon." If Crichton was out to get her sympathy he was failing, big time.

"Julian's murder has thrown us both completely. We only met tonight to, I don't know, sort out our heads. Then you of all people walk past."

"Eh, *run* past if you don't mind."

"Another reason why you'd make a rotten witness." He leaned forward. "Please, Maddy. No one's going to gain from this. Not the investigation, not me or Marion. Maybe the killer will. Give him time. But the person it's really going to hurt is Clare."

"You're all heart."

"Clare isn't a strong person. She really suffers from her nerves. She's being going through a particularly tough time these last few years. And now all of this."

"Every reason you give me not to tell, Crichton, is doing precisely the opposite."

"Why? It was a daft, almost innocent, liaison. We were both finding it tough at home. We took a little refuge in each other. It wasn't even a fling. And it was almost over. Jesus! This would *kill* my wife."

His eyes were wet and he was gripping the arms of his chair, knuckles turning white. She wanted to have sympathy for him. If it was all true what he said, it did seem unfortunate. Bad timing, bad decisions. Maddy had always thought of Bill Crichton as a nice man. Everyone agreed he was a nice man. But quite possibly based on no evidence whatsoever. Though the man was a bag o' washing before her very eyes, desperate and remorseful, she couldn't bring herself to like him. Still, she softened her voice:

"Bill. You're asking me – a procurator fiscal for heaven's sake – to withhold evidence. Evidence that any court would hold as material. You're asking me to perjure myself. Even if I was personally inclined so to do, professionally I couldn't possibly. You're going to have to resort to the deny-at-all-costs position. Your word against mine. Defender against procurator. Given the success of JCG Miller in recent years, I'd have thought you'd fancy your chances."

"I thought I could appeal to your heart. Common human decency."

"We're not in court now, Mr Crichton."

"I thought maybe as a woman…"

Maddy laughed outright. "That I'd *understand* you cheating on your wife? Your *sick* wife. Fuck's sake, Crichton, get a grip."

"Okay. One last plea. From the bottom of my heart."

"No."

"Give me a day."

"No."

"Let me tell Clare first. It's too late tonight. She'll have taken her sleeping pills. She's particularly vulnerable first thing in the morning. I'll have told her everything by tomorrow afternoon. You presumably wouldn't be in touch with the police until tomorrow. Just give me till close of play. I beg you, Maddy. I love Clare. This will damage her enormously. But if the police turn up at the door tomorrow, before I've had a chance to… There's no saying what she'll do."

Maddy got up and walked towards the door. "I'll sleep on it."

He didn't budge from his chair. "Thank you."

"No thank yous. I said I'd think about it. Chances are I'll be on the phone to Police Scotland HQ at 9 a.m. tomorrow morning." Crichton didn't know it, but she'd already cut him some slack – she had intended to call Alan tonight. "Now. Fuck off."

The following morning didn't work out as she'd planned. She didn't have to sleep on it. Her judgement had been called into question before – wrongly in Maddy's view. She couldn't afford for it to be doubted again. And anyway, every way she looked at Bill Crichton's predicament, her obligation, and her moral imperative, were clear. She did, however, decide to wait until she got into the office, and she would speak to whoever at Police HQ came to the phone. She was acting as a responsible citizen, not as a PF.

But sipping her coffee and eyeing the pack of fags with

three left in it, ten minutes before going out the door, Mamma phoned.

"Maddalena." That was a bad start. Rosa only used her Sunday name when it was serious, or she needed a favour, the two being indistinguishable to her mother. "I'm just down the road from you. In the Atrium. I need you to meet us for coffee. It won't take long."

"Mum, I'm on my way to work. Us? Who are you with?"

"Dante!" as if Maddy was standing in front of them and hadn't recognised him.

She groaned, inwardly. "Dante the repossession man? Mamma, I told you, I really cannot give him advice."

"But I promised him, *cara*! And I've dragged him all the way from Wishaw to meet you!"

Well at least it wasn't her patch. "On a Tuesday morning? At 8 a.m.? *Why*?" Then it dawned on her. Tuesday was Rosa's water aerobics class at the Western Baths. An early riser since her chip shop days in Girvan, she was always looking to fill in that empty hour between the cafés opening and the class starting. Dante hadn't been given an option.

"I have no advice to give him. And I'll be late for work. Tell him I'll search out someone who can help him. Give him a contact."

"You're a professional lady, Maddalena. You can turn up at work whenever you like. But you must talk to him now. They're coming today, or perhaps tomorrow, to throw him out into the street." This was a barefaced lie, and Maddy knew it. "And also, it turns out his lawyer, the one Dante blames for the whole sorry mess, is that man Milton. The one who was killed."

Maddy, having first warned that she could be of no use and that anything she might say should not be cited or even repeated, listened to Dante Marzullo's story.

Just before the banking crash Dante's violin-making business was doing well. As a guest of Julian Miller, his solicitor, at a concert – "Some group of four young men. Il Divo? Total rubbish." – Miller introduced him to a man called Ewan Church. This fellow happened to be a financial adviser. They became quite good friends and Dante ending up buying some of Church's financial products.

"The whole bloody lot has gone bust. And that *stronzo* Church, disappeared into thin air. Now they're going to take my house from me!"

It took a little time and patience getting the important information from Dante Marzullo. Luckily the Atrium café was quiet – the man raised his voice, a lot. Years of dealing with witnesses had taught Maddy when it was worth listening and when she could zone out. The special pleading, the irrelevant meanderings, dodgy explanations. Luckily too her coffee was huge. She'd been coming here for years and still forgot to ask for a small cappuccino. A medium-sized one was a soup bowl. The large was a bloody great cauldron with enough caffeine to give you hypertension. But it was good coffee, the staff were affable, and the place light and airy.

"Dante," she said, "if as you say the repossession of your house is confirmed and the sheriff officers have been in touch, then it has gone through an extensive procedure, full of checks and balances. You do know that it is an offence to give false information? If at any time you misled the lender – perhaps even inadvertently – then it is not a case of your inability to pay, but repossession on the basis of fraud."

"Fraud!" He shouted. "Exactly. That's what they're saying. Fucking fraud." Rosa, having kept quiet throughout the entire conversation, merely nodding her head vigorously at everything Dante said, and furrowing her brow dubiously at everything Maddy said, now spoke up: "Language, Dante, *per favore.*"

Dante, it finally transpired, had indeed overestimated "a little" the earnings of his business. "But only because that bastard Church advised me to. Said it was perfectly legal. Now he's gone bankrupt and skedaddled out the bloody country. Leaving me in the *merda*."

Marzullo's anger was volcanic. Here was another man clutching, white-knuckled, the arms of his chair. Crichton last night, by comparison, had been in control. Perhaps a little too in control she wondered now. Whereas this cousin three times removed looked and sounded hysterical. At any moment he might clutch his chest and die before their very eyes. Just as likely he'd grab a fork and stab it in the eye of any passing stranger.

"I'm afraid Dante," she tried to keep her voice calming but authoritative, "legally you haven't a case. You lied to the lenders. They're absolutely within their rights. I'm so sorry."

The man, overweight, almost as broad as he was tall, fiery red in the face, looked to the heavens above, praying to a vengeful god. "And you know the only man who could have told them that?"

"This Ewan Church," Maddy said.

"No!" Dante Marzullo screamed. "He fucked off ages ago." And anyway, Maddy realised, it wasn't in the financial adviser's interest to alert the bank or building society. "His old buddy. The man who set me up with him. The only other person who knew. Miller. I hope the fucker died in agony!"

"You're a hard man to track down, Mr Harkins."

Joe Harkins stood ankle-high in the mud at Belvedere – an over-the-top name if Russell had ever heard one. If this place was Belvedere then his own divorcee's flat in Anniesland was fucking Malibu. Harkins wore a dirty hi-vis jacket over a fleece, boots and hard hat. In his early thirties Russell guessed.

"No I'm no'. Mr Hughes has me running frae site tae site, that's all."

"You'd been informed we wanted a word with you. You could have saved us some bother if you'd popped in to see us."

"Sorry. Never thought of that. Nothing to tell ye's anyway."

"I'll be the judge of that."

Harkins led the sergeant over to a cabin by the site's entrance – a basic box that looked like an old container with a door punched in it.

"I'm not exactly clear what your position is," Russell said as they entered. "In Fulton Construction. Security guard? Boss's chauffeur? Handyman?"

"Aye."

"All of them?"

"Master of all trades, mate, that's me."

"Basically you do whatever Mr Hughes tells you to?"

"Oh man, I can see you're a detective right enough."

"That must get on yer tits a bit." Russell couldn't help himself. Anyone talked to him in a Glasgow accent – especially a male – and he'd find himself talking the same way. He couldn't, in all honesty, claim it was a throwback to his childhood. John Russell was born and brought up in a nice wee corner of Lenzie, went to a good school, and neither of his parents had strong accents. They'd never have said "get on your tits". Even Russell could hear that it sounded false. Harkins gave him a little sneery smile.

"Between you and me, big man, I'm an active mole in the revolutionary movement. Tam Hughes will be sent to a labour camp in Paisley, which is the nearest thing we have to Siberia."

"You're a funny guy, Mr Harkins."

"Listen, *cunstable*," the "o" on the word heavily stressed as a "u".

"Sergeant."

Harkins shrugged. "It's how the building game's always been. Especially in the last five years. Nobody's got any rights. Everybody just happy to have a job at all. Likes o' me, I'm non-skilled. So aye, sometimes I'm security and sometimes that means nightwatchman. Other times I'm a runner between HQ and the various sites. And when Hughes wants a lift, I'm the go-to man. It's *very* fulfilling."

"And Mr Hughes, he's a good boss?"

"Worship the ground he walks on." Harkins put on a kettle and, from a plastic bag, took out one teabag and one cup. "Nah. He's hunky-dory, really. You know the kind. Everything's work. Loves to tell you how he's never had a holiday in twenty years, never taken a sickie, doesnae know what to dae with hissel' at weekends. Which means, when I point out that I've worked twelve hours seven days in a stretch he looks at you as though you were mental. Or a woman."

Russell got the impression that Harkins did, in fact, find all that quite impressive.

"The night of Julian Miller's murder. Tell me what happened, from your point of view."

"I've already telt wan o' your bluebottles that." He sat down with his cuppa. "I drove Tam from here over to Miller's office in the Merchant City at the back ae six. Picked up Miller and drove them both up west."

"Just Miller? Not Mr Crichton?"

"Naw. Don't know how he got there. But he arrived just as I was dropping them off."

"Whose car were you using?"

"Hughes's. I could hae used my ain old Skoda but that's no really Mr Hughes's style."

"Once you dropped them off what did you do?"

"Came back here."

"Directly?"

"Well there were a few bends in the road. Corners an' that."

"If we could dispense with the jokes, Mr Harkins. In what capacity did you come back here? Watchman? Handyman?"

"Now who's got the patter? Watchman. I'm alternating nights with Davy Nixon. I let him go when I got back – around quarter past seven."

"How often did Mr Hughes meet up with Miller and Crichton?"

"Not a Scooby. Mibbe once, eighteen months ago, I drove them to another restaurant."

"Which one?"

"Fine dining isnae my forte. Place near where Miller lived? Wee country pub."

"Killearn?"

"Could ae been."

"The three of them always seemed to get on well?" It was cold in the container. Russell eyed Harkins's steaming cup of tea.

"Jesus, these questions are getting difficult. Pass. I run them there, pick them up..."

"And when you picked them up on Friday, what time would that be?"

"Fourish? And aye, they were in fine spirits. Naebody pulled a gun on naebody or called his mammy a hoor. It was just Miller and Tam. Your Crichton boy had slipped off earlier apparently. I waited in the car while Tam and Miller slapped each other on the back. You know what it's like after a few swallies. Best mates in the whole wide world. There was nothing to make anybody think your man was a couple of hours away from getting his heid blown aff."

"Then you ran Mr Hughes home?"

"To Giffnock, aye. Then he asks me to come back in a couple of hours and drive him two hunner miles to Hootsmonland for some wedding. I did that, came back," Harkins leaned over his cup towards Russell. "Then you'll never guess what happened?"

"Go on."

"I took the rest o' the day aff. In this outfit that's worth noting doon."

Russell got up. "One last thing. How long have you been with Fulton Construction?"

"Boy tae man, cradle tae grave. Nah, four year now."

"Perhaps next time we want to talk to you – and there will be a next time, Mr Harkins – you won't be quite the Scarlet Pimpernel."

"They seek him here, they seek him there, they seek him every fuckin' where. I'll be here for you. Don't you fret, cunstable."

So much of policing these days centred around the numbing whirr of the HOLMES room hard drives. Indexers, researchers, office managers staring silently at lists and spreadsheets. Coulter almost missed the grubwork of his early uniform days. But much as he distrusted that deadening electronic drone it produced results. A young officer handed him a printout of numbers and guided him through it.

"It's one of Mr and Mrs Miller's joint bank accounts."

"They have more than one?"

"Three that I've found so far. Mrs Miller has two in her own name and her husband had four. Nothing interesting in any of them, apart from this one. Look. Every month five thousand pounds is paid in."

"His wages?"

"No. He pays himself regularly from JCG Miller into one of his own accounts. And a damn sight more than that, sir. About fifteen thousand pounds a month. And then there's bonuses and shares and what have you."

It always astonished Coulter how much money people earned – people he knew, who lived in this same city as him.

"So where does the five grand come from?"

"It's a Bacs transaction. From an organisation called Abbott's. I keep trying to find out more about them, but I've come up with nothing."

"Abbott." It took Coulter a moment to remember. "DS Russell found a file from Miller's office labelled Abbott. Keep trying son. You might be on to something."

Around two hundred thou a year in straight salary alone. God knows how much when all the extras are added on. It genuinely puzzled him what people spent that kind of money on. Julian Miller had been in the habit of starting work at 6 a.m. and not leaving till seven at night. If Coulter had that kind of dosh he wouldn't sit behind a desk for thirteen hours a day. To be honest, he didn't know what he'd do. Most of his colleagues were grumbling that the retirement age had been upped. Coulter was relieved. His phone was ringing when he got back to his office. Maddy Shannon was waiting downstairs in reception.

"Thought I should tell you face-to-face."

"Oh dear."

"Lovely to see you too, Alan."

They took a seat away from the desk. She told him about spotting Bill Crichton and Marion Miller in the park. Coulter's first reaction was, these guys make all this money but they still end up skulking in the drizzle in public parks? She told him how Crichton had come to her house and asked her to keep shtum.

"That's madness."

"Yup."

"The reaction of a man panicking."

"Maybe. He'd thought it through though. Tried every tactic on me. Bargained, pleaded, then said he might still deny it all, the assignation with Marion and the meeting with me."

"Well let's see what he actually does."

"You going to bring him in?"

"I'm going to bring both of them in."

Coulter started to stand up, then stopped when Maddy remained still.

"Something else. And don't say 'oh no' again."

"Oh no."

She relayed the conversation she'd just come away from with Dante Marzullo.

"Okay," he said. "I'll have someone look into that. But if we ran a check on every citizen pissed off with a lawyer the force would collapse."

Maddy got up to go. "You told Maxwell Binnie about this?"

"Haven't managed to get to the office yet."

"You know what he's going to say?"

"Bill's little social call might just have robbed me of preparing the Miller case. Bastard."

"Maybe that's what he intended."

Maddy sighed. "I'll tell Binnie – it's a small town. I can't help it if people talk to me."

"He'll say you're getting in too deep."

In his office Russell brought Coulter up to speed on Joe Harkins. "His patter would bust your balls, but he's a nobody. We can forget about him."

DS Dalgarno had been working with the HOLMES team too. "Zack Goldie, the caretaker at Merchant's Tower, he's got a bit of a record. Nothing too serious. A couple of fights when he was a kid – he was in the Jordanhill Young Team."

All three of them burst out laughing. "There's a *Jordanhill Young Team*?!"

"What, do they fight with the Kelvinside Fleeto?"

"With sawn-off croissants?"

"You'd think they'd have the nous to change their name."

"West End Mad Squad?"

"Anyway," Amy tried to curb her laughing. "He got kicked out of medical school."

"That's not what he told me," Coulter said, rubbing his eyes.

"He was found with cannabis in his digs. Police in St Andrews looked into it, but let it drop. Probably personal use, but enough to make the uni decide he wasn't doctor material."

Coulter's laughter turned to a groan. Kill a lawyer and suddenly half of Glasgow looks guilty. "He led me to believe he'd quit because he couldn't stand the blood and guts."

"Not so."

How on earth were they going to keep a tab on all these persons of interest? "Crichton and Marion Miller should be here by now. I've put them in separate rooms. John, you and I will take Bill Crichton. Amy, find another officer and see what Marion Miller has to say."

"Just before we go, sir. One other thing. The firearms team recognise the serial number of the Glock Julian Miller was shot with. They've actually been looking for it."

"Stolen? From where?"

"Here. Us. Police firearms. One of a case of six."

"How the hell does Police Scotland lose six guns?!"

"Edinburgh. Not us. It was only noticed that six were missing when someone did an inventory. About a month ago. They got the thief, but he'd already sold them on by then."

"An officer?"

"Nah. Some flunkey in Stores. He's been sacked and charged."

"But we've lost sight of the guns?"

"Until now."

"And only one of them. No sign of the other five?"

"No."

"Well. It's something. Come on. We're getting there. Slowly but surely." He led them out the door. "Well, slowly."

Bill Crichton, Coulter decided looking across the table at him, was an unlikely choice for a fancy man. Marion Miller was a designer-clad, figure-conscious lady who lunched – or so she had seemed. Why risk a fling with your husband's business partner when he was smaller, shabbier, more nervous, and your man's junior? Crichton had the face of a man perpetually flummoxed by a hard crossword puzzle. Marion and Julian had made a set; Marion and Bill, an odd couple. Coulter decided to start with the money.

"You stand to inherit JCG Miller, Mr Crichton. Is that correct?"

"If I were advising a client, Inspector Coulter, I'd say you were in danger of exceeding your powers."

"In what way exactly?"

"Bringing me in here at such short notice. Leading questions."

"This time round, sir, you're not advising," Russell said. "We just want to check a few … omissions. Gaps in our previous conversations. You left earlier than the others last Friday night, and unfortunately Mrs Crichton is unable to say what time you arrived home."

"My wife doesn't keep well."

"So nobody," Coulter replied, "can vouch for your whereabouts between 2 a.m. and your arrival at the murder scene at seven. Can they, Mr Crichton?"

"If this is where your investigation has got you so far," Crichton was trying to look assertive, "you're clutching at straws."

"Oh I don't think so, sir." Russell meant it, Coulter could see that. His sergeant didn't like Crichton or Miller and, in his eyes, all the evidence was stacked against them. Russell would harry them into confession. Exterminate the nits and you get rid of the lice – one of the man's favourite sayings. Coulter kept his voice more equable: "We are given to believe that you and Mrs Miller have been conducting an affair."

Crichton looked directly at Coulter then at Russell, as if he still hadn't decided how to play this one. He plumped for hanging his head, a picture of repentance. "It's unforgiveable, I know. Clare is not a well woman. But that's partly the reason." He looked up at them both again. "I tried to explain to a colleague last night… It sounds such a cliché but really, it looks worse than it is. We were both having trouble with our marriages, we found a little comfort in each other. It was never going to last. Under normal circumstances nobody would have found out, and nobody hurt." He wrung his hands. "I assume it was Ms Shannon who told you this?"

"I'm not at liberty to say. You were spotted together in the Botanic Gardens last night."

"I can assure you again, Inspector, it has nothing to do with your inquiry."

"Unless," Russell leaned back in his chair, "Mrs Miller can vouch for your whereabouts at the time of the murder?"

Crichton smiled. "Another leading question. You are both professional enough to know that whatever I answer won't help. If I told you I was with Marion we'd simply both be under suspicion. Correct? As I told you before, I went home. My wife takes sleeping pills. It is, as you say, unfortunate that she didn't hear me come in."

In the interview room next door, DS Dalgarno and WPC Morrison sat back in their seats while Marion Miller, in a full-length leather coat, leaned over the table towards them. If anyone had come in it would have looked like *she* was interviewing *them*.

"Mr Crichton has a problem," Dalgarno was saying, "proving where he was early on Saturday morning."

There wasn't even a moment's hesitation. "Bill," Miller smiled, "from about 2.30 a.m. to 6.30 a.m., was warmly wrapped up in my bed. I believe the time of the murder was just before six? Let me think … yes, around then Bill Crichton Esquire, MA, LLB, was fucking me mercilessly. Will that do, ladies?"

"More detail than was strictly necessary, Mrs Miller."

"Oh dear. I seem to have shocked you yet again, Sergeant."

"Mrs Miller, I've read all the Irvine Welsh books and seen Frankie Boyle live." Only Alison Morrison laughed. "But thank you again for your candour. I don't suppose anyone else can corroborate your statement?" Before Miller had a chance she added, "And please, no unnecessary jokes about threesomes."

"Unless of course we were having one? But no."

WPC Morrison glanced at Dalgarno and the sergeant nodded. "Mr Crichton was in bed with you at six? We know your husband was in the habit of being at his desk by that time, but surely that was still taking a bit of a risk?"

"That's the fun of it, dear."

"And Mr Crichton shared your risk-taking vis-à-vis being caught?"

"Vis-à-vis? How quaint. Not really, even though I've told him that if Jules had caught us he probably wouldn't have cared. It might even have interested him. For the first time in years."

"Yet," said Dalgarno, "Mr Crichton remained with you." The tables had turned, the sergeant leaning towards Mrs Miller who had sat back. "It's almost as if he *knew* Mr Miller wouldn't be home."

Miller opened her mouth to speak, but for the first time words failed her.

"Shall we take a short break, Mrs Miller? After which I'd like to talk to you about you and Mr Miller's joint insurance policy. You have cover of six million pounds in the event of his death…"

Marion Miller gave a satisfied smile.

They'd agreed to break at the same time and Amy quickly told DI Coulter that Marion Miller had alibied Crichton. Reconvening, they asked Crichton to respond.

"Oh Marion." He shook his head. "I had hoped to keep her – and Clare – out of this. Well, it's the truth. But I don't see how it helps any of us. Is it at all possible, Inspector, that this be kept from my wife?"

"I've no intention of telling her, unless I have a reason

to, Mr Crichton. But I'm sure you know as well as I do that these things tend to come out in times like these."

"It would have been easier for all involved if you had just told us from the start, sir," DS Russell sneered.

"It would finish her off."

"Did Mr Miller know of your relationship?"

"Are you crazy?"

"So if he *had* found out…" Coulter had to hand it to Russell, it was a well-timed question.

"You mean … I killed him because…? Me shoot someone? I wouldn't know what end of a gun to hold."

Russell looked at him, then at Coulter. The inspector knew that his sergeant didn't believe Crichton, that Russell had made his mind up who had killed Julian Miller. John Russell had been right before.

Maddy got caught in a spectacular storm walking from Pitt Street to Ballater Street. The sky darkened as though a lever had been thrown in the heavens. And behold the floodwaters! All things that are on the earth shall perish. And not a cab in sight. Then an angel of mercy, in the shape of Doug Mason, was running towards her wielding an umbrella.

"Is that a *golf* umbrella?"

"Why? Would that make a difference?" He shouted over the roar of the rain.

"I'm a woman of principle, Mr Mason."

He had no idea what she was talking about but he kept it over her. Then the rain stopped just as instantly and miraculously as it had started.

"A kind thought," she said as he closed the brolly, "but too late. I'm soaked through. And actually I was rather enjoying it."

"You really don't like me, do you?"

"Take no notice. It's just the way I am." She realised he must have been coming out of his office. "They send you on an errand?"

"I've to find a lawyer with a heart."

"Good luck."

"How are things at over there? Have they made you a partner yet?"

"I doubt they will. Not sure they were ever going to."

"I thought you were Julian Miller's golden boy?"

"Even if I was – which I doubt – that particular game's a bogey now. Listen, we were very rudely interrupted on Saturday morning. I know you're spoken for but—"

"—But that doesn't usually stop you?"

"If I had wanted to take advantage I had the perfect opportunity. Isn't it just possible that a man can take pleasure in the company of a member of the opposite sex and join her for a coffee and chat sometime?"

"Not when they're as devastatingly sexy as us... I'd be delighted to join you for coffee. Maybe next week?"

"Excellent. So you'll stop blanking my calls?"

Maddy enjoyed the rest of the walk, over the river which looked energised by the downpour. The whole city felt redeemed, washed of its sins. The dome of the Central Mosque sparkled like the Koh-I-Noor. Dan had once told her, after they'd had a few drinks, that on special occasions it lit up and spun round. She'd believed it for weeks, even told other people. She still thought it a shame it wasn't true.

She had her meeting with Max Binnie and told him the bare facts of what she knew about both Bill Crichton and cousin Dante. Except she didn't say it was her cousin, nor how she had come by the information. Binnie showed no interest, riveted by the Crichton and Miller gossip.

"Really? Bill and Marion." She got the impression he knew them better than she'd realised. There was no need to tell him about Crichton's visit. She wanted this case, and Binnie might use anything he could to keep it from her.

Back in her office, after agreeing a date for the preliminary hearing of her fatal accident inquiry, opening a new file for a domestic stabbing that had just come in, and requesting a defence statement on the golfing assault, she reread everything she had on the Miller murder. The image of Julian dead in his office haunting her. He'd been a bulky, fleshy man, robust, red-faced, a lump of pulsating life. And then he wasn't. In an instant. The ruthlessness of his killing. Lucky, perhaps, that it was over so quickly, but there must have been a moment, a nanosecond when he knew the universe was about to collapse on him. Did he have time to see his killer? Did they speak? What of? Or did Death just walk up the stairs and claim him? Was he half expecting it?

It was how she worked. Go over the same ground again and again. It's amazing what you can miss first, or even second or third time. But nothing much came to her. Except for two names. In a report Coulter had given her there was mention of an argument between Tom Hughes of Fulton Construction and women by the name of Morag Boyd and Cathy Maguire. The report didn't say what the dispute was about.

It took her a few minutes to make the connection. Maddy had been involved in preparing a vastly complex and long-drawn-out criminal negligence claim against Petrus Inc. A multinational corporation, the case had been a nightmare involving laws and lawyers in the States, Saudi and Singapore. Years of work and nothing had come of the process in Scotland, neither in the criminal courts nor the civil. Finally it had seemed, should any real evidence be brought to light, that a civil case was more likely, so Maddy had dropped it, after wasting a lot of time. She searched deeper into her computer files.

There she was. Morag Boyd, a potential witness in a trial that had never taken place. Was there a connection between Petrus and Fulton? Or was Boyd a campaigner, making her presence felt whenever and wherever she could? Maddy had a vague memory of interviewing her. She didn't remember her as some kind of obsessive eco-warrior.

A nice wee woman, as she recalled. Worried, and doing her civic duty. A few more checks through contacts and there were the details. Morag Archibald Boyd, Robroyston, not far from Belvedere, Fulton's development site.

Amy Dalgarno offered Marion Miller a lift home. The woman fascinated her. Playing the pantomime villain, of course, for which she expected – and deserved – a standing ovation. Amy laughed at the idea – an innuendo Marion herself has probably used. But how deep did the act go? The sergeant, having to keep up appearances at all times, at least while she was at work, couldn't help but like the panache of this particular Wicked Queen. She reminded her a bit of Maddy Shannon, unable to resist the smutty line, the good-time-girl act. If Shannon, as Amy thought, battled her demons of weight and after-hours drinking, what were Mrs Miller's demons? Shannon was obsessed with work, brilliant if compulsive. There was more to Miller than the Merry Widow act. There must be.

It was a long drive out to Killearn and Amy knew not to point out her favourite climbs and cycles – the woman was not the outdoors type. So they sat in silence for most of the journey, Miller texting with the speed and dexterity of a teenager. Every now and then she'd laugh out loud at a message, but it felt just a little premeditated.

"So am I officially a suspect in my husband's murder?"

How could she not be? Though DS Dalgarno didn't believe it for a minute. Her story fitted and, no matter how hard the woman tried, she wasn't convincing as Cruella de Vil. And Bill Crichton? He didn't have the balls for murder. The pathetic creature was more terrified of his wife finding out about his bit on the side. What on earth made the colourful Miller plump for a pasty anaemic dud like him?

"You understand, ma'am, we have to investigate everything and everybody."

Miller nodded and went back to her texting. Dalgarno

sensed something pessimistic about her, the way she slouched a little when she thought Amy was watching the road. As if she was investing too much energy in a project that might not be worth it in the end.

They arrived at her house at the same time as Bill Crichton. He wasn't happy about DS Dalgarno seeing him, like it was still a big secret. There were two marked police cars already there, and a couple of uniformed officers were taking samples of soil from the garden.

"Good God," Marion laughed, "do they think I was going to bury him under the fuchsia?"

As they walked away together, Dalgarno standing by her car, Crichton frowned at her. "It's not funny, Marion."

"Bill, darling, it's absolutely hilarious." She put her arm round him which made him even more uncomfortable. "Come on, you need a drink."

As they walked away Amy couldn't hear his reply. She didn't need to, his body language said he wasn't coming in – not in full view of several policemen and Sergeant Dalgarno. Marion didn't feel the need to be so circumspect. "Running back to Clare, are we?" She let her arm drop from his waist and looked out her keys. "She has to find out sometime, Bill." Crichton stopped and, shoulders slumped, stared at the gravel path. "Don't be a coward on this one. She'll survive." Then opening her door she called over her shoulder. "A box of Kleenex and a phone call to Mummy. Tell her Bill. If you don't, I will."

Maddy and Alan met for a bite to eat at close of play. They used to go out their way, to Café Tibo in the East End, or St Louis in Dumbarton Road, so that they wouldn't be seen together. In their way they were like Crichton and Miller finding out-of-the-way spots, though so far they hadn't been reduced to sheltering under clammy trees in parks. And their liaisons were clandestine not for amatory reasons but professional ones. Fiscals and coppers cosying up was seen as bad form by both sets of colleagues. Now that there was a major incident on the go, all the more reason to keep a low profile.

Recently it had dawned on Maddy that the safest place for them wasn't far from the Crown Office and just round the corner from police headquarters. Hiding in plain sight, in the CCA. It was an interesting facet of provincial white-collar life that so many professionals wouldn't go near a place like the Centre for Contemporary Arts. So many of the moneyed middle class would never go to the Edinburgh Festival, or to the theatre. If artists still relied on bourgeois patronage Glasgow's cultural scene would be in a pitiful state. The golf courses and football terraces, however, would still be hoaching.

Just possibly Izzy, Maddy's junior, might go to the CCA, but only to see a particular show and, anyway, Izzy was too wrapped up in her own life and work to even bother mentioning if she saw Maddy there with DI Coulter. Until not so long back Dan McKillop frequented the CCA but he seemed to have become ever more professionalised and was now more likely to go to Gamba or the Ubiquitous Chip. Most of Coulter's colleagues didn't know the CCA existed.

Maddy resisted ordering a large Pinot Gris. She'd been good in so many ways. Not a drink or a cigarette since Friday night. There was a beer on tap that was only 2.5 per cent so Alan had a pint and Maddy a half. She'd also been a good girl trying not to get involved too early in the Miller investigation, despite it trying to reel *her* in. They pretended to talk about other things – Louis, Martha and the kids – but it only lasted until Coulter's food arrived.

"I could name you a dozen suspects off the top of my head," said Alan, picking at his salad – he'd still have to eat his tea when he got home. "The lovely Mrs Miller and her toy boy…"

"I'd love that, but, nah."

"You haven't been part of the investigation but you're

dismissing two prime suspects out of hand? John Russell would disagree. They can only alibi each other, either one or both of them could easily have been in Miller's office on Saturday morning. They had the opportunity, and the motive."

"Motives," Maddy scoffed. "Motives for Russell are like prayers were for my *nonna*. What motives? An insurance policy and inheriting the business? They're all loaded, they don't need the money."

"Crime of passion. Two lovers get rid of an inconvenient husband."

"From the little I know – as you're so keen to point out – about Marion Miller, she'd just have left him eventually. Or got a divorce. Doubt if old Jules would have cared much. Nah. Doesn't solve their problem. They'd have to kill Clare Crichton too." Maddy looked around, impatient for her food to arrive. "Killers are long in the making. Someone somewhere has been building up to this. The opportunity presented itself, but the decision was made a long time ago."

"You're teaching me how to catch a murderer?"

"Perhaps it didn't need to be Julian Miller. He just happened to be in the right place at the crucial moment. Maybe any lawyer. Or any man. Or any *one*."

"Thank you for the lesson. Shall we continue considering the cast of characters we *do* know?" Coulter smiled to cover his annoyance. Shannon could irritate him as much as she could everyone else. Yet he felt drawn to her, professionally as well as personally. "Tom Hughes or someone else at Fulton Construction? Zack Goldie?"

"The caretaker lad?"

"Don't think he'd have the energy to pull a trigger. Clare Crichton?"

"She'd be more likely to kill her ever-loving husband."

"What about your uncle Danny?"

"Cousin Dante? Long shot. Why talk to me? He'd keep a low profile. Then again he is a very very angry Italian man. You considered Stuart Anderson?"

"Who?"

"Husband of JCG Miller's conveyancing expert, Sam Anderson. They were with me on Friday night. They got a taxi back after midnight, to Bearsden. But Sam told me that Stuart didn't go to bed as usual, crawling in tired sometime the following morning."

"*Now* you tell me?"

"Stuart has a habit of slipping my mind. I was with him at the weekend, I've met him tons of times, but I can barely remember his face. Ever."

"Good face for a killer. I'll have him looked into. What does he do?"

"That keeps slipping my mind too. Civil engineer? Wee round fellow. Has he got a beard? Can't remember. Always pleasant enough, smiley, but then he fades like a ghost."

"Does he like gardening?"

"The earth found on the gun? No idea."

"Analysis will take another day or two. Meanwhile we're collecting soil from the Millers' and Crichtons' gardens. And Belvedere building site. See if we can find a match."

"Can't imagine Dante Marzullo being green-fingered, but who knows."

The CCA's borscht was as good as ever, thick as porridge, red as blood, spicy – the culinary equivalent of a tsarist brothel. She divided her attention between it and Alan's update on financial discoveries. Ownership of JCG going to Crichton, the Millers income and insurance policies.

"Then there's this payment that goes in regularly to the Millers' joint account." Alan pushed his plate away, half the salad untouched. "Five thousand a month, not a single withdrawal since it started."

"How long ago?"

"Three years? Originates in a company called Abbott which we can't find anything more about. But Russell saw an empty file of Julian Miller's labelled Abbott. We've sent people round to find out what happened to it, but Deborah

Hart – she's his secretary, or was – claims she's never heard of a client or associate by the name of Abbott."

Maddy kept her eyes on her borscht. "Could be any kind of dodgy dealing. We're talking lawyers and builders here." Coulter smiled and finished off his pint. "You know, I wish I hadn't said that. All these jokes about lawyers. We've no reason to think that Julian wasn't a perfectly decent honourable solicitor." The image of his shattered skull came back to Maddy, and she pushed the soup away. "The vast majority are. It's difficult work. Why does everybody hate us?"

"Us? I always thought you saw a big difference between you and private-practice defence lawyers?"

"I'm wobbling on that. I'm forever trying to put people behind bars. Miller and Crichton and Mason and the rest, they're trying to find reasons, trying to understand what makes people go wrong. Maybe they're about forgiveness, and I'm about retribution. Do you think I'm about retribution, Alan?"

"I'm not getting into one of your long theoretical discussions. Half the time they're just sticks for you to beat yourself up with. I'm not giving you handers."

Maddy had popped by her mother's flat before going home, forgetting it was her bridge night. Mr and Mrs Sweeney from the parish versus Rosa di Rio and some guy called Tam she'd met at the Western Baths. Maddy was pleased to get away so quickly but she was also pleased at how well her mum was doing. The woman whose life once had been shovelling fish and chips and giving the late-night Girvan drunks as good as they gave her. Up to her oxters in grease and trying to cope with her husband's drinking and high jinks. "That man's gas is never at a peep," she used to say about Packie Shannon. Giving up the shop, her divorce and finally, worst of all, losing her beloved Papa a couple of years back, Maddy worried that her mum wouldn't survive.

Everything she knew and lived for was in that trinity – the shop, Packie, and Nonno. All gone. But there she was, in her own wee flat in Glasgow, playing card games and socialising. Maddy just hoped that this Tam fellow wasn't going to turn out another Packie Shannon.

Dialling Louis' Skype she remembered that she still hadn't responded to her dad's Facebook request. When Louis didn't answer she checked the page. He now had the grand total of seven friends. But it looked as if he himself hadn't been back online. No doubt he'd come back from the pub, probably with someone who knew how to work Facebook, and had forgotten all about it ever since. So it was safe for Maddy to put in a friend request. The daft aul' eejit would never even see it.

It occurred to her that she hadn't mentioned Morag Boyd to Alan Coulter. She'd meant to. Did she forget on purpose? Why would she?

Louis messaged her just as she was about to close down the laptop.

"Hey."

"Hey yourself."

"Saw you were on online. Sorry, can't Skype. I'm in the office."

"Still forget about the time difference. So. What's crackin?"

"Crackin???"

"You know, whassup?"

"You've been here, Maddy. You know nobody speaks like that."

"Lots of people do. Fo shizzle."

"Dear God."

The badinage again, hiding behind jokes and words, pretending they weren't miles apart and maybe drifting further.

"So you coming over to see me or what?"

"Yes. Yes I am. But the only time I can get away is in a week or so, way before Easter."

"I'll see if I can get a couple of days off. Even if I can't…?"

"Then I'll have your dinner ready when you get home. Might be nice, though, to get a day or so out of the city?"

"It'll be early March. Rain, hail, sleet. Freeze your New York bawbag off you."

"I think I get the gist. I'm counting on you to keep vital parts of me intact."

"Fo shizzle, blood."

"Have you been drinking?"

"One half-pint of low-alcohol beer. Is that okay sir?"

"For a school night."

They thought of a few ideas – Arran, the Borders. Izzy's sister had a nice house overlooking Loch Craignish. Anywhere but Loch Lomond – he'd done that twice already. Louis suggested Girvan but Maddy mentally dismissed it. She wasn't sure if she could ever go back to her home town. And since all the tourists had opted for the Med and Ayia Napa the place was in existential crisis. The man would run for the hills. It would be a glimpse of her soul: Girvan in March.

He got called away. But Maddy was pleased. Louis Casci still thought it worth crossing the Atlantic to spend a couple of days with her in the Scottish spring. Scottish spring – more mythical than Brigadoon. She was also worried. They had developed a way of communicating from either side of the world's biggest ocean. Each time they had been together bodily – either there or here – they had to reinvent their relationship, start from scratch. One of these times it mightn't take.

She checked one last thing before turning her laptop off. Morag Boyd's address. Of course she wouldn't actually go see her. But she might. For the Petrus case, that's all.

DS Russell didn't get the impression that Debbie Hart was pleased to see him. Particularly so early in the morning.

"Debbie," Russell thought he should try and be friendly, "Did you get that Fulton Construction file for me?"

"I'm sorry, Sergeant. I spent all day yesterday searching and can't find it anywhere."

"Well that's very strange, isn't it? Given that they were such a big client."

"There definitely was one."

Bill Crichton finally arrived – a couple of hours later than he used to. He was even less pleased to see DS Russell. "Are we never to be left alone?" he glowered. Russell thought he was looking a bit dishevelled. From a night of banging Marion Miller, or from sleeping on the couch at home? Almost certainly the latter.

"Mr Crichton. I know I've asked you before. I'm sorry to hassle you." Debbie spoke to him like anything she said might cause him to break down and weep. "The Fulton file. You haven't got it, have you?"

"I told you Debbie, why would I have it? Jules dealt with them."

"I know, but it's not in his office anywhere."

"Don't ask me. *I'm* not a secretary." With a final glance at Russell he went into his office.

Debbie Hart was upset. "He was never like this," she whispered. "He's taking Mr Miller's death awful badly." He isn't half, Russell thought. Like he had a guilty conscience. Like he knew they were closing in on him. That *he*, DS Russell, was closing in on him. "The only other thing I can suggest is that Mr Miller took the file home with him," Debbie said anxiously.

"Was he in the habit of doing that?"

"Not really. But it did happen. If he had it with him on Friday night… It wasn't in his car?"

"No. Okay. Keep looking. We need to see that file. What about the empty folder labelled Abbott?"

"Another blank I'm afraid. But then I've never seen that one. I've checked with everyone and nobody has heard of a client called Abbott."

Debbie Hart thought of herself as the perfect PA but now

when it really mattered, when her boss had been murdered in cold blood, her systems didn't seem to work after all. She was frightened, feeling alone, abandoned and under pressure. Russell could see all that.

"This is a major problem, Deborah. I need you to find these files." Keep the pressure on her. If she was hiding something, even just a mistake, or covering for one of her bosses, he would know. "I'm going to have to go back to the station empty-handed. But I'll be back. And I'll keep coming back until I have the information I've requested."

Leaving, he noticed that Crichton had left his door ajar, listening in again? Lawyers. Forever trying to catch the police out in court, looking for errors, failings in their investigations, and they couldn't even keep their files in order.

While Russell was making his presence felt at JCG Miller, DI Coulter was in the station asking the HOLMES room manager to run checks on every registered company with Abbott in the title. Also, to add the name Stuart Anderson to his list, see if he came up with anything.

When Russell got back they talked about the possibility that Julian Miller kept work files at home. Coulter considered requesting a search warrant immediately, then wondered if he shouldn't just ask Marion Miller first. Then again, if she was involved with this in any way, it would give her a chance to hide or destroy anything of interest she had at home. Then again, she'd probably have done that already...

There was somewhere else they should check first. The two of them set out for Fulton Construction's Belvedere site.

Maddy had tried to phone ahead. But the number she had for Morag Boyd was unavailable. The information was five years old. Chances were Boyd had changed her phone and her number several times since then. Let's just hope she hadn't moved house too.

She went into the office, printed out some documents from the old Petrus files. She'd brought the car and left the office without speaking to any of her colleagues. Passing his office she caught Dan McKillop's eye. He knew she was doing something she oughtn't.

Driving north and east from the city centre, Maddy thought, was probably more educational than doing three years at University studying sociology. Skipping round past the Merchant City where trendy wine bars attracted very different customers to the century-old drinking dens next door, Glasgow was at its most mixed. But although the penthouses and studio apartments of Bell Street backed on to the single ends of the Gallowgate, their inhabitants very seldom mingled socially. A mile further on and the regeneration of the East End, in the wake of the Commonwealth Games, had meant a multimillion-pound facelift. It turned out like one of those botched jobs you see on elderly celebrities. Everything was too tight, the streets straightened, wrinkles combed out. The overall effect was that the life had been sucked out of the place, leaving it rigid and anaemic when there used to be raucous exuberance. Plant a few trees, cram in some houses nobody locally can afford, it didn't make up for there still being no jobs, no money. That couldn't be concealed.

Further out, all attempt at pretence was gone. Half-demolished houses, gap sites, crumbling factories and boarded-up shops. There were very few people on the streets she drove along. Maddy had no idea where the people who should be here were. She spent a lot of her life dealing with the misconduct and misfortunes these places fuelled and, much as she often liked the people, their mad energy and their endurance, she still couldn't grasp what their day-to-day lives were like. Back in Girvan when the late-night drunk boys saturated the chippie she'd welcomed the noise and the unpredictability, but was relieved when they were gone, back to lives that remained a mystery to her.

Louis had bought her a GPS gadget for the car. The posh English lady who directed her towards fantastical places like Sockiehall Street and Millengavvie was fun, but she'd never mastered the thing. It kept instructing her to drive into stone walls and over riverbanks. So she had to tour around a little to find Morag Boyd's house. It turned out to be on the second floor of a low-rise block, a 1960s concrete exercise in brutalism. On a dreich morning like this you half expected Soviet soldiers in great coats and furry hats.

She rang the bell, several times, but Morag Boyd wasn't home. Perhaps just as well. God – her mother would have told her – had made sure she wouldn't be. God didn't seem too bothered by tsunamis and earthquakes and wars, but He took time to make sure Rosa and her family didn't make little faux pas. She'd phone Coulter from her office and tell him about the connection between Boyd and Petrus and protests against Fulton Construction's site. Do things the right way.

Partially relieved, she was about to head back downstairs when she noticed the nameplate on the house next door was Maguire. Was that the name of the other woman who had been with Morag at Belvedere? Maddy decided to ring the bell anyway. If it wasn't her she could just ask the whereabouts of Mrs Boyd. But there was no answer there either. Although Maddy got the distinct impression somebody was in. A movement inside just as she'd rung the bell. She tried again. No answer. Then she opened the letter box and called in. "Hello?" Still no one came to the door. Perhaps she'd been mistaken.

Only going back down the stairwell did she notice that this block of flats was very well cared for. The steps recently brushed, a smell of bleach. Maddy was ashamed at herself for being surprised. Coming out the close she heard a door open above her. She crossed slowly to her car and eventually a man came out behind her, holding the hand of a little boy.

"Excuse me?"

"Not now. Sorry."

The man looked worried, and also genuinely sorry, giving her a sad smile. Whatever was worrying him was greater than his sense of civility and helpfulness.

"Just, I'm looking for—"

"—I'm in a rush."

He'd be in his late thirties, looking cold in jeans and denim jacket. The wee boy on the other hand was happed up to within an inch of his life – quilted anorak, scarf, beanie and gloves.

"Wee one late for school?"

He didn't stop walking. "I wish that was all it was."

"I could give you a lift. Somewhere."

He slowed his pace, not quite stopping. He seemed interested for a moment then looked harder at her and his expression turned to suspicion. She knew what he was thinking – that she was a cop. It happened to her a lot.

"We're fine."

Maddy met the little boy's eye. "Hiya. Off somewhere nice?" she smiled.

The man lifted the boy up – in a way only a dad can, Maddy thought – and walked off. "As a matter of fact," the man said bitterly, "we're not. Off somewhere nice."

She got back in her car. At the end of the street where she reckoned she should turn left to retrace her steps she noticed a sign for Fulton Construction. It looked like turning right would lead her past the Belvedere site. Turning the corner she passed the dad with his boy again. He'd been stopped in the street by a man presumably from the site. He was dressed in green wellies, hard hat, a hi-vis jacket with his name – Joe – printed on it, and the number 7, like a footballer's jersey. Joe was mussing the kid's hair and neither the boy nor his dad looked happy about it. Then the two men faced each other in what looked, from her car, a fraught conversation.

She found Belvedere – a massive pit in the earth, hectic with men scurrying and machines rolling at precarious angles – at the end of the street. She decided to drive round it, for no good reason she could think of. Probably yet more wasted time.

And nearly a fatal mistake. Driving past the front entrance to Belvedere she passed Coulter and Russell parking at the gate. She slid down in her car seat and turned her head away from them. Please God don't let them recognise her car. Russell wouldn't, but Alan had been in it a couple of times.

Her head turned the wrong way, she veered closer to them than she had meant to. Checking her rear-view mirror she was pleased to see she'd accidentally sprayed Russell's trouser legs with mud. Less pleased that he was staring right at her car, furious. Coulter hadn't noticed though. She might get away with it.

The two men made their way in silence through the gates of the site, Russell cursing under his breath and shaking his muddied leg. They were surprised at how much progress could be made in construction in just a day or two. Trenches they hadn't seen, or hadn't noticed, had sprouted concrete block foundations and now a team of brickies were building walls on them, already reaching their knees. The walk to Hughes's cabin was only a matter of a few yards but by the time they knocked on the door, Coulter's shoes and ankles were as sodden with gooey clay as Russell's.

"Has Fulton Construction," Coulter dispensed with the social niceties, "ever worked for or with a company called Abbott's?"

"No."

"Have *you* ever traded under the name Abbott?"

"No."

"D'you not want to think about that for a moment? Sir." Russell stared at him.

"I can think about it all day if you like, but the answer'd still be no."

"Can we see a copy of your accounts, Mr Hughes?"

"I only keep the ones for this site, Belvedere, here." Hughes hefted his weight out from behind his tiny plastic chair and desk, and opened an old tin filing cabinet behind him, while Russell stomped around the enclosed space making his presence felt, looking at the noticeboard, lifting cups and spoons. "If you want the whole company accounts you'll have to go to the office in town."

"I think you could maybe do that for us, Mr Hughes," Russell growled. "Seeing as how we're trying to catch who murdered your friend."

Hughes scowled but nodded.

"Do JCG Miller Solicitors appear anywhere in your financial records?"

"They will. Along with other lawyers. A company this size, Inspector Coulter, undertaking projects as big as this, has to deal with lots of lawyers. The law's a minefield for builders."

Russell's histrionic search of the cabin unearthed something after all, as much to his surprise as Coulter's. He picked up a torn, scrunched poster out of the wastepaper bin, smoothed it out and held it up. An A3 sheet with "Dump Fultons" scrawled in black and red marker.

"We're forever tearing those damn things down."

"Do you get a lot of this, Mr Hughes?"

"I explained to your lackey there a few days ago. If the law's a minefield, protestors are a pain in the arse." He sat back down and spoke slowly as if trying to make an obtuse child understand. "This is a phase two operation here at Belvedere. Phase ones are bad enough, phase twos double up on the cranks. There's more noise, more mess, more stuff in the newspapers. So, aye, we get a lot of that. Now is there anything else I can help you with, gentleman, only as you'll understand I'm a wee bit busy here."

Coulter turned to go, Russell standing his ground. Hughes simply ignored him, and the sergeant after a moment followed Coulter to the door.

Outside, Joe Harkins the watchman-cum-driver-cum-gopher was walking in through the front gate.

"Aw'right, Joe?"

Coulter smiled at Russell's sudden Glasgow accent.

"Back again, Wee Man?" In point of fact, Russell and Harkins were about the same height. The watchman could just as easily have said "big man". It was clear to both the inspector and the sergeant that he'd chosen not to.

"You seem to go off-site quite a bit, Joe," Russell grumbled.

"Places to go, things to do."

"You ever heard of an outfit called Abbott's," Coulter asked. "Builder, supplier, something like that?"

"Not that I can think of." Harkins responded with a little more respect to the senior officer.

"You had any trouble lately with protestors?"

"Just the usual. They put up their posters, I tear them down, they put them up again. It's fine. Just like the rest of life, eh? Pointless waste o' everybody's time."

"The women who were here the other day," Russell asked, "they local?"

"Chances are. Then again some of these people are pretty committed, right? So who knows."

The policemen left him standing outside the cabin, taking out a pack of cigarettes. When they were driving away they saw Hughes come out, glance in their direction, then take the lit cigarette from Harkins's mouth and smoke it himself. Harkins didn't look happy about it, but took his pack out his pocket again.

By the time they got back to the station they'd already been given the news. About ten times. Calls to both their mobiles, texts, car radio. William Crichton had had a fall and was in intensive care at the Royal Infirmary.

Crichton had come home at lunchtime. "Dead on five past one," one of the constables who had been posted outside the Crichtons' house told Coulter proudly. The young

WPC with him nodded gravely. "Then – we were at the front of the house – there was this, like thud, and—"

"Son. Start from the beginning. Before the beginning. Start at four minutes past one."

The two of them were still flushed with excitement. It was the girl who settled first. "Mrs Crichton had brought us out a cup of tea, and we were standing at the doorway drinking it."

"Kind of her. Never thought she was the type."

"Surprised us too. She didn't really say anything, just stuck the two cups in our hands."

"It was minging. Some herbal stuff," offered the lad Coulter now remembered was called Eddie Something.

"She'd been in a bit of a state all morning. We saw her through the window, pacing, and the phone to her ear but never talking."

"So far as we could see."

"Then Mr Crichton's car pulls up. He leaves it outside on the street though there's a garage at the back."

"He walks right past us, face like thunder. Don't think he even saw us."

"Then there was an argument."

"We couldn't hear all of it, but they were shouting so we heard bits, like."

"He goes, 'Who told you?'"

"And she goes 'You're pathetic, Bill!'"

"We reckon, sir, she'd found out about him and Mrs Miller."

"Do you now? What about him and Mrs Miller? You been listening to station gossip? Just stick to the facts, Eddie."

"She shouts," the young WPC – Morrison, wasn't it? – took up the story. "'Julian pokes you with a stick for years and now *this*!' She'd been preparing lunch when he'd come in. We went round the back to see what we could see. She had the knife in her hand and she's screaming like crazy at him."

"'I swear Bill I could kill you.' Those were her precise words sir."

"Very attentive. Well done. Then what?"

"He leaves the room," said Morrison.

"But we couldn't see where he went."

"Except he must've gone upstairs. Because five minutes later there's the thud we heard."

"We didn't think anything of it at first. But then it was really quiet."

"Like eerily quiet, you know?"

"And I'm not sure what made us do it, but we went round the side of the house, where the driveway leads to the garage. And there he was. Lying on the ground."

"A window was open directly above him. In the attic, the third storey."

"There was blood everywhere," Morrison said, paling again at the memory. "All around his head. And he was lying there in a really weird position. We phoned the ambulance and the station."

"She must have heard us on our phones, 'cause she came out."

"Where had Mrs Crichton been just before then?"

"We couldn't say for sure, sir. We lost sight of her after he went upstairs."

"When she comes out she hardly reacts. She just stares at him, lying there. Then she looks up at the open window, and all she says is, 'When he has a fly smoke he sits on that ledge. He thinks I don't know.'"

At the hospital no one could shine much light either on how Mr Crichton fell or what his chances of recovery were. Coulter and Dalgarno had to wait in the corridor like worried relations. Clare Crichton was being seen by another doctor, her blood pressure apparently plummeting, having fainted when she reached the hospital with her husband in the ambulance.

Coulter had done this countless times, waited outside intensive care and other wards. Thankfully, so far, mostly in the line of duty. And yet he fretted, worrying about the state of whoever was being treated, no matter what they had done or how much the inspector had been hunting them down. He wasn't, he thought, too afraid of his own death, more the circumstances in which it might occur. One day it would be him in there. Martha, or the kids, the whole family sitting in these seats as his life ebbed away. Or perhaps it wouldn't be like that. Maybe it would be a backstreet at night, alone in the gutter. His heart suddenly exploding, or a bullet from nowhere, from out of the sodden night. Or long and wasting, slobbering in a home somewhere. Sitting here you were attending on Death and no matter who the victim was you shared something with him; you were dying too. Your turn next. Dalgarno and he barely spoke and avoided each others' eyes.

Eventually the consultant came to see them. Coulter had met him before. Every inch the professional: groomed, soft-spoken, detached but not uncaring. Gavin Hood was highly respected, well liked. But that practised demeanour put a shiver down Coulter's spine every time. "My best estimate at the moment – spinal fracture, fractured skull, one leg and one arm broken. Probably a collapsed lung. In short, Inspector, multiple wounds to the head and back, organ damage. Possibly brain damage too."

"What are his chances?" Such a limp question. Coulter was as practised as Hood. Did his voice put the fear of death into people too? Of course it did – he was a policeman.

"Hard to say. He needs a lot of work. We'll start on him now. It's possible that each of his injuries will heal. At best it will take a long time. He'll be a very lucky man if one or more of his injuries isn't life-changing at least."

"Falling from a third-storey window. Bad I know. But those seem like very severe injuries for, what, thirty, forty feet?"

"I agree. He must have fallen with some force."

"More than just tumbling off a ledge?"

"You're the detective, Inspector. If you're asking me if his injuries are consistent with being pushed, well I couldn't possibly say. Throwing himself down would increase the impact. But so too might tripping, falling headlong."

Clare Crichton was given the all-clear to talk to them. Though once they had found them a room in the hospital and she sat down, Coulter wondered if it had been the right decision. She moved a little too slowly, apprehensively. Her face pale, eyes blank, seeing and not seeing, like an ancient Greek statue. Dalgarno, Coulter noticed, was very good with her, guiding her into her seat, talking quietly, soothingly, all the while.

"This is very difficult for you, Mrs Crichton." Coulter tried to mimic Amy's murmur.

"Clare," she said, automatically.

"Do you have an idea, Clare, what might have happened?"

"He fell from a window."

"Do you know how he might have fallen?"

"I'd warned him about it before. He kept cigarettes up there. Had one every now and then. When he was feeling anxious."

"About Julian Miller, this time?"

"Well of course. What else?" Then those blank eyes began to moisten, and she turned her head towards Dalgarno. "It was me. I killed him."

"What do you mean, Mrs Crichton?" Coulter asked.

"We'd just argued. A terrible, terrible argument. I suppose you all know, but apparently my husband was having an affair with Marion."

Coulter waited a beat, then: "What made *you* think that?"

Clare Crichton paused for a second too. "She told me."

"Marion Miller? When?"

"An hour, less, before Bill got in."

"How did she tell you, Clare?" Dalgarno asked quietly.

"She phoned me. Just like that. And just … said it. Then hung up. What kind of woman does that?"

"So when he came in, you rowed."

"That's putting it mildly. After everything I've done for him. Standing by him. And he's screwing her over his office desk, or whatever, while little wifey's home making dinner."

Although her words were bitter, they were spoken flatly. Rehearsed, Coulter wondered?

"And he went upstairs?"

"I presume so."

"Did you *see* him going upstairs?"

"I was cooking in the kitchen. He stormed out. The next thing I know your officers are shouting into their phones."

"A terrible accident," Dalgarno said tenderly, though Coulter knew she was fishing.

"Yes it was. It couldn't have been anything else."

"Like what, Clare?"

"Well it was either that or he jumped out, but that can't be right."

"Why not?"

"Well, first of all, if he'd wanted to kill himself, he isn't stupid. He'd be more likely to be badly injured than dead. It's not that high."

WPC Morrison had said that she showed no emotion looking at her husband's body lying in a pool of blood. She spoke now, too, matter-of-fact.

"Bill isn't the suicide kind. He's scared of blood. Cries like a baby when he cuts his finger. It takes courage to kill yourself. Bill isn't a courageous man." She stopped and stared at the blank wall behind Coulter. Then, an afterthought: "And he certainly wouldn't kill himself on *my* account."

Hearing the news, Maddy got in her car and, heading for the hospital, took a last-minute decision, veered off the motorway to pass by the Crichtons' house. They lived in a mews cottage in one of the lanes off Cleveden – the kind of house Maddy had often dreamed about. Perfectly secluded, but still a few minutes' walk from the pubs and cafés of Byres Road.

A policeman and woman, standing close together, talking animatedly to one another were at the gate. They looked like a young couple excited on their first date.

"Hullo. Maddalena Shannon. Procurator. I was passing, thought I'd take a look at the exterior."

They knew who she was, and not asking to be let inside made it easier for her to pass without questions or checking with their superiors. "Whereabouts did Mr Crichton fall?"

They pointed to the side of the house. This wasn't a mews at all, but an old stables, at the back of a house that could serve as a small castle. It had been beautifully restored. If this was the Crichtons' doing they had good taste, and deep pockets. The area Bill had fallen into had been cordoned off – like it were a murder scene. As she'd hoped, nobody else was there yet. Clare Crichton would still be at the hospital, and so would Alan and his team.

Bill Crichton's blood was congealing on the driveway paving, black and crusted like a giant skint knee on the path. He'd lost a considerable amount of blood. Looking up, the window he had fallen from was still open, a saltire of police tape across it. These old structures had high ceilings. The first floor in particular, where the horses had probably once been stabled. Maddy winced at the thought of falling from such a height. And those paving slates looked unforgiving.

Standing back and straining her neck she could just about see inside the window. White walls, what looked like the top of a desk, a phone on it. No drapes but a blind, rolled up closed at the top of the window. There was a little ledge. It might even have a window seat on the inside. Could Crichton have been sitting there? It wasn't raining, or particularly cold, but it was still Glasgow and

February – unlikely he'd want to sit outside. Could he have been smoking? She looked around for a cigarette butt or ash but couldn't see any. He might have been leaning out to get a signal – depending on your provider you often had to get near a window or a door in the West End to use your phone. No sign of a mobile on the ground, and he'd hardly have put it back in his pocket when he was falling.

Returning to the officers she tried to get some information out of them. It confused them. They knew the procurator was important but equally didn't want to get into trouble for saying something they shouldn't. You learn early in the police to keep information on the inside. The only thing she hadn't known, from the message DI Coulter had left for her, was that Crichton had returned home only ten minutes or so before he came tumbling out the window. What had brought him back?

Retracing her route along the motorway Maddy thought about desperate men. What bothered her was how well, in her experience, they hid that desperation. Crichton, the night he had come to see her. His world was falling apart. Boss and mentor murdered in cold blood. Which meant his affair with the boss's wife would come out. He'd seemed genuinely concerned about what his wife might do when that happened. Professionally and personally everything had turned to shit. Yet he still sought to be in control, manipulate the situation. How many others were doing the same? Was Julian Miller a desperate man before he was shot? Lawyers, builders, businessmen – all known for living on the edge. Pushing to the limit.

She texted Coulter from the car. Five minutes later they were standing on the High Street outside the old gates of the infirmary. He told her about the argument between Clare and Bill moments before he fell. How Clare looked to Coulter to be in deep shock. Perhaps had been since Miller was killed.

"So all bets are on?" She said. "She elbowed him out the window."

"Possible."

"Did you ask her?"

"No. But I will."

"Or he threw himself out." They must look like a couple of smokers, standing outside the hospital. She patted her pockets but had left the nearly empty packet at home. Just as well.

"He'd had to have really dived, judging by the wounds he sustained. Forensics will have an idea about that."

"Or he fell, badly."

"That's my feeling. For the moment." Coulter didn't look convinced by his own words.

"Spectacular timing. Just as his company's in a mess and his wife's caught him playing away."

They stood for a while lost in their own thoughts. Around the door stood a clutch of patients, some of them in pyjamas and dressing gowns. One of them, an elderly lady leaning on a Zimmer frame, sucking deeply on a cigarette. Behind her was a woman with a young boy. Not unlike the lad she'd seen with his father outside Morag Boyd's flat. The mum looked exhausted, shoulders slumped, staring down at him. As she looked up and their eyes were about to meet, Maddy quickly turned her head away.

A couple of hundred yards down the road was the old Glasgow Cathedral, and beside that the Museum of Religion. She'd seen Dali's *Christ of St John of the Cross* in there a few years ago. A painting she loved, though she'd been told by people who knew about such things that she wasn't supposed to. It was kitsch, Dali looking for another headline, nothing more. But for Maddy it had solemnity and anguish in equal measure. Christ crucified filled the evening sky; below, a tiny fisherman not looking up at Him, not even aware of Him. It seemed an appropriate image, here at the edge of Glasgow's East End on a smudged winter night, sick kids and worried mums, talking about a man who was fighting for a life he maybe didn't even want.

"No point standing here," Coulter said, turning up his collar. "My head's just going round in circles. Might as well do that on a comfy pillow."

"Accident, murder, suicide. Whichever it turns out to be, it complicates the situation."

Coulter closed his eyes and sighed. "Doesn't it just."

Alan Coulter eventually got home. He sat and poured himself a whisky. What a way to live. Dead men, near-dead men. Suspecting everyone of everything. Hospitals, doctors, gory details about fractures, punctured organs, brain matter. His neighbours did ordinary jobs. Taught kids, sold cars, operated cameras. None of them, though, would escape the blood and guts. In the end it would touch them all.

Policing wasn't such a bad way to live, he decided. Or convinced himself. It was honest. It looked life – and death – in the face and dealt with them even-handedly. Every day he saw how bad, or frightened, or vengeful people can be. What they are capable of. Most folk turn away from all that. Concern themselves with the latest Vauxhall, debate diesel versus petrol, play golf and ride carbon-frame bikes, go shopping. The charade that saves them from thinking about the bits of themselves and others they don't want to see. It was Coulter's job to think about little else.

Over the river Maddy sat and looked at the copse of trees outside her window. Chiaroscuro. Branches picked out by the orange street lights against a shining black sky. Like a painting. Tiny lives being played underneath it. She thought of contacting Louis but decided she'd be too distracted. She should call her mum, but wouldn't be able to deal with the chatter and cleverly concealed criticism. She tried to picture Dali's crucifixion in that blackest of skies, but couldn't quite.

The fag packet was lying on the coffee table, within reach. She smoked one, instead of having a drink. She'd make up for it by going to the gym tomorrow. Or maybe the next day. Sucking the sour smoke deeply she checked Facebook. Dad had answered. "Hey Flutterby. What do you think? Your old fellow on social media. When you coming over to the Oul' Country?"

Flutterby. What he'd called here when she was little. When he was big and loud and funny and threw her up into the sky and could do no wrong. She couldn't think how to reply to his message.

Southside, Coulter's reverie was brought to an abrupt end, his mobile making him jump. There was something he had to see. Russell picked him up half an hour later.

The two uniforms positioned outside the Crichton house, older than the rookies who'd found Bill Crichton earlier, should have known better.

"We just sat in the car for ten minutes."

"To get out of the cold."

It wasn't cold. It was boredom. Coulter knew that, could remember. Sitting in the car you could put on the radio. He had some idea there was a match being played tonight. A Scotland friendly? They took him round the side of the house to the spot where Crichton had landed. There, in the middle of the stain of dried blood, lit up by the officers' torches, was a gun. A Glock G19. The same model that had killed Julian Miller.

"And look. There, sir."

Beside it lay a single bullet.

II

It's all about relief. Mine and theirs. The trigger is pulled and two people are put out of their misery. Though one of them only temporarily. The deed is done, duty fulfilled, and the body relaxes. You can stop holding your breath. The duty discharged: both bullet and barrel.

A body lies lifeless, and you would think it would be earth-shattering. But it's not. It has, when it's done, about the same weight as turning out the bedside light, or turning off a car engine.

What is most striking is the silence. The big bang of the gun and then a hush. A peaceful hush.

There are worse ways to kill a human being. Grind them down, over years and years. Send them the wrong way, perhaps with a smile, towards their certain demise. Bury them alive, slowly. Make them kill themselves. Betray them, sometimes with a kiss.

A trigger, a barrel, a bullet – it's clean, quick, easy. Very easy. The mechanism does it all for you. So well designed, simple to use. It knows what it's for even if, for a nanosecond, the hand holding it does not, or suddenly questions the logic.

And then you leave. Just walk away. Put on the old mask. No need to think through any plan, just go about your business as usual. If, one day, the gun decides to change direction and point itself at you, well you know now how it works, and how simple and clean and quiet it is.

Who knows where the blaming begins and when it ends. If ever.

The job is done. You feel, not elated, not agitated. Just relieved.

Until the next one.

A signature killer. What does that tell you? Maddy pedalled like crazy on the exercise bike, adrenaline surging. That they want to be caught. They want the world to know that this is their work. She'd never come across it before in her own career, but she'd read about it. Didn't Jack the Ripper leave some clue behind? She couldn't remember what. Then there was some lunatic in the sixties, somewhere in the States, who posted clues, zodiac signs or something, to the newspapers. Must ask Louis about that.

He was the reason she was doing an extra spin class: shed a few pounds, and quickly. He'd be here in a week or so. She told herself it wasn't actually for *his* sake she was doing it. Fuck that. She is who she is and he can like it or lump it. The lumps were the problem. For her, not him. She just wanted to feel good. She was going to have to get naked, and playing Hide the Sausage was more fun if you weren't trying to cover up the splodgy bits, turning off the light.

Maxwell Binnie had spoken to her like the Miller case was definitely hers and it was live. Probably he was just keeping her happy – she had too many connections to prepare a case. But just in case, she had to start moving on it. Even if it was just to hand it over to Dan or Izzy. It was a fiscal's fate anyway. Do all the hard work then the rights of audience were handed over to an advocate depute who got all the glory in court and more money for it than she'd see in the months of preparation.

It was her job to think it through, be ready to build a case for Learned Counsel. Let the police do the investigating of course, but good practice to keep up with events and think independently.

She turned the resistance up a notch higher.

They might just be taunting the police, society. But, in the long run, didn't the taunters want to be caught too? She could picture it in her head. Some sicko, proud of the death he'd brought, the pain and chaos he'd caused.

Standing self-righteously in court, a knowing smile on thin lips, believing he was privy to some great plan, some profound understanding the rest of us aren't. This was turning out to be a high-profile case – the newspapers were obsessed with it, carrying crazier theories every day – lots of dosh sploshing around, the cream of the legal profession would be fighting each other to defend the bastard. It was down to Maddy di Rio Shannon to put the fucker away, forever.

She looked at her fellow spinners. She was definitely pedalling faster, with more resistance, than the older super-fit woman. Young Tricia was glancing over at her, smiling, but surprised. Now that she was conscious of actually going hell for leather Maddy realised she was overdoing it. Her heart was racing and she was wheezing for breath.

"Doing good, Maddy," the trainer said. "Keep it up."

"I think I'm going to be sick."

"Excellent. Just do it after the class."

A couple of the women from the running group were in Mario's Plaice after, and Maddy joined them, happy to have her mind taken off her tiredness and queasiness. They had all ordered tea. Maddy had been looking forward to a black pudding roll, maybe even a quick fag after. But she ordered tea too. Probably sensible, a big jag of caffeine while her heart was still thudding might be a bad move.

"We're having a wee session a week on Sunday night in the baths bar. Come along, Maddy."

"What's the occasion?"

"Doing the women's 10K that afternoon."

"If ever there was an excuse."

She was beginning to warm to these people, laughing and prattling happily. "Do I have to do the race too to come along?"

"Course not."

But then they started talking injuries – Achilles tendonitis, shin splints – and she got bored. If she went along after their race she'd just feel guilty. The fat lass at school with a note from her mum to excuse her from sports. Which made her think she'd better call in on Rosa. At lunch-time she was meeting Doug Mason, another promise she was beginning to regret. She told the running ladies she'd try to make it along, excused herself, paid, and walked up through Hillhead, keeping well away from the Botanics and Kelvingrove.

DS Amy Dalgarno had been right. There was another side to Mrs Marion Miller. The swagger was gone, the unholier-than-thou smirk. Where Clare Crichton had been wan, dazed, Miller's tears streamed down her cheeks, the perfect hair and make-up mussed and streaked.

"Is he going to die?"

Coulter answered. "I'm afraid we don't know that yet, ma'am."

"He's in the best of hands, Mrs Miller," Dalgarno offered.

"Mrs Crichton said you phoned her?" Coulter remained firm.

Marion sat on the same seat as before, big enough to hold two of her. "Bill was right. She did go mad."

"How mad exactly is that?"

She dabbed her eyes, aware now that her make-up was running, trying to fix it but only making it worse. "Clare's ill. Has been for a long time. She takes these turns."

"What kind of turns, Marion?" Dalgarno asked.

"I don't know. Flies off the handle. Shouts and screams. The way Bill described them it was like some kind of fit. Scary."

"And you think she took one of these … *turns* yesterday?"

"I don't know."

"What did she say on the phone? When you told her?"

The woman winced, remembering. "I should never have done that. I just thought … it would be easier for everyone. Best to just tell the truth. Get it out in the open."

"What did she say?"

"I didn't give her much time. I said I was sorry. There was nothing any of us could do about it. It just happened. Then I hung up."

"Mrs Crichton was silent throughout all this?"

"Completely. No sniffing or gulping. She *knew*. I've told Bill that, several times. She knew."

"How would she know?"

"I don't know. Bill's not as good, not as practised, at keeping secrets as I am. I think maybe Clare sensed that something was going on. Maybe put two and two together. I wasn't sure. Just a feeling. But yesterday on the phone, I didn't think she was surprised. It's so hard to tell with her. She's … strange." Dissolving into tears again, she said, "I should have told Bill I was going to phone her. I should have warned him!"

She got up and began pacing the space between the back of the chair and the huge window with five bays. The room was so large that when she was right over at the window Coulter felt as if he almost had to shout. "Mrs Miller. You have to see the situation you're in here. Your husband has been murdered, and now your boyfriend is critically ill in hospital."

"That's ridiculous!" A glimmer of the old brash Marion. "It's clear now, isn't it? Bill and I had nothing to do with Jules's murder." She gave into the tears. "I've been so stupid!"

"In what way?"

"I was glad. Happy. About everything. Yes, even my husband's death. I was even glad you suspected us, Bill and me, of having something to do with it. This was my chance, at last. Of course *I* knew we were guilty of nothing. But you threw us together. And I thought, this is it, this will bring everything to a head. Bring Bill and me together. Get everything out in the open. And it was working. Like a charm… Until I told *her*. I should never have spoken to that crazy bitch!"

Miller was still at her window as they walked down the path. Was she watching them? Making sure they were leaving? The woman confused Coulter. He bought her distress, and her astonishment, at Crichton's accident. She seemed genuinely convinced that Clare Crichton was capable of just about anything. But was that her plan? Point the finger at her rival?

"I know we're supposed to keep perspective," Dalgarno said. "Don't make judgements. Until yesterday I was willing to give her the benefit of the doubt."

"But now?"

"This is going to sound prissy. But I think she's morally bankrupt." Dalgarno smiled at her own phrase. "I sound like some old-time minister. But really. She doesn't blink an eyelid when her husband dies. Not even a tear for the *way* he died. She just sees it as a chance to get one over on Clare Crichton. Then phoning her? For why? For sheer pleasure, I reckon."

"But does she have a point? Is Mrs Crichton angry, deranged, enough to kill?"

"In a fit of rage? She charges up the stair after him. Sees him sitting there. Can't stop herself."

"None of this explains the gun and the bullet."

"Maybe it doesn't have to. Maybe it's unconnected with what happened yesterday morning, *inside* the house."

"Someone, somewhere, had Bill Crichton next on the list? And was beaten to it?" Coulter opened the car door, but didn't get in. "We need three – no, four – things. Clare Crichton's full medical history. Did JCG Miller ever have a client that dealt with guns?" He glanced back at the vast landscaped garden. "And the results of those soil tests."

"And the fourth?"

"A drink."

"Some hope."

Maddy was asking the same kinds of questions. Rosa busied

herself making a sandwich for them both. She was used to her daughter thinking out loud and knew not to ask too much, just make the odd remark to show she was listening.

"They think there might have been traces of soil on the second gun too. Maybe from the gloves the killer was wearing. That would suggest the killer had set out to shoot Crichton. Didn't know that he'd fallen."

"Or maybe it's just soil from the Crichtons' own garden? Do you have to walk across it to get to where they found the gun and the bullet?" Rosa didn't look up from her sandwich-making.

"There's a path but yes, it'd be quicker to cross the little front lawn. I don't suppose anyone intent on killing has much respect for victims' gardens."

"You want provolone?"

"What? Oh. Please."

"Your cousin Nicola says provolone is a southern cheese, but I told her they have it in Elba too."

"Right… According to Coulter the first gun at least was from a stolen cache. Sounds like the second one too."

"There you go. A little half glass of wine with that?"

"Go on."

She had her foibles, Rosa, but by God she made a good sandwich. All those years throwing chips in a poke, was she dreaming about a little Italian bistro where she could make panini and crostini and sandwiches like this? Home-made pesto, a dash of puttanesca, it tasted like heaven. It tasted like girlhood holidays in Elba.

"You been in touch with Dante?"

"There's nothing more I can do for him, Mamma."

"Of course there is. You're an expert."

"I've done what I can."

Rosa sniffed, disappointed at a di Rio's lack of concern for one of the *famiglia*.

"Can't you, for once, trust my professional judgement?"

"I usually do, bella."

"No you don't," Maddy tried to make it sound light, jokey. "You like to disapprove. You know you do."

"Ay!" Rosa waved the remark away. "Without me, you'd be dead." One of Rosa di Rio's favourite ripostes.

"The wife."

"What?"

"The wife of the crazy fellow who got himself thrown out a window. The gun just appeared in the middle of the night? With two police on watch? It'd be easy for her to open the back door and put it there."

Her old mamma was right. So it would.

Maddy was having a second glass of wine an hour later with Doug Mason. Walking from her mum's to the bar she'd smiled at the idea that maybe Doug was the very man she could practise with before Louis got here. He'd be only too happy to oblige – at least, she hoped – and she couldn't care less what he thought of her bingo wings and love handles. But it was a very different-looking man who was waiting for her in The Belle on Great Western Road. Casually dressed, to the point of unkempt, he looked drained, and she told him so.

"This is my devil-may-care weekend look."

"It's good. I like jaded and scruffy." She chinked his glass. "You must be getting worried at JCG. The male of the species there seems to be near extinct."

Mason smiled, but Maddy realised she had misjudged. This wasn't the Doug Mason she'd woken up next to a week ago. The wisecracking, the innuendoes, all gone. Death acts like caustic soda, stripping away the veneer, the masks we don to face the world. One of his bosses was murdered a week ago, the other's life was hanging by a thread. "Sorry. That was insensitive."

"I'm a solicitor," he kept smiling. "Can hardly complain about insensitivity."

"You liked him didn't you? Bill."

"Yeah. I did. He was smarter than Jules ever gave him

credit for. It was Bill, not Julian, who kept the company going, making us feel like a team."

"He was working yesterday morning. You must have seen him, just before…"

"I said hello when I got in. Didn't really speak to him after that."

"What do you think, Doug? Would he kill himself?"

"If you'd asked me yesterday, I'd have said absolutely not. What makes anyone take their own life?"

"In Bill's case, circumstances?"

"He told us all, the day before yesterday, about him and Marion." Doug managed another smile: "The look on poor Debbie's face! She'd never heard the like." The smile faded. "Must admit, though, I was pretty taken aback myself. I mean, your best friend? Talk about shitting on your own doorstep."

"And yesterday morning. Did he seem any more upset, or depressed, than before?"

"As I say, I never really talked to him. But he was searching for something. We could all hear him opening drawers and filing cabinets, swearing to himself in his own office. Then he was in Julian's doing the same thing. Then back to his own again. Debbie kept asking what he was looking for. He just said 'nothing'."

Doug asked if she wanted another glass of wine, but she declined. They sat for a while longer, trying to talk of other things – Louis, Doug's love life (less colourful, if he was telling the truth, than Maddy would have guessed). But they were both probably thinking the same thing. Bill Crichton goes into work, searches madly for something, doesn't find it, and rushes home. Ten minutes later he's at death's door. Were the two things connected?

"I'd better get going," she said, draining her wine. Mason's face fell. Had he thought they'd spend more time together? More likely, Maddy thought, he just needed company of any kind. She had no reason to rush away, except that tragedy and mystery affected her in a different way – she needed to be alone, to think, to let the gloom inside take over. Like when you're sick, pulling even a clammy sheet over you helps. The answers to dark questions lie in dark places.

"Why on earth don't we have the soil analysis yet?" Coulter was getting grumpy now. Wasn't everything supposed to be more efficient these days? All those computers grinding away day and night, researchers and managers and IT specialists. The entire Scottish police had just been reorganised into one national force, the fanfare promising prompt, joined-up responses to every crime. It seemed to the inspector that the more technology and management the slower everything got. Crawford Robertson, newly promoted under the new regime to deputy chief constable for the whole of Scotland, was on his case as much as he'd ever been. Coulter needed answers before his next meeting with the boss.

"They had to send them to some place in Aberdeen," DS Russell told him.

"The James Hutton Institute," Dalgarno clarified. "They emailed an interim report on Friday. But now they're checking the gun and bullet left at Crichton's house, so it'll be a day or two yet. If there are traces of soil they'll have to compare them."

"And what about the stolen guns?"

Again, it was Dalgarno who had the information. Russell stared out the window of the meeting room as if she already knew. "Firearms team can now confirm that the Glocks definitely come from the stolen case of six. They'd already been looking in the Glasgow East area. Fits a pattern apparently."

"What, we've misplaced guns before?!"

"From police arsenal but also from other sources, a lot of them ending up in the east of the city." She tapped her screen. "Here. Anywhere between Springburn and Shettleston."

"Which would include Fulton's building site."

"Where in these areas have they turned up?"

"Under-the-counter sales in dodgy pubs. A Colt Cobra snubnose was used in a shop robbery eighteen months ago."

"Then ask the robber where he got the gun, no?"

"They never caught him. Or them, rather. Two of them, probably young. Shopkeeper put up a spirited fight, as they say, and the robbers ran. He managed to wrangle the snub-nose off them, though."

"Great. John, find out what you can about gun dealing in Springburn pubs. Go to them. Go to them all. Give me a name, a clue, anything. Who's selling who Glocks on a weekly basis!"

Russell and Dalgarno got up to go. "What's the latest on Crichton?" Coulter asked.

"Far as I know he's still under the knife."

"Poor bastard."

"Poor bastard my arse," said Russell, leaving. "Whether he was pushed or jumped, we're going to find out that he deserved it. Mark my words."

Coulter would have loved to disagree with his sergeant. That's how the dynamic worked between them. Russell reached for an early conclusion while his boss played a waiting game. Usually the latter strategy worked better. But in this case, Russell might very well be right.

Crichton, by all accounts bullied by Julian Miller, starts an affair with his partner's wife. Greedy wife. Things get out of hand, Julian is killed. Coulter doubted very much that Bill Crichton himself pulled the trigger, although he had – as Russell liked to point out – both the opportunity and the motive. Neither he nor Marion Miller could prove their whereabouts last week. He's a lawyer, he knows how the bad guys get guns. Still, Coulter couldn't imagine the scene. Eyeball to eyeball, in cold blood? Could Marion shoot someone? Her husband? With Crichton by her side? Slightly more possible. Whatever, Crichton finds he can't stand the heat. His girlfriend spilling the beans to his wife was the last straw. Agitated, confused, he takes a sudden leap... Maddy Shannon could make a case out of that.

Except she wouldn't. She doesn't buy it. Dan McKillop would be more likely to go for it. Then everybody would be happy. The fiscal, Maxwell Binnie himself. Deputy Chief Constable Robertson. The newspapers. Maybe even Marion Miller, if she was the genuine femme fatale. Crichton takes the blame, snuffs it or lies in a coma for years, unable to speak up for himself. Mrs Miller walks away with the insurance money, and the company.

Maddy had decided to hop on a subway at Hillhead, go into the office and do some digging. COPFS was quiet. No Dan or Max. Manda was quietly working on something down the corridor and they said they might go for a drink when they were both finished. In her own office Maddy searched for another mobile number for Morag Boyd, but couldn't find one. She'd drive out later and knock on the woman's door again. She opened every file she could find that mentioned JCG Miller. Looking for anything that might connect the company to the guns trade. Any case they had defended where someone had been shot, or threatened. But there was too little to work on.

Then she noticed a cross reference between JCG Miller and the old petrochemical criminal negligence case she'd spent years working on.

Ten years ago the multinational corporation took local advice from JCG over an inquiry by the Scottish Environmental Protection Agency. From the little she could see in her own files it was all straightforward. Toxic leakage had been detected in groundwater in North Lanarkshire. She managed to find articles on the Web relating to the case. Polychlorinated biphenyls – substances used apparently in coolants for electrical goods – had been found, albeit in low levels, in a stream adjacent to an open landfill site. JCG's advice – in a report that was delivered to, among others, Forbes Nairne, before he was a lord – seemed fair to her, simply stating the law as it stood on dumping and outlining the responsibilities of both Petrus Inc. and Costello Laboratories, a local company, now defunct, but at the time partially owned by Petrus. Julian Miller himself had seemingly prepared the report and he had been careful not to show prejudice towards either the environmental agency or the multinational.

Still, all the more reason to track down Morag Boyd. There was no mention of her involvement in the Lanarkshire case, but she had been cited as a potential witness, perhaps in her capacity as an environmental campaigner, in a civil suit – which was why Maddy had had no direct contact with her – against Petrus. And now she was protesting at Fulton's construction sites.

She put Morag Boyd's name into her search engine. After a page or two she found an article about the woman being thrown out of a meeting in Maryhill Burgh Halls three years back. It was a day of talks on environmental health – everything from food safety to air pollution. It seemed that Morag hadn't been the main troublemaker, but a woman she was with, a Catherine Maguire. Ms Maguire had made herself very unpopular. According to the two-paragraph piece in the *Evening Times* she had used "abusive and threatening language" before being asked to leave. Maddy checked back through her notes. Maguire was the other woman Coulter had seen with Morag at Belvedere construction site.

She'd forgotten about the drink with Manda, who'd contacted Dan. The pair of them came into her office just as she was leaving.

"Listen, guys. Sorry but something's come up."

"I don't care," Dan said. "It's probably something you shouldn't be doing anyway. At least not on a Saturday night."

"And what, going to the pub is something I *should* be doing? Didn't work out that way last Friday."

There was no getting out of it. She went with them to Blackfriars and made sure she was at the bar first. She got wine for them and made sure the spritzer for herself was mostly sparkling water – she needed to drive out to Morag's house.

"I know you, Maddy Shannon. You've gone all intense. Which means not only are you going to go all vanilla on us, you're going to do something really stupid."

"This Miller thing. I know it's close to home and everything," Manda smiled kindly at her, "but shouldn't you back off a bit? For the moment."

"No, no, Manda," Dan said. "Let her go. Way things stand she's still first choice for generalissimo when Max keels over, which is any day now. One more mistake and that job's mine."

Dan beamed at her, but Maddy knew he was half serious.

"You two have no idea what I'm doing. As a matter of fact I'm concentrating on an entirely different case."

"Are ye, aye?" Dan laughed.

"What?" Manda asked.

"Petrus."

"Still *that*?" Manda shook her head. An obsession of Maddy's.

"Petrus is it?" Dan said knowingly. "Even from this distance I can see a connection with Miller and Crichton."

"Then get your eye tested."

"So. A case, ten years or more on the go, all but shelved… Where do you need to rush off to, on your own, on a Saturday night?"

"I'm not rushing anywhere. I'm here drinking with you, am I not?"

"You've hardly touched that drink, which looks to me, by the way, suspiciously like fizzy water. If you're not going anywhere in a hurry, stay there and I'll get you a proper drink."

She had a choice. Take the huff, and get out of there now. Or give in and get a proper drink.

"Margarita."

Three margaritas later she walked with Dan and Manda to Queen Street station. When they went to get their trains she waved them off as she walked towards the subway station. When they were out of sight, she veered off and hopped in a taxi.

Probably unwise to knock on Morag Boyd's door at eleven at night, four drinks down. Was Morag the kind of woman who'd go to bed early on a Saturday night? Maybe she'd be out on the town. In which case, no damage done, apart from two taxi fares.

Thankfully the driver wasn't in a talkative mood. A problem in Glasgow, the need to make an instant, common bond – nobody's the boss here, a' Jock Tamson's bairns. Fine, except you ended up talking rubbish throughout the entire journey. But this guy said he was in for a tough night when the clubs come out, and slid his driver protection screen shut – mutual protection, from half an hour of inane conversation.

The Glasgow night hadn't quite yet come to the boil. The street lights and shop signs sizzled in the smir, reminding Maddy of Blue Nile songs. *The neons and the cigarettes... Do I love you? Yes I love you...* Lassies in peerie heels tottering, midriffs bare to the chill, looking for love, or a fight, whichever came first. The taxi stopped at a red light beside two young men who gawped absently in at her. They looked like they'd just burrowed their way up from hibernating underground and hadn't got used to even this half-light. Leaving town and the bright lights behind, the night got blacker, the streets wetter, slick and glassy.

The Belvedere site was like a moon crater, the massive hole in the ground more conspicuous than the new foundations half hidden in the night. There was a light on in a cabin. The nightwatchman presumably. The light flickered several times as someone crossed in front of it. To and fro, to and fro.

She paid the taxi, the rain more assertive this side of town, and the driver took off with more urgency than Maddy felt was necessary.

Climbing the stair, she could hear voices above. "I wouldn't trust him as far as I could throw him," a woman was saying, a touch of anger in her voice.

"It's only a job. Man's got to earn a crust."

"Aye, well, some of us know where to draw the line."

Turning on to the landing of the second floor, Maddy saw that the voices were coming from Morag's next-door neighbour. Cathy Maguire's house. She had to cross by the door to get to Morag's and, as she did, it opened wider and the man she'd seen with the little boy was backing out.

"I'll see you later, Cathy."

He almost ran into Maddy. "Oh, I'm sorry," she said.

"You? What you doing up here?"

"I'm looking for a Mrs Morag Boyd?"

Cathy Maguire, hearing the voices, came out into the hall. "Who's that?"

She'd be in her late forties, tall, her long black hair, dyed, hung down her back. Her eyes were naturally black and, right now, bristled with irritation. She stepped past her neighbour, taking control of the situation. "Can I help you?" She had a smoker's voice, pleasingly husky like an old jazz singer's.

"I was just telling this gentleman I'm hoping to catch Morag Boyd next door."

"What d'ye want her for?"

"You wouldn't be Mrs Cathy Maguire, would you?"

"You fair know a lot of names. Any chance of us knowing yours?"

The words were direct, dismissive, and the eyes still burned, but she put a smile on her face and relaxed her posture. A well-practised line in passive-aggression.

"Maddy Shannon. I'm from the procurator fiscal's office. I was just hoping to—"

"You work long hours, Maggie, hen. Nearly midnight on a Saturday?"

Maddy tried to smile back. "Well I was passing, so…"

Maguire gave a throaty, almost cheerful laugh. "Passing my aunt Fanny."

"Okay. I wasn't. Just, once I've got a bee in my bonnet… I'm interested in your protest against Fulton Construction."

That got Maguire's interest, but she kept up the chutzpah. "ID."

"Right, yes. Hang on." Maddy looked in her bag for something that might satisfy the woman.

"Ach leave it. If you pulled out something official looking I wouldn't believe it anyway. Kenny," she said to the man, who had been standing there throughout, keeping as still as possible. "Away in and tell Morag we've got company. I'll bring her through in a minute." Kenny nodded to her, then again to Maddy as he squeezed past. "Mon through," Maguire said.

The living room was a surprise. The usual items of furniture, a telly, coffee table, the smell of smoke not completely disguised by fresh air sprays. But the walls were covered in posters. In pride of place, over an electric fire with one bar lit was a naïve-style portrait of an American-Indian woman with the words I, *Rigoberta Menchú*. Maddy remembered a little about Menchú. Didn't she win the Nobel Peace Prize? For indigenous peoples' rights. Then there had been what seemed to Maddy at the time some kind of smear campaign. On the wall by the door there hung a photograph of Maguire laughing joyfully amid a group of African women dressed in kaleidoscopic robes and headwraps. Cathy seemed to be the star of the show. Next to that a photograph of an inconspicuous if kindly looking elderly gent. The caption read, "The population doesn't know what's happening, and it doesn't even know it doesn't know." Reading that, Maddy thought she recognised the face now as Noam Chomsky's. There were a couple of Yes posters from last year's referendum, including one that Maddy had never seen before. The Joan Miró Spanish Civil War print with the "Aidez L'Espagne" redrawn to read "Aidez L'Ecosse". Finally her eye fell on a black-and-white poster. A woman, her face completely hidden by a kind of balaclava, only her furious eyes showing, holding a machine gun, ready to fire.

Maguire and Maddy sat facing one another across the coffee table, on which were a pack of Rothmans and a lighter, and an open jotter full of hectic writing.

"Well, I've been visited by the polis, social workers, councillors, you name it, but never by a procurator fiscal." Looking at her now, Maddy decided she was probably actually in her fifties, but striking, somehow younger looking despite the fags and what was obviously a long life of fighting. "I'm no' even sure I know what a procurator fiscal is." Maddy knew that was a ploy. She had the feeling this woman knew a lot about most things. "Does it mean I'm going to get arrested?"

"Do you think you should be?" Maddy calculated that Maguire was up for verbal fisticuffs. For a moment she thought she was wrong as the woman's eyebrows knitted tightly. Then Maguire gave a long loud guffaw.

"Oh aye. Definitely. Sorry. My manners. Can I get you a cup of tea?"

"No thanks."

"Something stronger?"

"I'd love to, but better not. I'd take a cigarette though?"

"Be my guest. I know the script – pretending to yourself you've given up and smoke OP's."

"OPs?"

"Other people's. It's fine. Help yourself. I do it all the time."

Maddy lit up, the dry, dingy smoke at once depressing and quenching. Cathy Maguire folded her arms: "So. Explain."

"I just wondered what your gripe with Fulton Construction is."

"No, Maggie, hen. I said *explain*. This is my house, I'll ask the questions."

"Okay. Your name and Morag Boyd's came up in a report concerning the murder of Julian Miller—"

"Funny how when a lawyer gets killed you all leap into action. Carry on."

"I recognised Mrs Boyd's name from a case I'd been preparing a few years ago. Petrus? A petrochemical company."

"Aye, I know all about them. But so what? Morag complained about Petrus and now we're on the case of Fulton. I can see that that might be a wee bit interesting. But you're a fiscal, not a policewoman. Yet you come across town – twice. Aye, I know you were here a couple of days ago." Maguire gave a contemptuous little smile. "Call us a close-knit community."

"I'm in charge of this case, Mrs Maguire."

"Cathy. Not that I'm trying to be pally. I just think you people hide behind formalities. Deal with me as I am."

"Okay." Maddy stubbed out the half-smoked ciggie, causing Cathy to frown.

"You're 'in charge of the case'." Her frown turned to a look of amusement. The woman knew it was odd. "Fair do's. And it stands to reason that me and Morag murdered Miller."

"Of course not! I'm not saying that."

"But you're thinking, *maybe*. Why else would you be here?"

"I'm simply trying to put the pieces together, Cathy."

"Two working-class women. With a chip on their shoulders. Schemies. Inured to violence. Hey presto. That it, Maggie?"

"Actually, it's Maddy."

"Aye, it would be." Cathy Maguire got up, pocketed her fags and lighter. "C'mon then. We'll go see Morag. Dinna fret. We promise not to stick a kitchen knife in your heid."

Maddy followed her out of the house and through the open door into Morag Boyd's. The two houses were mirror images of each other, but Morag's hallway was brightly painted and cluttered with clothes and shoes, including a child's pair and a small backpack. In the main room Morag was sitting watching TV with the sound turned down. The lottery quiz show. The walls were more brightly painted than Maguire's, the whole room more traditional. Hanging on the walls were family photographs. Amongst them only one, small, picture. Beautifully coloured in reds and ochres it bore the words, "The Wee Yellow Butterfly". Maddy thought it might be the cover of a book.

"Morag," Maguire announced brightly, "this woman tells me you killed Julian Miller."

Morag gave a tired smile, but couldn't think of an answer to that.

"Seems Cathy likes her jokes, Morag." Maddy went over to the woman who did not stand up. "My name's Maddy Shannon. I'm from the procurator fiscal's office."

Morag smiled and nodded. She wasn't being offhand, Maddy thought, she simply looked too exhausted to get up. "Hello."

"I hoped maybe you could answer a few questions? They might lead to nothing, but it's worth a try."

"Sure. Carry on."

"Do you remember Petrus, Morag? You were involved with a campaign against them."

"There's your connection right there. Petrus used to own the pharmaceutical factory on Creggan Street."

"They weren't actually the owners," Cathy Maguire said. "The company was called Costello Laboratories. Petrus were both a supplier of materials and a buyer of end products. They had minority shares in Costello." Maguire was clearly the meticulous researcher of the two.

"We're pretty sure, but, that they were the real power," Morag said.

"Five years ago dangerous levels of toxic waste were documented. Not enough, however, for any of you people to do anything about it."

"I tried," Maddy said. "Morag, you were involved in the attempt to bring a criminal case against Petrus."

"Cathy too."

"We came up against a couple of problems. International companies like Petrus are hard to pin down. Where were the decisions taken? The responsibility trail was muddled to say the least."

"Well that's what they do, big conglomerates like that. Supranational – isn't that what they cry it? They're bigger, and more powerful, than any government, so they get away with bloody murder."

"It wasn't just that. It was hard to make any indictment stick. I personally led a whole number of discussions on whether or not, under Scots law, a company could have *mens rea.*"

"I mind that," Morag said, sitting up in her chair.

"Can an organisation, in and of itself, have evil intent? In criminal law we need a body, an accountable human being. I tried all kinds of angles – if we could prove a crime had been committed, then who benefitted from the proceeds of that crime? In the end of the day, although the criminal case is still technically open, it was decided that complainants should pursue the matter in the meantime through the civil courts."

"Where it was kicked into the long grass again."

From outside the door the voice of a young boy called out "Mummy!"

"Coming son," Morag called back. But before she could get out her seat, Kenny put his head round the door. "It's okay. I'll see to him."

"Thanks, Ken," Morag smiled at him. "Tell him I'll be through soon." Maddy looked closely at her, and thought she probably was the woman she had seen at the Royal

Infirmary with the little boy. Kenny, before leaving the room, glanced at Maddy. When she caught his eye, he nodded to her again, left and closed the door.

"What I'm interested in now is if there is any connection between Petrus and your protest against Fulton."

"Costello Laboratories was closed down, for no apparent reason—" Cathy said, interrupted by Morag: "Though we like to think it was the efforts of people like us that got them running." Cathy took up the story again: "Fulton acquired the land – what, three years ago now, Morag?" Morag nodded. "And started building on top of the pharmaceutical factory. We're very far from convinced that they sealed that site properly."

"Do you have any proof of that?"

"Not directly," Morag began, but Cathy Maguire put her hand up. "I think that's enough for one night, eh? It's the weekend and this woman here wants to say goodnight to her boy."

"If I could just ask a couple more things…"

"With all due respect Miss – Shannon? – you've been less than useless to us in the past. I'd like to think that you're now on our side and want to help. But I don't. I don't believe it for a single minute. Quite possibly you *think* you want to help. But that's not how it works. Not how the system works. What you really want to do is find out who killed Julian Miller."

"No, that's not—"

"Why'd we want to kill a lawyer?" Morag asked, looking genuinely curious.

"Nobody's saying you killed anyone!"

Cathy stood between the two of them. "I'll see Miss Shannon out, hen. If we meet her again it'll be on our terms. *We'll* ask the questions." She went to the door and held it open for Maddy. "We know how it works. You don't give a tuppenny fuck about the likes of us. Shall we?"

As Maddy followed her to the door, her eye caught

again the poster on the wall. Under the caption, "The Wee Yellow Butterfly", written in smaller letters she read "The War Without Bullets".

Coulter phoned home and was glad when Kiera answered. Martha could handle his absence, even on Saturday nights, these days, but when one of the family was round it made him feel better.

"I've done as much as I can here. I'll be home soon."

"No problem, Dad. I've set Netflix up for you and Mum. We're halfway through ep one of *True Detective*."

Coulter only understood half of what that all meant, but was aware of a certain irony. He got his coat, checking out the window to judge the weather. A smirry night, his favourite kind. A good night to walk home, an hour of thinking, or better yet, not thinking, just walking. But it wasn't to be.

"Sir." WPC Morrison came in and stood by the door. "There's someone downstairs I think you'll want to see."

The someone in question was a student-looking young guy, waiting for him in an interview room. The lad's hair was gelled back, cut into the bone at the sides – Coulter's father would have approved.

"Mr Daniels. You want to talk to me about Zack Goldie?"

The boy looked worried. "I'm not sure I should be doing this."

"Whatever it is, son, believe me, you should."

"Zack's a friend. I really like him."

"But?"

"This is hearsay. I could be landing him in a whole bunch of shit he doesn't deserve."

"But."

"Zack's a really chilled guy. But like a lot of guys like that, when he *does* blow a gasket…"

"Sparks fly?"

"Listen personally I've never seen him do anything really crazy. Can this remain confidential, between you and me?"

"I can't promise that, Mr Daniels."

"Gabe."

"Gabe. But if what you want to tell me amounts to nothing, there's no reason why Zack should know you ever spoke to me."

"Okay," but the lad didn't look convinced. "I first knew Zack at uni. But we still hang out sometimes. Some other people don't like him, have tried to warn me away from him."

"We've heard he can have a bit of a temper."

"Oh. Right. Well that was it really."

"Can you give me any particular examples, Gabe?"

"Like I say, I've never seen it for myself. But I know that he did once walk into a party, already tooled up. He'd brought a kitchen knife. Apparently he just came into a busy room and said to this guy, 'I'm going to kill you tonight.'"

"Who was this?"

"Guy called Josh. Josh Callaghan. Not really one of my crowd."

"I take it he didn't kill him?"

"No. Josh is a big guy, you know? But he'd seen Zack lose it before so he got out of there quick style."

"And why did Zack pick on Josh Callaghan?"

"Way I heard it, it was a stupid reason. Zack'd been kicked out of uni for dealing weed. His parents hired some lawyers to defend him and Zack was pretty sure that'd do the trick. When it didn't, when the lawyers failed … and Josh was studying law."

"He took a dislike to lawyers?"

"Big time."

"And it was enough that Josh was studying law for Zack to want to kill him?"

"He wasn't really going to kill him, man. Sir. He just wanted to noise him up. But when I heard about the Miller murder…"

"That was over a week ago, Gabe."

"And I've been trying to figure out ever since whether I should tell you or not."

"You did the right thing. Finally. And, yes, it's highly unlikely Zack had anything to do with what happened to Julian Miller. But the incident with Josh, it wasn't the only time Zack lost it?"

"I've heard he's done a few crazy things like that. But always just talk, you know? When he's had a drink, a smoke."

Coulter got up. "I'll get you a car home, Gabe. But we'll need to take your details first."

"Is that necessary?"

"'Fraid so, son."

Maddy took her mum to morning Mass. Years ago she'd read a book, couldn't remember its name. By Marina Warner? Warner had been a young intellectual leftie atheist when, on holiday in Paris, she'd wandered into Sacré Cœur or Notre Dame and was suddenly reduced to tears looking at a statue of the Virgin Mary. The rest of the book questioned why the image had such an effect on her.

Sometimes Maddy felt the same thing. The forgiving face of Christ in the Stations of the Cross, the picture of Our Lady. They were in Rosa's favourite church, Our Lady of the Immaculate Conception. Maddy disliked the name – out to deny women their sexuality, the whole whore/Madonna thing. But the rhythm of the prayers, the small congregation murmuring, the holy pictures and the faint smell of incense, all seeped under her skin. In a place like this you could too easily forget all the other stuff – the hierarchy, the crazy rules about sex and sexuality, the secrecy. In the hands of the wrong people it led to catastrophe. Like two boys dead in a park.

But now all she could feel was a kind of longing. Probably for childhood, the nuns at school, all the lovely stories and picture books about saints and angels. The old certainties.

She remembered being at a do somewhere and talking to an older man refusing a drink. "I keep away from alcohol to stay closer to God," he'd said. Maddy had had a few already and couldn't stop herself from saying, "I drink to keep away from Him."

Sometimes she should keep her big mouth shut.

After delivering Mamma safely home she went back to her own place and dug deeper still into old Petrus files. There was nothing she hadn't read twenty times in the last week.

Taking Mamma to church made her feel more receptive to Dad. God knows why. Packie Shannon had, to put it mildly, an idiosyncratic relationship with Catholicism. When Maddy was growing up he had supported her mum by bringing Maddy up in the faith, going most Sundays to Mass with them. But his boredom, and occasionally his irritation, was plain to Maddy even when she was very little. Once in a while, when he'd had a skinful, he'd come home at night and rant about priests being in the pay of oppressors and imperialists.

He had similar contradictions about the chip shop. On the one hand he was canny, fiscally precise and scrupulous about takings, declaring his tax to the penny. But he'd regularly seethe about the small-mindedness of petty capitalism and the bourgeoisie. Packie Shannon was the only Catholic atheist reactionary socialist in the world. Later, when Maddy began reading up on politics she laughed at her dad being the very embodiment of dialectical materialism, busily sowing the seeds of his own destruction.

"Hi Dad. Can't see me making it over to Ireland in the near future. Very busy here."

Phoning was out of the question. Talking one-to-one had been mutually proscribed since he and Mamma split up. Over twenty years ago now. Bloody hell. Rosa would see meeting him as an act of high treason on Maddy's behalf. There had been virtually no communication between father and daughter for a year or two. Then there had been the odd furtive phone call, but they always ended badly, either with Maddy railing at him all over again for abandoning them, or Packie slagging off her mum. More silence, then for a while Dad wrote her letters.

That was when he was playing his trump card against Rosa, going off to live in Italy. *Her* country. Gleefully mounting his own emotional imperialism, colonising Rosa di Rio's most treasured sense of self. Those letters had been surprisingly tender, but they came just when Maddy, a rookie fiscal, was trying to amputate her entire past. Thereafter there had been stabs with new technologies. Emails, then short, mostly droll, texts for a bit. And now he'd discovered Facebook.

"Mamma's fine." She'd always made a point of referring to Rosa. Partly to keep him somehow part of the family, but more to keep the punishment fresh and bitter. Feck knows when she'd get a reply – Dad seemed to check Facebook once a week at best. Perhaps he'd already moved on from it. Maybe he's already sending her Snapchat or Instagram messages. Packie would love being ahead of his daughter technologically.

She decided to reward herself with an afternoon glass of wine and an email tête-à-tête with Louis. Closing down all her Petrus files she remembered that one of the judges involved along the line was Forbes Nairne. That was good news. It would give her an excuse to pop in on him and talk professionally. Dan McKillop was good at playing the networking game. Maddy would take a leaf from her colleague's book. And who knows, Nairne might even help her find a connection between Petrus and the Miller case.

Halfway through describing to Louis – in veiled terms, no names: email trails might prove compromising in the future – her thoughts to date on Miller and Crichton, the protesting ladies and Fulton Construction, Samantha Anderson phoned. She'd be in the West End this evening, if Maddy fancied meeting for a drink.

There was no way she could avoid it – her job, the little social life she had, her time alone, all seemed to involve alcohol. Ten years ago she hadn't worried about it. Yes, she was younger, but it seemed now that hardly a day passed when there wasn't a new set of guidelines or an expert putting the fear of death into everyone. Dan McKillop told her recently that he couldn't care less. "Better than dying of fuck all." Maddy wished she could share his insouciance. If it were true, that you could drink and smoke and eat to the point of dropping dead, she'd sign up for it. But that wasn't what usually happened. Usually you got a stroke or a heart attack or cancer. Dying was one thing; being *half* dead for years terrified the bejesus out of her.

Not enough to stop her nodding when Sam, at the bar in the Chip, said, "Large one?"

"He might as well have not bothered going home," Sam said, once they'd found a seat. "Stuart. The night we were round at your place. Turns out that once I'd gone to bed, he went out for a walk. Some walk! He walked right back into town again."

"From Bearsden?"

"Stuart likes walking, but at two in the morning?"

"He told you this?"

"My brother did. He drives in every morning early to work and thought he'd passed Stuart on the way. Before six in the morning! When I asked Stuart he admitted it."

"What made him do that? Must be, what, five miles or something?"

"He said he just started walking. No destination in mind. Suddenly realised he was at the top of Byres Road."

"What did he do then?"

"Says he turned around and walked right back home again."

Maddy remembered the story of her great-grandfather. He'd walked from poverty-stricken Elba all the way to Scotland. Set up the café in Girvan and, two years later, walked all the way back to Italy to collect his family. Stuart's journey was hardly as epic.

"He's not coping at work."

"Sorry. I always forget. What does Stuart do again exactly?"

"He's a project manager in facilities management."

"Ah."

"No, I haven't a clue what he does either. Manages, I suppose. He's always worrying about staff, and sales, and reading spreadsheets. I sometimes think *he's* not sure what he does." Sam finished off her glass, when Maddy was less than halfway through hers. "He's always so … distant. He never was a great talker, Stuart, but now he hardly says a word. To anyone. I used to think he was the strong silent type. He *was* the strong silent type." Maddy found that hard to imagine: had there once been a prototype Stuart, leaner, pre-baldy, made of sterner material that had deteriorated over time? "But the strength seems to have gone. When he's not staring at reports, or walking round in circles, he … well…"

"What?" Maddy asked.

"He cries. He cries all the time, Maddy."

Maddy wondered why Samantha Anderson was telling *her* all this. She hardly knew the woman. As far as she could remember she'd spoken more to her in the last week than at any time before. Sam gave her a sad smile.

"I'm sorry. I know what you're thinking. Because I don't know who else to tell. Not my 'friends' such as they are. That's all about how well we're all doing. How perfect our families are. Are you on Facebook, Maddy? It's horrible. It's one big boasting billboard. I can't tell my 'family'. We don't have kids. I have one brother. In London. We send each other Christmas and birthday cards. End of. Stuart has a sister and a brother, but they all hate each other. And certainly not anyone at work – we don't even talk about what's happened to Jules and Bill." Maddy poured half of her glass into Sam's. Sam immediately drank it. "So. You. I have no idea why. You remind me of a ... priest or something."

Maddy laughed. "That's just the Italian name."

"No. I don't mean priest. I mean confessor. Do you get female confessors? I hope you don't mind me saying but there's something, I don't know, kind of wounded about you, Maddy. That makes it okay to confess to."

"You mean someone worse off than yourself?"

"Not worse, no. But wounded, and coping."

Maddy didn't know how to react. Considered one way, this woman, whom she hardly knew, was happily drinking her wine and insulting her. Even if she didn't mean to. Put on the professional face – that seemed her only option.

"What time did Stuart get back from his walkabout?"

Sam was surprised at the question. "I have no idea. I got up late, hung-over. He was back when I went downstairs. Mid-morning?"

"At work, Sam. You ever come across a company called Abbott's?"

The woman looked deeply disappointed at Maddy changing the topic. What had she expected? A counselling session? Three Hail Marys and absolution? Perhaps she'd hoped Maddy would respond in kind and spill out admissions of her own, the two of them getting drunk and crying, hugging each other. Bugger that.

"No." But Samantha Anderson didn't even think about it.

February. In Glasgow *that's* the cruellest month. No sunlight since November. The challenge of Christmas. You've survived January and you need, you really *need*, light and warmth. February gives you nothing. It's the Limbo month. Four weeks of purgatory. Everybody goes a bit crazy. But, walking back alone to her empty flat, try as she might to cut Sam some slack, Maddy's heart just hardened. She couldn't reciprocate Sam's kindred spirit. And she liked her husband less.

The doctors had decided to put Bill Crichton into a medically induced coma.

"Just what we need," Coulter moaned.

"What is it?" Russell asked.

Amy had just returned from the hospital, taking off scarf and hat and gloves. "You shut down all brain functions with anaesthesia. Crichton has intracranial hypertension – trauma caused by the fall. The brain heals better if it's allowed to rest. At least that's the theory."

"But it might not work?"

"No."

"How long for?" Coulter sighed.

"A Dr Boergmann told me of a case where the patient was kept in a coma for six months."

"Six months!"

"Did it work?"

"I didn't ask. But apparently that's unusual. Depends on how long it takes the swelling to go down. He hopes no more than a few days."

"Even then we don't know what state he'll be in."

"He might not even survive, sir."

Russell picked up the phone. "I'll get Zack Goldie to come in."

"No. I'd like to see him in his natural habitat."

Russell groaned. "Waste of bloody time."

"Who I do want brought in are these protesting women from Belvedere." Coulter looked at his screen. "Morag Boyd and Cathy Maguire. I'll ping you over the details."

"Where did you get them from?" Russell asked, suspicious. Rightly so. Coulter was reading from a long email from Maddy Shannon. Stuff she should have told him days ago. She tried to make it sound like she'd chanced upon the pair of them – something about researching another case. Coulter didn't believe it, so no chance Russell or Dalgarno would. Was he going to have to rein Maddy in? For her own good, as well as keeping colleagues off his back. But she was good at this. She might go about things the wrong way, but it was like having another – keen, talented – officer on the case. Unpaid.

"Oh, stuff's coming thick and fast, John. HOLMES, beat reports, you know…"

Then again, it nettled him that she didn't trust him. She could easily have talked over her hunches, given him the names and the information he needed and let him, the detective inspector, do his thing.

"You got any further with East End gunrunning?" He turned the tables on Russell.

"Going over again this evening. Uniforms are asking around too."

"That's our best lead. Track down those guns, we get our killer."

Two easy steps. If only.

Zack Goldie lived with his mum and dad. Or rather, he lived in his parents' granny flat, the top floor of a massive Victorian villa in Dowanhill. He was clearly under instructions not to change anything. There must once have been an actual granny, the hallway and living room old-fashioned. A telephone table in the hall, with a phone and a chair. Antimacassars on the backs and arms of a sturdy three-piece suite in the room. Family photographs, many of them in black and white, in frames on the mantel and little tables in each corner.

"I knew one day it'd come back to haunt me." Zack sat down, looking out of place on the floral-patterned sofa. DI Coulter and DS Dalgarno remained standing. "And it wasn't because he was studying law."

"Why then, Zack?"

"Because, at that point in my life, I was a psycho. Not literally," he said quickly. "I'd flunked uni, was drinking, on snow—"

"Cocaine," Amy said to no one, but for Coulter's benefit. Which rankled. He knew that one.

"Just a couple of months. Did one or two stupid things like that. Now everyone's got me down as some kind of gangsta."

"So why pick on Josh?"

"Because he's an arsehole? Will that do, Officer?" When it clearly didn't, Zack sighed deeply. "You know how there's people in your life that bug you? But they're friends of friends or whatever, so you just put up with it. When you're in tailspin, drinking and snorting, suddenly you can't hide it any more. Callaghan always acted the big man. I just wanted to scare him I suppose. Did that a couple of times back then."

"And what about Julian Miller, Zack. Did he bug you?"

"Seriously? Because I once went a bit mental at a party you think I'm a killer? Jesus. I hardly knew Miller."

"You used to run with a gang, Zack." Amy made the question sound like a childhood hobby. Zack looked at them both in turn.

"I'm beginning to see things the way you do. A series of minor events, two and two together... Yeah, me and my pals got lifted once for paint-spraying. I was twelve for Chrissakes."

"Okay." Coulter sat down on the wool-covered sofa. "Why did you tell us that you left medical school, when in fact you were thrown out?"

"I'm such a prick." The lad's self-loathing was building by the minute. "Because I can't bring myself to say it... That, and my parents don't know. I'm sorry."

"You can see why we're here, Zack, can't you?" Coulter was feeling sorry for him, but he was right – it didn't look good.

"You find Mr Miller, dead in his room. As far as we can tell you were the only other person in the building that morning."

"Apart from the killer!"

"Then you lie to us. Then we find out that you have a record of violent behaviour."

Zack stared open-mouthed at him. "Oh, dear Jesus."

It might have been a real prayer. Coulter didn't mention to Goldie, but the results of his fingerprinting and tests for soil on his shoes had come up blank. Zack Goldie, at best, was a long shot. "We're not going to take you in right now, Zack. But go nowhere. We'll check in on you every day."

"Anything you can think of that might help," Amy offered, "tell us."

Coulter got up. "Like for instance, you ever hear Mr Miller or anyone else at JCG Miller mention a company or a person called Abbott?"

"Abbott?" He thought for a minute. "Rings a bell… Oh. Yes. I was coming in one day, just as the other guy, Crichton, was arriving. He was taking a whole pile of files and folders from his car to the office. He dropped a couple. I picked one up. Full to bursting it was. I wouldn't have noticed except that he got flummoxed and grabbed it off me. Then made a wee joke – 'Pretend you never saw that.' I remember it was labelled Abbott because my dad and I used to watch *Abbott and Costello* on the telly, when I was wee."

Costello. It was Coulter's turn to think. Wasn't there, in amongst the stuff on Petrus that Maddy had sent to him, mention of a company called Costello Laboratories?

WPC Morrison was taking Clare Crichton to the hospital, under instructions to stay with her throughout her visit. The woman said nothing on the way, staring out the side window, back of her head towards Alison. At the Royal Infirmary a car was leaving the only available space, so the policewoman waited. Clare Crichton didn't however, and got out.

"Just wait a sec, Mrs Crichton?"

But she didn't. Without looking back she walked quickly, head down, directly towards reception.

"Shit."

The old man took an age to park. Alison Morrison ran to

the entrance. Just as she was going in a man brushed past her. Middle-aged, heavy built, face like a basket of dirty laundry. She'd hardly have noticed him – it was probably true what DI Coulter had once said to her, nobody over fifty exists for anyone under thirty – had he not glanced at her uniform then too quickly looked away again. Nothing unusual in that, the public's general response to the police. But she thought she recognised him. It took her to ask for William Crichton's room at the desk and get into the lift before she placed him. The guy from Fulton Construction. Hughes?

Bill Crichton was in a private room within a ward. She asked a nurse if he had had any male visitors today.

"He has visitors now. And, yes, there was a gentleman. He just left."

"Did he say who he was?"

"Family member, I think."

Alison thanked her and went to Crichton's room. Inside there was not only Mrs Crichton, but Marion Miller too. The two women stood at either side of the bed, staring at each other. Completely motionless and in silence. Alison wondered how long they had been like that. Their faces seemed set in stone, each, at first glance, as expressionless as the other. Even when the policewoman stepped inside they maintained their positions. The wife and the lover, acquaintances, at the very least, for over twenty years, united now in grief and betrayal. This stand-off was about seniority – which of them had most right to remain in the room. The partner of many years or the new companion. Who loved him most, who cared most, which of them suffered most and had more to lose?

After what seemed like nearly a minute, Marion Miller's face slowly dissolved into a grin.

"Your shot."

She was trying to look unconcerned, but it didn't quite work – the smile quivered at the corners and her eyes glinted less with arrogance than with tears. But she straightened her back, turned smartly around, passed Alison without a word and went off down the ward, heels clicking.

Clare Crichton stood in the same position for another half minute, still staring at the woman who was no longer there. Then she looked down at her husband, showing no emotion. He looked like a power multiboard adaptor, wires and tubes coming from every part of him. His mouth, stuck to his chest, under his sheet, on both wrists. There was a bandage over his forehead and monitors at either side, beeping and humming. Not having been in the force for long, WPC Morrison hadn't seen too many men struggling for life. She found the sight not so much frightening as just weird. Almost comic, like at any moment this extra from a medical TV show would sit up and ask for his make-up to be refreshed.

Clare Crichton sat down. Put her hand out to touch him, then withdrew it again. She made herself more comfortable in the little hospital chair, and tried again. She laid her palm on his shoulder, as if keeping it in place, her eyes fixed somewhere just over his bandaged head.

Alison sat in a chair in the corner of the room. What was etiquette? Was it okay to take out her phone? Text. Play *Minecraft, Angry Birds.* Check Facebook? She looked out the window where there was only a watery flavourless sky. She wondered what the point of staying here was. The man couldn't speak, and the woman was hardly likely to blurt out a full confession in front of her. Clare looked in such a dwam that Alison felt she could phone her boyfriend and chat and laugh and the woman wouldn't even notice.

"If you must stay here," Clare glared at her, "at least be decent enough not to look so bored."

"I'm sorry, I—"

"Go on, take out your phone. That's what you want to do, isn't it? Bill was the same, he wasn't alive unless he had that bloody phone in his hand. Now I know why."

WPC Morrison texted in that she was presently with Mr and Mrs Crichton and that Mr Hughes of Fulton Construction had been in earlier.

Maddy, having prepared notes for her preliminary hearing and trying to secure a first diet for Drummond versus Garner and Menzies of Giffnock Golf Club, was having her coffee and looking through maps online. Ordnance surveying wasn't her strong point, especially on screen, and she had to screw up her eyes, nose almost touching the glass or plastic or whatever it was made of. She'd found, throughout the Petrus case, difficulty in making head or tail of the architectural and site maps. She liked the look of some of them, thin straight lines, faint and perfect.

Dan McKillop came in, cycle helmet under his arm, lime-green jacket over his suit.

"Doesn't go with the tie, Dan."

He'd taken up cycling to work last spring. Maddy had burst out laughing when she first saw him mount his bike. He was so large and burly that the bike looked like a kids' toy. Watching him pedal off was a circus act, a bear on a mini cycle.

"Proud of you, though. Still at it in February."

He slumped down on the seat opposite her. "It's not easy, you know."

"I'm sure."

"The actual cycling is fine. It's this city. Everybody's that pass-remarkable. I had my lights on the other night – it's still dark by five. Two guys came out a pub as I was passing. "Haw, Billy, it's the Starship Enterprise." Fair enough I thought. Then his pal piped up. "It's transport, Cap'n, but no' as we know it.""

Maddy laughed.

"Then this morning my front wheel was rubbing a bit. So I dismounted and got down and had a look at it. This apprentice jakey – in his twenties but he was getting the hang of it – stops, looks down at me and goes, "Fix your bike right. Ya fucking prick."

After she stopped laughing, Maddy said it seemed reasonable. "Look at it from his point of view, Dan. He's walking down the street. He sees a fucking prick fixing his bike, and he offers encouragement and advice. Bikes are dangerous things."

"What're those?" Dan nodded towards the screen.

"Come round. Look. You can verify this. Three maps. This one is the Belvedere development site now, or at least the plans submitted eighteen months ago. This is the same area before construction started ... and *this* one is five years ago."

"What's the big grey area in the middle of that one?"

"I can see you'd be as much good orienteering as me. That, Daniel dear, is Costello Laboratories. Partially owned by Petrus International. Cathy Maguire is right."

"Who she? And about what?"

"You remember, nearly ten years back, the toxic leaks and illegal dumping we managed to connect with Petrus?"

"*We* nothing, all your own work, sweetheart."

"Polychlorinated biphenyls, and all sorts of other muck. God knows what Costello got up to in there. They closed down not long after we started snooping around. Cathy and Morag – the protestors at Fulton Construction – seem to think the site was never properly sealed."

"So what now? Nothing you can do but let Coulter's mob know."

"JCG Miller played a small role in all this, advising Petrus. They delivered their report to Forbes Nairne."

"Don't."

"But it's best that I talk to him, no? I know all about the Petrus case. I know the law. I know Nairne."

Dan got up. "I'm going to look at fancy houses in the *Herald*. I feel a promotion and a big wage rise coming up."

Maddy watched him close the door behind him. Perhaps

he was right. She should just hand over all the information to Coulter. Let him decide what to do with it.

Morag Boyd was waiting for them in an interview room, Coulter and Russell walking and talking.

"Nice night out with a couple of the lads from Glasgow East Command."

"Touring the pubs? Get anything?"

"East End's fair changed. New shops and bakeries and stuff all along Duke Street. Looks like, these days, dads don't leave their weans outside pubs wi' a bag of smoky bacon, but sip cappuccinos in cafés while Rufus and Arabella nibble paninis under the awning."

He laughed but Coulter felt there was something recited about the line. No doubt one of the local coppers had given him it and Russel's now claiming it as his own. "And the guns?"

"Everyone tight-lipped. Some punters seem to think that kind of business has moved west and south. I *did* however hear a name mentioned. Joe Harkins."

"The Fulton watchman?"

"He hangs about out there, has done for years. And when guns were mentioned everybody went a bit *too* tight-lipped." They arrived at the interview room. "Want me to bring him in?"

"Maybe. Maybe see what more we can find out first."

Coulter looked in through the glass in the door. A middle-aged woman was sitting up straight in her chair, waiting. She glanced at her watch, tapped her worn-down shoes and sighed.

"Just one of them? Where's the other?"

"She's Boyd," Russell said, "the other one – Maguire – couldn't see the point in taking up both their time."

"Oh couldn't she?" Coulter opened the door and put on his most hospitable smile.

Now that he was sitting across from her, Coulter saw that Morag was not middle-aged. It had been her clothes – still buttoned woollen coat, thick black tights like the ones Martha wore on cold days, sensible shoes – and her posture. But her shoulders rose a little as she spoke to him, and she tried to smile. Out of habit, Coulter thought, common manners.

"Thanks for coming in, Mrs Boyd."

"No problem." Again, the response was etiquette. She was as disconcerted as most people are in a police station.

"Forgive me if I get the business out the way first. Basic questions we have to ask everyone. Can you remember where you were, Mrs Boyd, a week last Friday night/Saturday morning?"

"Your colleague already asked me that. My son was in overnight at the hospital. We stayed with him."

"Our colleague?" Russell asked, already knowing the answer.

"Aye, the woman. Shannon?"

Russell rolled his eyes.

"All night?" Coulter pretended to take notes: this would all get checked out and reported back to him.

"Yes."

"You say 'we' Mrs Boyd. You and your husband?"

"Kenny, aye. You can check with the nurses. And the night porter."

"Between what times?"

"We'd have got there around, dunno, maybe half fiveish? We were a wee bitty late checking him in, then we left for work about eight?"

"You both left together?"

"Yes."

"Where do you work, Mrs Boyd?"

"In the café in Barmulloch Community Centre. It's a part-time job. Which suits the now, what with Jason and everything."

"And you got there at what time?"

"Before nine."

"Were you first in? Did you open up?"

"No. Molly's the café manager and Christina the centre director. They were both there."

"And Mr Boyd?"

"He was wi' me. He's a painter and plasterer and he's got some work now in the centre, sprucing up the Wi-Fi area of the centre's library."

"Thanks for all that." Coulter closed his notepad. "I know you have troubles of your own." Morag Boyd gave him a very slight forgiving hug. "You wouldn't happen to know where your friend…" he made a play of reopening the pad, "…Catherine Maguire, was at that time?"

Morag stiffened a little. "Eh, Friday night she was down the Canal. Our local. We were supposed to go too, but with Jason… There'd've been plenty of folk there."

"But in the morning…?"

"Cathy's no' an early riser. Especially after a Friday in the Canal."

"I see. Thanks. Shame she couldn't make it along herself."

"She couldn't. Telt me to tell you she'll speak to you whenever if it's still necessary."

"It might be, Mrs Boyd. Now, the following Tuesday afternoon…"

Morag's manners couldn't stop her from sighing.

Ninety minutes later CDI Coulter was walking down Saltmarket with Maddy Shannon. There was tension between them, and she knew he was annoyed with her. So what's new? Most people are, generally. She'd like to think she had no idea why that was but, truthfully, she was pissed off with herself half the time. Sergeant John Russell hated her. If she were him, she'd feel the same. Bloody woman always overstepping the mark. She sometimes caught herself in a bar or at a meeting, her voice too loud, talking too much, ugly big guffawing laugh. Even Dan, she reckoned, could get his fill quickly enough. Her mum too. Louis? Who knows. But Coulter – Maddy wanted *him* to like her.

"Alan, if you want to see him yourself, I'll cut off here."

"No. No. You're right. You'd have to fill me in on years of this Petrus thing. And you know the guy. I hear he likes you."

Thank God somebody does. From a distance of course – the man barely knew her. She was annoyed at herself for feeling a wee thrill of pleasure, though. The big important judge *liked* her. Well, didn't loathe her. Yet.

"So. Morag."

"Much as you said," she could hear the irritation in his voice. "She and her comrade think Fulton Construction have been up to dirty tricks."

"*Is* that what they're saying?" There she goes again. That note of keening insistence in her voice.

"Well isn't it?" Coulter was swallowing back his exasperation.

"I'm not sure they do know that. I think what they're saying," she tried, without total success, to keep her tone pleasant, informative, "is that the Costello chemical factory site might not have been properly sealed. Whether that's Fulton's doing, or Costello's, or Petrus, or any number of partially owned companies and interests…"

"In that case," Coulter seemed surer of his ground, "why direct their protests at Fulton and Belvedere?"

"Where else are they going to direct it?"

"DS Russell agrees with you."

"There's a first."

"He thinks we're hassling ordinary decent folk, when we should be focussing on greedy snobs of Killearn and Cleveden."

"Man's not all bad."

"And the Boyds' alibis pan out. They were sitting at their son's bedside in the Royal Infirmary at the time Miller was being shot, and both were at work in the community centre when Crichton fell. Staff in both places vouch for them."

They crossed the bridge in silence. Maddy resisted the urge to put her arm through Alan's. Where did that notion come from anyway? Trust me. *Like* me. You older professional man you.

"By the way," Coulter said. "Costello's. There's a missing file somewhere called Abbott. Connection?"

They were directed through to a room that Lord Nairne had more or less commandeered as his own. You can do that, claim public spaces, if you've got "Lord" in front of your name.

Maddy watched the two men size each other up. They'd met, somewhere along the line, never socially, always in a courtroom. Both, Maddy could see, were decided about their rank – Nairne had the title, was twenty years older and, on the occasions they had met, he was the guy in the high chair wearing a wig, poking questions at the middle-ranking policeman. He could afford to be magnanimous. Which he was, sitting back in his seat and ushering them in with a wide sweep of his arm.

"DI Coulter, good to see you, man." Then, with an even broader smile, "Miz Shannon, come awa' in!" Which, she knew – and the old man no doubt knew too – peeved Alan. "Shame it has to be over this ill-fared business." Nairne was old-school. The type of judge who traces his ancestry back to Lord Braxfield. "He'll be nane the waur for a guid hingin'" and all that malarkey.

"Miller, and now Crichton. Ach."

"You knew them both well, sir?" Coulter poshed up his voice a little, sitting a bit too far back in his chair, not succeeding at looking comfortable.

"Crichton not so well. Julian's been in front of me far more often."

"Good lawyer was he?"

"Aye, knew what he was aboot." Then a little smile. "Sometimes overplayed his hand."

"Was he good in the other sense?" Maddy had meant to keep quiet but, as so often, her mouth took on a life of its own.

"*What* ither sense would that be, Mizz Shannon?" He flicked an indulgent smile towards Coulter. Alan, she noticed, flicked one back. The wimmin, just cannae keep it zipped.

"You know – *good*. Fair."

He replied to the inspector. "The ladies like saints and sinners, eh? Guid men and bad boys."

"Kind of comes with the territory, don't you think sir?" She was relieved that Alan backed her up. "Isn't that what the law is all about?"

Now Nairne turned to her. "I just see people muddling through, lass. Sometimes getting it right, sometimes badly wrong. The way o' the world, Mizzz Shannon." Each time that "miz" was more pronounced.

"A murder and either a possible second murder or suicide," Alan said. "What would you call that, Lord Nairne – a bit unchancy?"

This meeting was turning out to be different from what Maddy had expected. The tables had turned: it was her and DI Coulter now against the grand old man of the law. She really did have a terrific talent for screwing up her career. Her only friend in the judiciary and now here she was riding shotgun to the local sheriff.

"The Petrus case..." Coulter began. Maddy helped him out. "Fiscal stopped work on the case five years ago. Petrochemical company. Costello Laboratories. Alleged illegal dumping."

"I mind it well."

"Fulton Construction Ltd," Coulter took up the baton, "are now building on the old site in Glasgow North East."

"Nought unusual aboot that. Land often gets built on, change of use."

"You read files and reports at the time, Miss Shannon tells me. We were hoping you might be able to shed some light on the matter."

"Ah I'm an aul' man, Inspector Coulter. And I've read several thousand reports and pleas and debates since then. But if memory serves me richt, you" – he looked directly at Maddy – "and the fiscals didna have near enough to proceed with any meaningful charges."

"I'm not so interested," Coulter interrupted him, "in Petrus. But in Fulton. Part of the evidence gathered, and which you took a judgement on sir, related to whether or not that site had been properly decontaminated before building the new houses began."

"Like I say, I cannae mind all the wee details, but we adjudicated at the time, if you remember Maddalena" – this was a new tack, using her Sunday name – "not to proceed to assize. It was thrown out at debate stage."

"Where can I get hold of the file you read, sir?" Coulter asked.

"JCG Miller should have the original. Three years ago, wasn't it? Just possibly it could have been destroyed – though I wouldna recommend that myself. Nae doot I'll have a copy – belt and braces, eh? I'll have it dispatched to you, Inspector."

"Thank you."

"Am I right in saying, Lord Nairne," Maddy tried to look meek, asking a simple ladylike question, "the complainants were a group of local residents?"

"Headed up by a bit of a nippy sweetie. A Mrs… Mrs…"

"Boyd," Coulter suggested.

"No. No memory of that name. No, a Mrs…"

"Maguire." Maddy said. "Cathy Maguire."

"That's the wifie!"

The meeting was over more quickly than they had planned for. Lord Nairne lost interest in the conversation. He returned to his reading, and only gave them a peremptory wave goodbye. At least it meant they had time on their hands. Maddy persuaded Alan to swing past Belvedere.

"I think we're wasting valuable time here." Coulter kept his eyes on the road. He was a careful driver. The one time that she had driven *him*, she thought he might give her a ticket.

"It's always bugged me how the Petrus case has been all but discarded."

"Then you might make some headway. But it's a waste of *my* time. Even if there's unfinished business, maybe even at Belvedere, what's it got to do with the killing of Julian Miller? We're too many stages removed, Maddy."

She didn't answer. She had a feeling he might be right. That she was getting two cases mixed up in her head.

As they travelled north a rare hint of winter sun welcomed them – like the sky was yawning but had every intention of dozing off again. The site was going like a fair. Must be nearly a hundred workers going about their mysterious business in cranes, tractors, on foot. You could begin to see the layout of the new scheme. Embryonic houses, budding streets and walls. Coulter parked but didn't get out the car. "They keep going at this rate, you'll have a hell of time getting back under the foundations."

The idea worried Maddy. "Maybe we don't have to. Maybe they can tell what's under there without actually knocking the whole place down again. Geiger counters or something."

"Isn't that for radiation?"

"Oh, yeah. But who knows – they might even pick some of that up."

"Unless of course the place *has* been properly sealed."

"So I'm wasting my time too?"

"Have to say, Maddy. Sounds like it's all been looked into. Courts and environment people were satisfied."

"So it would seem."

They both jumped a little when there was a knock on

Coulter's window. Tom Hughes, in full construction site regalia, was staring in at them.

"Just enjoying the view?" he shouted in. "Seriously, do you people not have any work to do?"

Coulter waited a moment before opening the power window.

"I hear you took some time off yourself this morning, Mr Hughes."

"Did you, aye?"

"Nice of you to visit a sick friend in hospital."

"Actually," Hughes put on a sad face, "My wee granny. She's no' weel."

"Mr Hughes, we *know* you went to see Bill Crichton."

"Oh right enough. I did pass by. After. Waste of time – man's a vegetable. Now if you don't mind, I'll get on." He walked away, then called back, "Want me to bring you out a picnic blanket?"

Coulter rolled the window up again. "Shit."

Maddy knew what bothered him was being seen with *her*. Why is the investigation leader hanging about with the fiscal? She reckoned, but didn't say it, that Hughes, even if he'd recognised her, was unlikely to know enough about the law to make that a problem.

They drove along the side of the site – nearly a mile, flat as a pancake, the natural shape and contours of the area lowered, elevated, reworked. That's what humans do, Maddy thought, pummel and restructure the lie of land. The *lies* of the land, she thought, once builders get their hands on it. Covering over the truth, burying the past. As they curled round the wide bend, new houses to their left, old houses to their right, they saw Hughes's watchman.

"Joe Harkins," Coulter nodded towards him.

Harkins was deep in conversation with another man, roughly the same age, dressed in civvies but otherwise he could be Harkins's brother. Mid height, wiry, unshaven, sallow skinned.

"And *that*," Maddy informed Alan Coulter, "is Kenny Boyd."

"Morag's husband?"

"Definitely him."

"Well, well," said Coulter, and drove off, happier now that the jaunt had perhaps been of some small value after all.

Maddy thought it was time she made someone's day. For her own reasons – but Doug Mason didn't need to know that. They met in Cafe Hula. A little bit of the West End that had got wedged somehow in Cowcaddens. It was her favourite morning and lunchtime meeting spot. Even better, on the odd occasion she managed it, to just sit and read, looking across at the Theatre Royal, and dream of a time when she might actually have a social and cultural life.

"Funny how things just carry on," Doug said getting stuck into a massive sandwich. "No Jules, no Bill, no idea who'll take their place. No one even certain who has the power to make those kinds of changes. We're all programmed, aren't we? We get on with our allotted duties until someone tells us to stop, here's your P45."

"Marion Miller? Wouldn't she be effectively in charge of the company now?"

"You're talking like poor Bill's kicked it. If he does... Possibly. There is an executive board. I believe Marion has a notional place on that, though I've never heard of her attending any meetings. The others are just hired-in people, to sign off the books, advise on staff development, that kind of thing."

Maddy deconstructed her sandwich – you'd need a mouth the size of the Clyde tunnel to bite it. "We're all hoping that dear Bill will make a full and hearty recovery. Doug, listen, I'm pretty sure this was before your time, but JCG Miller were hired, about three years ago, to answer a case made against Costello Laboratories, and possibly

Fulton Construction, by local residents around Belvedere."

"You're right. Before my time. I don't get it," he stopped eating, "why all the interest in these builders? The only connection I can see is that their boss happened to be dining with Bill and Jules the night before."

"Turning sleuth are we, Doug? And before you say it, I know, I know."

"What? That you like to dig about – pardon the pun, in this instance – in cases yourself? I'll have you know, I've always defended you, even before I met you, on that issue. That's what lawyers do! We have to, don't we, to understand? To know where we go next. In my case, how to defend an accused, in yours how to prosecute him. I don't see the problem."

"People actually talk about that?" Maddy was horrified. "Shit." Not so horrified she couldn't finish her lunch.

"Don't get me wrong. You're not the first topic of conversation every morning in every solicitors' in the city. But I have heard it mentioned, yes."

They chatted on about the murder, about Bill, work in general, and it took her a moment to realise that Doug had – impressively, she thought – brought the topic of conversation subtly round to relationships, and him and her.

"Let me speak plainly. I fancy the absolute arse off you."

"Why, sir, your words are like silk."

"But, alas, I know I must suffer alone for all time. You are spoken for."

"I've never understood that phrase. Let me reply in kind… You've got a nice tight butt, a promising career, and a stylish line in shoes, Mr Mason. You're a lying bastard – whatever it is you might 'fancy' it certainly ain't my arse – but let that lie for the moment. The truth is, even were I free, my jo, to court you, you'd find me a total fucking nightmare. The man I do have keeps a safe three thousand miles away."

She left, smiling at his offers of consolation should she

and her beau ever go their own ways. He was a bit of a prick, Doug, but as bits of pricks go he had his good points. Mainly that butt and those shoes.

Back at the office she got through as much work as she could. Sheriff and Summary stuff that she'd neglected badly. A few minor infringements of trading standards (two Southside pubs), several benefit frauds (she hated those – they made her think she was on the wrong side after all) and a complaint against the police (desperate stuff by a poor soul of a man).

There was a lot she could be doing but when Coulter emailed her Nairne's copy of the protestors' file she turned all her attention to that. For a couple of hours she read as carefully as she could, comparing times, dates, background data, precognitions, to her own files on Petrus and Costello. It was all disappointing. She'd been hoping for something new, something no one had spotted, not her or the Environment Protection Agency, or Nairne. But there was nothing. She could see why the case had been thrown out. She was spending far too much time chasing ghosts.

She talked, in passing, to Manda and Izzy, and once to Maxwell Binnie himself, about the Miller and Crichton case, but it was as plain as day that nobody was interested. Until it was time for the Crown Office and Procurator Fiscal Service to leap into action it wasn't their concern. And neither should it be hers.

"The soil's from a garden, a well-tended one." Bruce Adams, crime scene manager, read wearily from his notes. "Composites suffused with weedkiller."

"The sort of stuff you get at a garden centre?"

"I wouldn't know, DI Coulter. I'm more of a bowling man at weekends."

He bloody would be. "That's the stuff found around the murder scene? What about from the Millers' and Crichtons' gardens?"

"Still waiting for that report."

"For Christ's sake. How long does it take to poke about in a wee bit of garden crud?"

Russell pointed out that if it was indeed normal garden soil, then it would probably match. "But so would anyone's, no?" Then he laughed, "If it is just common or *garden* soil." This time the joke was his own, and that doubly delighted him.

"No, Sergeant," Adams looked as if boredom might grind him to a complete halt any minute, "the science is a bit more discriminating than that."

"You think?" Coulter said. "After all this time, I do hope so."

Adams shuffled off. Russell did the wanking gesture behind his back. Coulter just smiled. "Kenny Boyd. Anything on him?"

"Fifteen years of age," Russell read from his screen, "done for attempted break-in. Children's Panel and the house-owner dropped it. Social Work and the school took over from there. Seems to have kept his nose clean since. Or, more likely, he's got better at not being caught." He scrolled down. "Twice fined for driving with no insurance, but he seems to have wangled his way out of those too."

"What does he do? I mean, do we know where he works?"

"House painter and decorator, I'm told."

"Who by?"

"Gave his wee pal, Joe Harkins, a ring."

"You told him I saw them together?"

"I did."

"How did he react?

"Never realised you could shrug over the phone. Kenny, he says, finds his own work. Sounds like odd jobs to me. Including, wouldn't you know, gardening work. Fulton Construction have hired him in the past. Contract stuff. No doubt he's hoping for a bit of painting and decorating once the Belvedere houses are up."

Coulter held up an empty coffee carton. "I'm going for another shot of caffeine. Want one?"

Russell shook his head. "HOLMES boys have got some interesting info on Mrs Crichton. Clare – née Ross – was sectioned in New Craigs Psychiatric Hospital in Inverness. When she was a teenager, and only for a short while." He read from his screen: "The lack of any further medical records would suggest she had made a full recovery. Her case notes from 1987 diagnosed her as having social anxiety disorder."

"Who sectioned her?"

"GP, and parents, apparently with Clare's consent."

"See if we can speak to anyone who treated her back then."

"I'm on to it. I've said all along, the woman's a pure dafty."

Coulter pretended not to hear, opening the door. But Russell wasn't finished yet.

"Oh and Mrs Goldie came to see me. She's worried about Zack."

"What did you tell her?"

"Usual spiel. Not making any accusations, line of inquiry, blah blah. She says, hasn't the boy gone through enough, finding a dead body like that, without the police threatening him and making a meal out of nothing? Tell you one thing but – Mrs Goldie? Tits out of *Baywatch*, face out of *Crimewatch*."

Coulter closed the door behind him.

Was it possible that Stuart Anderson didn't just walk to Byres Road that morning, but further, all the way into town? To Merchant's Tower. Maddy microwaved a shop-bought vegetable moussaka, kept the cork firmly on the bottle of wine sitting tantalisingly on the worktop, and let her thoughts roll, not trying to organise them in any way.

The times fitted. Samantha had no idea what time he got home. He could easily have gone into town, done the deed, and maybe got a taxi or a train home. But why would Stuart Anderson want to kill Julian Miller? It was his own work that agitated him, not his wife's. A tryst between Sam and Jules was ridiculous. Sam was a nice enough looking lady, but shagging on the boss's table? No way. She didn't seem Miller's type. Then again, maybe everything in a skirt was Miller's type.

Was Stuart Anderson capable of such a cold-blooded crime? Who knows? He was a total mystery, not only to Maddy, it seemed, but to his own wife. Presumably he was a semi-decent organiser, so planning and executing the job might be a skoosh for him. Acquiring the guns? He wouldn't know where to start looking. No. She dismissed the idea.

She settled down in front of her laptop and Skyped Captain Louis Casci of NYPD. His email said he was working from home that afternoon. It was five past seven here, so five past two stateside. Louis was already smiling when the webcam came on, sitting at his kitchen table, a mug of coffee in his hand. Maddy remembered that table, even that mug. The whole layout of the little flat in Queens.

"I wish I was there with you."

"No you don't. There's a storm coming. They say it's going to dump more than six inches of snow on us."

"Great. I love snow."

"Not in this city."

They talked idly about nothing in particular, like an old married couple chatting in one kitchen instead of two. But he had bad news for her: he didn't think he could make it over to Glasgow in the next few weeks after all. She was disappointed, of course she was, but she couldn't help feeling a bit of relief too. Just the hassle of it all, getting the house ready, getting work out the way, organising interesting activities for them both. She felt a physical pang of not being able to touch him. Only now that the visit was in doubt did she realise that she was as horny as hell and had been really looking forward to the sex. To hell with interesting activities, she could shut shop and the two of them go at it like bunnies night and day.

"Some kind of virus," he was saying. "Half the force is down. Once you get it it seems to take about a month before you're back on your feet. And the work is building up as it is."

From that point on the conversation took a darker turn. His story sounded right, but when you're halfway across the world, how could she know, for sure? She felt guilty about deciding to check the net later, see if there were any reports of viral outbreaks in New York City. Maybe he just didn't want to come over.

They both tried to steer away from it, but the always to be avoided but inescapable relationship discussion had decided it was going to get them. Dump itself on them, and a damn site more than six inches' worth.

It was like driving at night-time, you followed a narrow beam of light that only showed you a few yards up the road, no notion of what was all around you. Then you ended up somewhere with no map of the journey you'd just made. Out of the blue, it seemed, they were talking about difficulties between them, bringing up old squabbles, blowing them out of proportion. Even the possibility of breaking up. How did they *get* here, and so swiftly?

"What are you saying, Louis? That we take a break?"

"What are *you* saying, Maddy? But maybe we should consider it."

"How the fuck can you take a break from a relationship which is one long, three-thousand-mile break as it is?"

She remembered a line from an old Gerry Rafferty song: "Talked all night and left it all unsaid." But that wasn't the problem with these kinds of rows. It was not knowing what the other person was saying. Reading between the lines where maybe there really was only blank space. Not knowing what you were saying *yourself*. Reinterpreting your own words, suddenly attaching meaning to moods and thoughts that had meant nothing half an hour ago. Becoming suspicious of every word.

She was exhausted at the end of it. Couldn't remember what she had said. Some of it wasn't nice. Voices had been raised but she couldn't say exactly over what. At other times they had soothed each other, but that only served to irk them both more. Which of them was the soother and which the soothee? Louis had been the calmer of the two, she thought. Maybe too calm. Maybe not seeing the importance of this discussion. Maybe he didn't think it *was* all that important. Maybe it had always been a more casual thing for him.

When they had first met each other, nearly five years ago, they had fallen together like pieces from a flat-pack kit. It had surprised and delighted them both. Before, they had been stiff, odd-shaped bits of wood with no purpose. Suddenly they were a comfortable sofa bed, a solid set of matching bedside tables. She'd thought they still were, despite all the downsides, the lack of bodily contact – or rather the intermittent lack followed by a superabundance of it. She opened the wine.

How flimsy relationships are! Shoogling on a base of a rocky conglomerate of assumptions, hopes, promises, feelings; the lies of the land again. And how quickly it can all subside. Two hours before switching off his face on the screen they had been laughing and joking. By the end of it she had heard herself saying: "I'll give you a week. A week to think about it."

"Okay," was all he'd said.

She was scouring the house searching for a cigarette in a pocket or bag somewhere, then, as if the fates had decided to take her out to play with tonight, Mad Packie was on Facebook. "I'll be over in Glasgow in a week or so. Can we meet, Flutterby?"

Jaysus Murphy.

In the morning she phoned Cathy Maguire. Her voice an accurate representation of her mental state: rigid, harsh, a brittle shell to protect her emotions. The two women agreed to meet at the far end of the Belvedere site. The minute she'd made the arrangement she wished she hadn't.

She drove, her body rigid too, so much so she could feel the strain in her neck. Keeping blinking to a minimum – she'd be dammed if even a passing motorist spotted watery eyes. There's staying strong, and there's white-knuckling it. Think about the case. Not him.

For as long as she could remember work had been her therapy. In primary school she'd burrowed her head deeper in spelling exercises and times tables when Mamma and Dad started arguing. In secondary she got her head round subjects that baffled her when there were problems in her personal life: fallouts with friends, weight gain, boys. From university on, the law was her escape, her therapist. Hunt down the bad bastards who smudged the world with their greed and cruelty and stupidity. Somehow it felt like revenge, too, on her parents, her body, her disappointments. Now here she was, beginning to feel indifferent about the murder of Julian Miller and Bill Crichton's little accident. Rich, self-satisfied lawyers – why the hell was she going out her way to find justice for *them*?

What in God's holy name had happened last night? A standard Skype session had turned into a car crash. Not that any of it was new. They'd simply voiced problems, fears, she'd had since day one. She'd suspected Louis had them too, now she knew for sure. And they'd allowed those doubts to take over. Like a sudden wind had ripped off the top of their house; something you couldn't see, couldn't touch, control, was blowing them apart. It wasn't a fair fight.

She couldn't contemplate the possibility of a rival, a real flesh-and-blood woman within Louis' reach. No, it was merely the configuration of any relationship, magnified by distance and a bloody great ocean. Where they had got to, where they were going. Both late to this romance it felt time was running out, yet the ache she felt now was as intense as a first love affair. But what truly annoyed her was that she had handed him all the power. Take a week to think about it? What the feck had got into her? She'd forgotten that love affairs involve power.

Lovers like to believe that power and control belong to the cold worlds of work, politics, probably the lesser relationships of other people. Your own love life was all trust and passion and mutual understanding, no leader, no follower. It's not true. And now she'd handed him on a plate every scrap of dominance and influence. She didn't think he'd manipulated the situation – she prayed he couldn't have – to get to precisely this point, win the strategic high ground. Surely to God he wasn't relishing it? Maybe still hadn't even realised that she was now a plaything in his hands.

She was at Belvedere before she knew it. She spotted Cathy Maguire on a street corner, up a little hill, looking down over the site. She was with someone else. A man, but he had his back turned, lighting a cigarette or on his phone. She couldn't see how to drive into that street so she parked by the temporary fencing surrounding the site, some way away from them.

Louis wasn't emotionally unintelligent. He was a cop – the workings of the human mind and emotions were his domain. He must understand the impossible situation he'd placed her in; how much he'd weakened her. Yet no sympathetic email or text had arrived. No wee note to level the playing field between them. She'd said she'd give him a week. She wasn't going to revoke that now. But come on, if there was anything between them, if he was a caring man, he'd ease her passage through that eternity-long seven days. If he doesn't, and soon, she might be taking a decision of her own first.

Cathy Maguire and Kenny Boyd must have thought she was a nutjob: so lost in her thoughts, head down, she almost barged into them before seeing them.

"So tell me, Miss Shannon," Cathy didn't give her time to recover. "Are you here to help us, or frame us? Maybe you still don't know yersel'."

The woman was right. What was she doing here? What did she hope would come of it?

"I just want to get to the truth, Cathy."

"The truth will oot?" Just like Maddy's *nonno* used to say, but his Scots-Italian accent made the idea sound less cynical. "Ye shall know the truth, and the truth shall make you mad."

"You just make that up?" Kenny asked, more bewildered than impressed.

"Aldous Huxley." Cathy informed him. Kenny didn't seem to recognise the name.

Though they were only a few feet above the flattened ground of the site below them, it felt like they were standing on the summit of a small mountain. Cold northerly gusts blew their coats and hair, chip pokes and general litter tumbled around their feet. Cathy pointed out across the valley below like a general surveying the battlefield.

"See? The site extends right up to our gardens. And underneath it, the dump. Right on our doorsteps."

"It's a windy day," Kenny said, not looking at Maddy. "On a still day, you can smell it. Specially in the summer."

"Where's Mrs Boyd today, Kenny?" Maddy asked.

"She's wi' Jason."

"That's your son?"

"Tell her, Kenny."

Kenny looked long and hard over the view before him. Past the site, over condemned tower blocks, towards Glasgow University tower and the distant spires of the affluent Park area.

"He's got a tumour on his spine."

"I'm sorry." So it was Morag and Jason she'd seen at the Royal Infirmary the night of Bill Crichton's accident. "How is he?"

"How do you think?" Cathy snapped.

"Touch-and-go," Kenny said, turning to her for the first time. "They're going to operate."

"When?" Maddy asked.

"Soon. Sooner the better."

"You see now?" Cathy almost shouted. "They're still poisoning us!"

"You think Jason's tumour has something to do with the dump?"

"My dad died of emphysema. Three months ago. Cancer rates in this area are sky-high. Emphysema, liver damage, disability in babies, all of them way higher than the national average. Naebody's counting any more, not officially – you've all lost interest in us – but I can assure you that things haven't got any better since they were supposed to have decontaminated and sealed it up for Fulton here."

"There must have been a lot of disappointed people round here since the case failed."

"Well you'd know. You had a hand in it."

"Not me, Cathy. I was collating the Petrus case – Costello Laboratories were just a footnote in that process. And Fulton started building long after we'd stopped pursuing the matter."

"Hear that, Kenny? We're a *footnote*. Wee Jason's in italics at the bottom of a page." She turned to Maddy. "Some old geriatric judge takes it up his hump tae not sour his sherry with our wee lives. Disappointed hen? Oh, much, much, more than disappointed."

"I can understand people being angry at everyone involved. Including JCG Miller."

"Oh here we go. Back to the mental murderers of Glasgow East." She stared, furious, at Maddy, then turned to Kenny. "What chance did they have anyway, the lawyers?

Up against multi-internationals, the entire petrochemical lobby?"

"Hang on, hang on." Maddy was confused. "*Against* Costello and Petrus?"

"That bastard Tom Hughes. Ruthless. Greedy thug. I wouldn't be surprised if he'd done Miller in just for trying. Just for speaking to us at all."

"Sorry, Cathy, are you telling me that Julian Miller *represented* you?"

"Hear that Kenny – Miss Shannon doesn't seem to know much about us at all. Who'd have guessed."

"But I thought – *we* thought... Christ."

Coulter and Russell stood facing each other like kids in a playground. Amy, between them, wondered if she should chant "Fight, fight!"

"I gave *you* the job of going through Miller's and Crichton's files, John!"

"And I gave them to the legal boys, to HOLMES, and left a copy on *your* desk!"

"How could you not have noticed that they were representing the protestors?!"

"I'm a fuckin' policeman, not a lawyer. How come your pal Maddy Shannon didn't know till now? She's all over this like a case o' hives. Can't an assistant depute procurator fiscal tell the difference between defence and prosecution?"

That stumped Inspector Coulter, but he stood his ground. It was Amy who broke the deadlock. "Isn't the question – if you men don't mind me saying – not how we or COPFS didn't know, but why nobody at JCG Miller knew. Or told us."

Coulter stepped back. Russell rolled his shoulders as if, being the second to move away, he'd won the fight.

"Julian Miller was dead before he could tell us. Bill Crichton can't speak. And, anyway, they *did* tell us – in the files and records. Which *you*," he wasn't going to let Russell get away with this, "were the responsible officer for!"

"You're forgetting that they lost the Fulton file."

"And then there's that Abbott one," Amy said, trying to help. "And there's someone else who could have told us. Tom Hughes. Why wouldn't he mention that JCG Miller were on *his* side?"

Amy was the only one of the three being professional here, Coulter thought. He and Russell were acting like a couple of badly trained pit bulls; she was calm, thinking it through.

"Get him in here!" Once you start shouting, it's hard to stop.

Now he'd have to go and pass the news of this blunder up the line. Blunder? Catastrophe. Crawford Robertson will go nuts. The deputy chief constable will lose no time in pointing out that, while Detective Sergeant Russell was at fault, *he*, Detective Inspector Coulter, is where the buck stops.

Why is that? Why doesn't it stop at Robertson? Go all the way up the line. Not that he'd actually say that, of course. And anyway maybe it did. The DCC had committees, boards, councils to report to. And the press loved hauling him over the coals. Geez, this was going to be one hell of a meeting.

Having phoned the site, Amy and John Russell made their way into the city centre. Tom Hughes was in Fulton Construction HQ today.

"Shysters," Russell said. "JCG Miller. All lawyers. Do anything for money."

He was still smarting from the row with Coulter. Face still flushed, but a hangdog slouch to his gait. Amy could see he knew he'd screwed up big time.

"*That's* where we should be looking. The Millers, the Crichtons – mark my words, Amy, this is going to turn out to be a sleazy wee tale of greedy lawyers and greedier wives. I'm beginning to feel sorry for Hughes and his mob. They know we're wasting our time and theirs."

And that did indeed seem to be the way Hughes looked at it. He led them into his office. Russell had been to the HQ before, Amy hadn't. On the second storey of an old red sandstone Victorian building in Wellington Street. A bit crumbly on the outside, not much better inside. But it was clearly a bigger company than she'd realised. Twenty or more staff here alone she reckoned.

"What now?" Hughes barked.

Russell kept his voice meek and soft. "Sorry, Tom, I know this must be a hassle. But listen, we won't keep you long. It's just something ... that we realised a while back, but I never got round to asking you. The lawsuit that was brought against you and Costello Laboratories—"

"First, it wasn't a lawsuit as you call it. It was a report, and the law said it was all in order. Second, if there had been an actual lawsuit it would have been brought against Costello, or one of their holding companies, not us. They were responsible for decontamination, not us."

"According to the report," Amy said, "or what I've seen of it, decontamination was a specialist job for Costello, but the final sealing was part of Fulton Construction's contract."

"A technical detail."

"Anyway," Russell gave Amy a warning look, then smiled again at Hughes, "what we wanted to confirm with you is that JCG Miller were acting against Fulton Construction."

"Correct."

"I'm just surprised you never mentioned that."

"You never asked. And I assumed," Hughes was beginning to put two and two together, "that you lot had done your homework."

"We did notice," Amy stepped closer to Hughes, and away from Russell, "that Fulton have had JCG Miller on your books as advisers for nearly ten years. Since before the decontamination issue. Isn't that unusual, sir? Your own solicitors acting against you?"

"You know, hen, you need to brush up on your law.

There's nothing illegal in that. Or even unusual. They have lots of clients, we have lots of clients. Glesga isnae that big a place. Sometimes you find yourself playing for the other team against your pals."

"Thank you for your co-operation, Mr Hughes. Though, if I may say, this isn't a *game*."

Hughes glowered at her.

"Cheers, Tom," Russell said, rushing out, "Sorry to bother ye."

The magic hour, at this time of year flaxen and filmy, brews slowly into a thick greeny light. The slightest hint of aurora borealis over Glasgow's splintered skyline. The air a cold draught of hills and wilderness just beyond the stone and concrete of the city. Depending on your state of mind, it's either dreamy or nightmarish.

WPC Morrison was back on duty in Bill Crichton's room. Police work can be dull, but this was driving her mad. She wondered if Clare Crichton was just ahead of her in the breakdown stakes.

The woman had taken to singing to her catatonic husband. Fair enough, but Elton John?

"I miss the earth so much, I miss my wife…" she half sang, half spoke it. "And I think it's going to be a long, long time." She played with his hair, but Alison felt it was just for something to do. She never *looked* at him. "Your eyes have died…" Alison was pretty sure that was from a completely different song.

Then Marion Miller arrived. All kitted up. Every single time she brought grapes and sweets which WPC Alison Morrison shared with the nurses afterwards. And books. One for herself and one for Bill, which she put on his chest then took away with her at the end. She never read her own book either, eventually picking up magazines – *House & Garden, New Scientist, Heat* – from the pile beside Alison's

175

chair. The two unread books, the policewoman noticed, were called *On the Heroism of Mortals* and *Aliyyah*. Marion also had her phone at the ready, texting in spurts over the two or three hours she stayed, alternating that with refreshing her make-up. The woman had an impressive arsenal of lipsticks, powders and creams. Unlike Clare she seldom ever spoke – and certainly never sang – to the man motionless on the bed.

It was the same rigmarole every time. Clare Crichton would be there first, from mid-morning. Marion would take over in the afternoon. Late evenings until after nightfall it was back to Clare again. And every time, at the changing of the guards, Mrs Crichton kept Mrs Miller waiting. The wife saw the floozy outside the door, made a point of hanging on for another half hour at least, while the bit on the side stood outside, pretending to text. When Clare finally did give ground they passed each other without a word or a glance.

Maddy sat in her kitchen, staring into space, coat still on. She'd been like that for nearly half an hour. She didn't know which body blow to concentrate on. Her and Louis. Her dad suddenly threatening to pop up. Worst of all, getting the wrong end of the stick at work. If nothing else Alan Coulter will think less of her. Read everything carefully – it had always been a golden rule.

But what did it mean, Miller acting against Fulton? Maybe nothing in particular. It wasn't unheard of, friendly solicitors who ended up on the other side of the table from their usual client. And did it shine any light on either the murder, or the pollution cases? Her brain went round in circles: Louis, Miller, Packie, Fulton.

She nearly jumped out her skin when her mobile rang. The Beach Boys' "Barbara Ann" would have to go.

"It's Alan."

"Listen. I'm sorry. I've been thinking—"

"Forget that now. As representative of the Crown Office and Prosecution Service you have the right to come round here."

"Where?"

"The Millers' house. Killearn. I'm standing in the living room right now, looking at the dead body of Tom Hughes. He's been shot through the heart."

The night outside, for Maddy rushing to her car, felt distinctly nightmarish.

III

We all hide, don't we? Hide from the world, behind a hundred masks. Who we are to our mothers is not the part we play for fathers. I am a completely different person with friends to the child the teacher once knew. We're mysteries to ourselves: how many times a week, a day, do you tell a different story to yourself? About yourself.

We look back on our lives and can't trace the journey that brought us here. What made us do the things we did.

But something drove us. Some self-regulating system that understands the whole of everything? Determined chaos. The butterfly effect.

We can't know ourselves, so nobody knows us. You think you do. Your brother, colleague, friend. The man next door. To you, he's a gent, picking up your post, always a smile on his face. To his neighbour on the other side he's noisy, nosy, a peeping Tom.

Nobody knows me. They all think they do. Have me summed up. But where am I when they're not around? A whole secret life they would never imagine – a lover, a spy, an Internet troll, closet drinker? Where do I go, when they're not looking? Do I … lie out in the rain? Hide under the stairs? The bookworm in the library, reading, perhaps, about the Big Bang. Assignations in dark alleys, being instructed in the use of firearms?

I don't know myself. But *something* does. Some

innate force, maybe, a fundamental imperative. Not forcing me – I am not using that coward's defence – but guiding me.

Each step is made clear to me, at the key moment.

It never failed to fill her with trepidation. The police cars and ambulance, lights flashing, the scurry of professionals and the rubberneckers gathering. Death was only a few feet away, inside that elegant, upmarket house. She had a feeling that one day it would be her, lying there, twisted and lifeless, terror etched on her face. Inspector Coulter came out to meet her, his finger lightly and briefly touching her arm.

"In the office, upstairs. I'll show you."

They stopped at the main door. A middle-aged man, with the look of a reformed villain about him, spoke to Coulter. "If he broke in, he knew what he was doing. Look. The wiring for the alarm's been neatly detached. No cutting. He had precisely thirty-five seconds to find the box, open it, and disconnect the wires without setting it off."

"How about the door? Doesn't look as if he kicked it in."

"No. Either someone opened it from the inside, or he had a key. Or," the man, built like a tank, pointed at the Yale lock, "he picked it. Can't be sure right now, but see they wee scrapes there? Again, skilful job." The wee chunky man looked impressed.

"Tricks you learn in a lifetime in the building trade?"

On their way upstairs, joining the traffic of men and women going up and down, some with the spacesuits on, some in uniform, others in civvies with clipboards, or cameras, or talking urgently into mobiles, they passed the open door into a spacious lounge. Sitting on the couch, her head in her hands, coat still on, was Marion Miller. A uniformed policeman was offering her a cup of tea but she wasn't hearing him.

"Have we confirmed what time she arrived home?" Coulter asked Amy Dalgarno, standing by the door.

"Her times match with WPC Morrison's. She left the Royal at twenty past midnight. Got here just after one."

Coulter nodded and continued on up the stairs. He

hadn't directly invited her but Maddy followed anyway.

SOCOs and forensics were still at work in the office. Maddy and Coulter could only peek in. She could just see, to one side of the room, the bulky cadaver of Tom Hughes. He, too, hadn't got round to taking off his coat. He was lying among a guddle of papers, ring binders, books. Looking around she saw they'd been swept off shelves and the top of the large desk at the back wall.

"He was looking for something."

"Or someone was," Coulter corrected her. "We don't know if the search was done before or after he was killed."

"No sign of the gun this time?"

"It'll turn up, and soon. It was left in plain view for us at the Crichtons'. Some bastard's playing musical coffins."

Bruce Adams came out to see them. He pushed up his goggles and unhooked his Piccola mask – Maddy thought that his face had more expression when it was covered – and spoke to Coulter, half turning his back on the fiscal.

"First impressions. He's facing this way, right arm outstretched. I reckon he was over by the desk, heard the killer at the door, made a rush at him, trying to grab the gun."

"How clean was the shot?" Maddy asked.

Adams answered Coulter. "Looks neat enough to me. Certainly close to the heart if not bullseye. Holloway thinks he died pretty quickly. No sign of scratching or shuffling."

Holloway, police doctor and pathologist, was bent over Hughes's body, getting a photographer to take close-ups of skin, hair, nails. Doc Holloway: in his mid fifties, balding and ruddy, he was the least likely gunslinger ever.

"No chance it could be the other way round?" Coulter was really just wondering out loud. "Someone else was doing the looking, pulling everything off the shelves, he comes in … they dance around each other, swap positions…" He wasn't even convincing himself. "Have any other rooms been ransacked?"

"No." Adams's words were like turds falling into a toilet.

Thank God he had few of them. "This was Julian Miller's home office."

Maddy spoke the words that, this time, Coulter kept to himself. "So Hughes was looking for something work-related."

They chimed in together: "The Abbott file."

They made their way, like squeezing past late-night shoppers in a mall, down to the living room.

"How did he get here? Hughes. I didn't see a car outside."

"Left it out of view?"

As they were about to go in the living room Coulter tugged one of the constables' arms. "You know Detective Sergeant Russell? Minute he gets here tell him to get every car within a half-mile radius checked. Registrations, makes, the lot. And a door to door – did anyone hear Mr Hughes arriving, or his car."

Maddy thought that Marion Miller was still sitting there alone, the cup of tea still sitting untouched beside her. The room was so large it took her a moment to spot DS Dalgarno, almost swallowed up in a colossal couch. Dalgarno nodded to them both and gave Maddy a quick half-smile. She was less resistant to the PF's presence, but not so bold as to let any of her colleagues know it. Quite right.

"Marion, you've met Detective Inspector Coulter." Maddy hung back near the door and Amy took the hint not to introduce her. "Are you okay? Is there anything I can get you?"

Mrs Miller didn't react to the question. Coulter took a different tack from his junior officer. He marched over and stood directly in front of her. "Mr Hughes a regular visitor is he?" His tone was cold, accusatory. It seemed to rouse Miller out of her stupor.

"What? I'm sorry. I..."

Maddy watched Coulter; he was pissed off. This case was having a bad effect on everyone.

"I hardly know the man." Miller looked up at him, a slow and tired student struggling with the classwork. "But he has been here before, to see Julian."

"Mrs Miller. Your husband's been killed. Your boyfriend's fallen out a window, and now a house guest has ruined the carpet. What was he doing here?"

If Coulter's intention had been to rile her, it worked. Marion Miller shot up out of her chair. "I have no idea!"

"You just came back from the hospital and found him?"

The woman stomped off towards the door. "You think I did this? Killed Julian too? And, what, persuaded Bill to jump out his window? Maybe I assassinated JFK."

"You're up to your oxters in bodies, Mrs Miller!" She didn't stop to answer but stormed out the room.

Maddy decided it was time for her to leave too. She'd been lucky Russell was late. No point in pushing it, best to leave the police to get on with their work. She slipped quietly out the room while Coulter and Dalgarno were deep in a confab. As she did, she noticed, because it looked out of place, a medal on a ribbon lying on an occasional table by the door. Odd, it was exactly the same as the one she had in her office, gifted her by some forgotten client. Marion and Julian didn't have kids, though it was the kind of bauble you might give to children at a school sports day. Clare and Bill were childless too. All these people too caught up, like herself, in work, or too aware of their own inadequacies to want to reproduce themselves. She couldn't imagine Marion Miller running races, even less so Jules. Yet there, in a room otherwise furnished in meticulous and expensive fashion, was a medal just like hers. There must be millions of these cheap trinkets littering most homes and offices she decided, as she slunk past the various professionals in the hall, and out into the night.

The rain had come on, her wipers clearing the windscreen of water but not her eyes. Glasgow at night, sleek and inky and not quite empty. She didn't feel like driving straight home, so she turned up streets on a whim at the last moment. She wondered how many of the few cars she passed were doing the same. Going round in circles, heading nowhere in particular. Staying away from, rather than going to, some place. She thought of Stuart Anderson: it's a risky thing to do, just roam. You may end up in the wrong place at the wrong time; you may do something you hadn't intended to. Or people might think you have.

Back at the Miller house everything they were uncovering just begged more questions. Adams came out into the porch where Coulter and Dalgarno were bringing Russell up to speed. He'd dozed off watching a Rangers game on the telly, hadn't heard the phone or the radio.

"Pack of fags, four left in it." He held it up, bagged, for the others to see. "Lying under Hughes's body. Looks like they fell out his pocket, but it could also be the killer's."

"Rothmans," Russell peered at it in the meagre light. "Hughes was MD of a big construction company. Those are about the cheapest ciggies you can buy. Not his style, surely?"

"Let's hope we get prints from it," Coulter said.

"And soil," Adams said. "Traces of it on the stairs and the office floor, by the door."

"Gloves again."

"Unless Mrs Miller was doing some gardening in the last couple of days."

"And then went up to her dead husband's office?" Coulter was sceptical. "Three men went out to dinner the Friday before last. Now two are murdered and the other one's in a coma."

"I've had nights out like that," Dalgarno said.

Nobody had slept much, and tempers weren't much better than they had been last night. The murder weapon had been found, early in the morning during the fingertip search, by a constable. It had been pushed down deep into branches of a bush in a garden three doors along.

"Glock 19?"

"From the same batch," Russell said.

"What kind of murderer, with a long list, throws away his gun every time!"

"One who thinks each killing will be his last?" said Amy.

"So something's actually happening out there, now, between these people? The shooter's reacting to events? But we've had these people under our noses for the last fortnight."

"We're not actually surveilling them." Russell felt they should have been. "Stuff could be happening under those noses of ours. In their houses, on the phone."

Coulter turned to Amy. "First Glock was in a bin in the car park of Merchant's Tower. We couldn't miss it. The second was actually laid out for us—"

"Though it wasn't actually used."

"But making it clear it would have been? But this one... Pushed down into a shrub. That looks like some kind of attempt at concealment. Different MO?"

"Not a very great attempt," Russell said.

"In which direction was this shrub? East, west, of the Millers' house? Where was the killer heading, straight after? Back to a car?"

"He would have to, there aren't any buses in and out of Killearn late at night. It's not on a train line."

"Unless, of course it was a local. Like Marion Miller." Russell snarled her name. "Stirlingshire's own Tina fucking Turner."

"Her times fit, John."

"Aye but do they, Amy? She floors it all the way back from the Royal. Does it in under half an hour. Plenty of time to pull a trigger, mess up a room, and phone us."

"We're all assuming here," Coulter sat down, "that we're looking for *one* killer. Maybe it's not. Could be a game of pass the pistol."

"In a prearranged order?" Amy subconsciously copied

her boss and sat. "Or, like you say, each killing leads to the next—"

"—a different killer each time. Somebody, somewhere needs to talk. Christ they're falling like flies and we're nowhere!"

"Crichton," Russell said.

"Amy, go see the doctors. Tell them we need to wake Rip Van Winkle out of his beauty sleep."

Maddy had ended up at her mother's house. She had no idea why. She'd parked, opened the door quietly with her key, taken off her coat and lain down on the couch. She'd woken a couple of hours later, the February early dawn pushing dingily against the window.

She'd made a pot of tea, not worrying about making a noise – Rosa di Rio had always slept the sleep of a cherub. She'd taken it in to her and finally, almost an hour later, Mamma emerged, in a green satin chemise, face shining with cream. How could it be that her sexagenarian mother looked more glamorous than she did, even first thing in the morning?

"Ai, Maddalena," Rosa looked at her pityingly, "you need to get more sleep. Or something."

Should she tell Rosa about Packie? Her parents hadn't seen each other in twenty years, more. Since Dad walked out there had been virtually no communication, except through lawyers and third parties. Maddy had never told Rosa when Packie had got in touch with her. It had taken her mamma years to get over the hurt, the shock, and now, when the woman seemed to have nearly forgotten, he was threatening to turn up in Glasgow. He probably won't, anyway, so no point in creating a fuss. And even if he did, and Maddy did see him, Rosa wouldn't have to know.

"Dante has disappeared."

"What do you mean, disappeared?"

"Disappeared. Gone. Hey presto, whoosh."

Maybe she *would* send Mad Packie to her – God knows the woman loves bloody drama. "What, into thin air?"

"Exactly! Your cousin Gina says his house is like the *Mary Celeste*. No sign of packing a suitcase, but he's not been home in weeks, doesn't answer his phone. Puf!" She clicked her fingers. "Just like that. No more Dante."

"Weeks, Mamma? You and I were with him last week."

"Well, days." Rosa poured herself another cup of tea.

"How many days?"

"I don't know! I'm just telling you what your cousin Gina said."

"And when did my cousin Gina tell you this – about my cousin Dante?"

"Last night." She sat down across the table from Maddy. "And it's your fault."

"Oh gawd. Here we go."

"If you had helped him… Maybe he wouldn't have done it."

"Done what? No, don't tell me."

"Run away. Jumped in the river, blown his brains out for all I know."

Maddy rolled her eyes. "He'll turn up." Maybe Dante really was family – a tendency towards overreaction. "And anyway there was nothing I could do to help."

"If you want to believe that."

"I thought you said I was working too hard? But I have to run and help every member of the extended di Rio clan?"

"I didn't say you were working too hard, dear. I said you weren't getting enough sleep. Look at you, big black eyes, puffy face. Just as well your boyfriend is far away."

If Maddy had come round, without admitting it to herself, for maternal support and solace, Rosa was delivering precisely the opposite. She got up to go, and her mobile pinged a text. She glanced at it – from Louis. She decided to wait till she was out of her mother's sight before reading it. This was the worst place on earth to receive more bad news.

She walked down Queen Margaret Drive, the text still unread. Like a bill, or a court order, you can't bring yourself to open. There was, she noticed, just the barest hint of spring in the air. Sun somewhere, buried deep in cloud, like a shy child hiding in its mother's skirts. The trees over the Kelvin showed signs of budding, covered in tiny green plooks. She wasn't in the mood for spring. It was like hearing a happy song when you're miserable – it just makes you more miserable. She passed the old BBC which a millionaire had bought as his private home and built a bloody great wall round: Piss off, I'm rich; ordinary smelly people Keep Out. One night she'd come here and piss on it. Then, to really rub in her self-loathing, one of the jogging ladies came sprinting past. All Lycra'd and defined, she waved merrily, ponytail and glutes bobbity-bobbing, shipshape. Maddy mustered a grim smile in return, and thought: at least she's flat-chested.

She'd go home, get a quick shower, change. It was still only 8 a.m. She'd be in the office the back of nine. But on Kew Terrace the not knowing became too much to bear. Making sure there was no one around, like a housebreaker scoping the scene, she took out her phone. Before she'd even brought the message up she could feel tears welling. Tears of misery, of rage, self-pity; a potent blend of all three.

"Sorry. This is unfair. You okay? Thinking of you." *Smiley face*.

It's ridiculous. You're forty, Maddy. Nine vague words and a wee drawing and suddenly, in a flash, you're as skittish as a puppy? You're screwing up an important case, possibly two; your job's on a shoogly nail; you're mum's a pain in the bahookie and your dad's about to make an unwelcome return. You look like shit, apparently, and feel worse... Yet here you are skipping along the road, a song in your heart.

At about the same time, DS John Russell got some good news too. One of the snitches he'd been given by the local East End boys, and on whom Russell had been leaning hard finally came up trumps. When he got back from the meeting – the price being a fry-up in a greasy spoon on Shettleston Road – he ran straight up to tell Coulter. The sergeant wouldn't have liked that he had something in common with Maddalena Shannon: that he, too, was acting like a child, eager to please the teacher, hoping that the dunce's hat would be replaced by a gold star.

Unfortunately Coulter wasn't in his office, but upstairs seeing the chief. He'd be in a hellish mood when he got back – having failed to please his own teacher. So Russell got on the phone and set things up himself. The only problem was that Coulter would see the news as reason to go further down the Shannon line of contamination and protestors. A blind alley, to Russell's mind.

As anticipated, Coulter came in like a goalie who had just let the ball slip from his hands.

"Robertson doing your nut in, boss?" Russell never called Coulter "boss", but he made an exception in this case. Teachers' pets are respectful.

"I haven't given him much choice, have I? A fortnight in, two corpses and a mummy, and I've got nothing."

"Well *I've* got something."

Coulter didn't look hopeful.

"Joe Harkins received a delivery of firearms about a month ago, and passed them on locally."

"Who told you this?" the boss's eyes lit up a little.

"Publican. He's reliable." Russell wasn't going to share his informants.

"Reliable enough to put it in writing?"

"Doubt it. We don't need him to, do we." It wasn't a question, and Coulter knew he was right.

"The Glocks?"

"He doesn't know. But he does know that a deal was made, on his premises. And another one a few days later."

"But we do know there was more than one gun?"

"The way Harkins was throwing his money around after, must've been."

"Who did he buy them from? Who did he sell them to?"

Russell shook his head.

"It's not much. But it's the first break we've had. Thanks, John."

Russell shrugged, concealing his delight.

"You suggested bringing Harkins in before. Looks like you were right."

"Nah. We'd have got nothing out of him. We can now, but." The sergeant checked his watch. "And … he should be here about now."

Coulter actually smiled. "Top marks, my man. Let's go."

Amy Dalgarno reckoned now that DI Coulter should have done this. Consultant Neurosurgeon Mr Hood was talking very politely to her, but behind the charm his god complex was in full working order. The inspector in charge of the investigation might have got further with him than she was. A mere sergeant. A lady one at that. If he'd talked to her in that way in a bar she'd have thought him a lounge lizard.

"DS Dalgarno, I appreciate your situation, but I'm afraid your objectives are not ours. The well-being of Mr Crichton is our sole concern and the only circumstances that influence my decisions are medical ones."

Amy said that she appreciated that, of course she did. Could Mr Hood at least give them some idea of when Bill Crichton might be brought out of his induced coma? "Other lives might depend on it. Sir."

"And I appreciate *that*, Sergeant. You must be aware, however, that even if we have had any success with this procedure, it is still highly likely that the patient will be of little use to you for some time to come. If ever. It would be a crime, don't you think, to rush things, risking Mr Crichton's chances of recovery, perhaps only to discover that he has nothing of use to tell you?"

Amy's experience of doctors in her personal life was that she was in and out before you could say "urinary infection". Yet Mr Hood appeared to have twenty minutes to spare to joust with her and subtly tell her how important he was and how weighty were the decisions he had to take, on a daily basis. In the nicest possible way, it has to be said. At the end of the consultation, as he was walking to the door, he said: "As a matter of fact, we are meeting today to take a decision. There is a reasonable chance that we will discontinue Mr Crichton's regime in the next day or two." He opened the door. "I wouldn't get your hopes up, though, if I were you."

He left Amy sitting in the nurses' room. Why the hell hadn't he said that at the start? That's all she'd wanted to know – when Crichton was being brought round. The man knew all along, yet felt it a good use of his time to talk round the matter.

WPC Alison Morrison came in just as Amy was leaving. Until last night someone had been posted by Crichton's bed, one of Alison's colleagues covering between her shifts. Coulter, or someone, must have decided to dial down on that, the expense of it not giving them anything. For the moment, though, Morrison was still stuck with it.

"Can't be fun, sitting watching a sleeping man all day."

"Most boring thing I've done. The only entertainment is watching the wife and the girlfriend crossing over. "

Amy laughed. You would think, in such a man's world, having female colleagues to talk to would be good. The sergeant liked the constable well enough but there was no particular spark between them, no meeting of minds. Rank, it seemed, outweighed solidarity in all things. Amy knew that other women in the force, Alison included probably, thought her "manly". All that cycling and hillwalking, happier talking about Garmins and derailleurs than shoes or boyfriends. The police didn't attract many girly girls but some of the women wanted to reclaim some femininity.

Fair do's. WPC Morrison struck Amy as being not so much more womanly than her, just younger. Amazing the difference seven or eight years makes. The few downtime conversations they'd had Alison talked about phones and clubs, and had asked her who Ben Macdui was.

"You never get anything from them – the Mrs Miller and Crichton?"

"Not a word. Literally. They're like two weans in a huff with each other."

"Must all seem like a waste of time? Hopefully it won't last too long. Think they might be bringing him round."

"Any chance you could ask them to give me whatever it is they're pumping into him. This doing nothing but sitting is knackering. *I* could do with a fortnight's snooze."

Maddy never checked Facebook at work. She didn't check it all that often at home, but the office was no place to catch up with school chums' holiday snaps. She made an exception today, not having replied to her dad's message. Social media was annoying these days anyway. Too much cod philosophy and worse, political barking. The exciting flowering of energetic debate over the period of the Scottish referendum had given way quickly to depressing sectarianism. People who were essentially in agreement over the big issues – Trident, NHS, Europe – had taken up dogmatic positions along party lines. SNPers screaming at Labourites and vice versa. It seemed to Maddy that having two left-of-centre, three if you include the Greens, was a good thing. But human nature preferred division to unity. Scotland: a land united by its schisms: east versus west, Highland, Lowland, Gaels and Sassenachs, island versus mainland, Catholic cats and Proddy dogs...

Her good mood hadn't lasted as long as it took her to shower. Louis was just being nice and, as her *nonna* used to say, it's nice to be nice. But something vital, something structural, had changed in their relationship. A lever had been pulled. She had a horrible feeling that there was nothing left now but a series of miserable heart to hearts and the slow dismal slide to the final sad farewell. She thought of sending him a message now but had no clue what to say. That, in itself, was a first.

And there was Packie Shannon's message, unanswered, hanging in mid cyberspace. "Can we meet?" She had no answer to that either. She was right – it's always a mistake to go on Facebook during work.

This file – if that, indeed, was what Tom Hughes or someone was ransacking the Millers' house for – what could it contain? It couldn't be the documentation delivered to Lord Nairne. That had been read through by police lawyers, and herself. There was nothing so dangerous in it to make someone ransack a house – and die, or kill, in the act.

"Tom Hughes was a wanker."

"That reason enough in your book, Mr Harkins, to kill him?"

Fulton's factotum was still in his hi-vis jacket, but instead of his hard hat he had a beanie, which he kept on in the interview room.

"If I made the laws… But I don't."

"Mr Harkins," Coulter and Russell sat side by side across the desk, "a black Audi A3 was seen driving down Mr Miller's street last night."

"An Audi in Killearn? Whatever next."

"Joe," Russell smiled, "feel free to light up if you want."

Harkins looked at him then at Coulter. "You're not suggesting, surely, that I break the law."

"Just give us your fag packet."

Harkins looked bemused, shrugged, and put his cigarette carton and lighter on the table.

"Rothmans."

"'Give you extra length.' That's what the old adverts used to say. Not that I've had any complaints."

"Mr Harkins, I really don't have time for your banter," Coulter pulled his chair in closer to the table. "Nor do you. A packet of Rothmans was found beside your boss's body last night. We're taking prints from it as we speak. But I'm willing to bet that yours is on that pack," Harkins's brow furrowed for a moment.

"And the Audi, *I'm* willing to bet," Russell mimicked Coulter's body language; they'd done this double act before, had it down to a fine art, "was Mr Hughes's own…"

"…and we all know he was in the habit of getting you to chauffeur him around."

"You were there last night, at the Millers', with your boss."

"And with crud from the site on your boots."

"Maybe your gloves too."

"So it's odds-on you killed him."

"Whoa, back up there boys—"

"But let's leave that for a moment shall we? While you ponder on that and we wait for confirmation of the prints, we've another interesting topic of conversation."

"Just to pass the time."

"You received a case of guns—"

"Glock compacts, G19—"

"Certainly more than one. A month ago."

"And sold them on a few days later."

Throughout, Harkins switched his eyes from one police-man to the other, like watching a game of tennis on telly. An exciting one, judging by how the man's pupils were dilating.

"Who telt you that? It's no' true."

"Oh Joe," Coulter sighed, "let's not do this, eh? We know it was you."

"In the Brewery Tap. One of your locals. You shouldn't piss on your own doorstep, Joe."

"Who told you this? 'Cause I've heard the rumours too. And the way I was told it, any shooters floating around the city come from *your* arsenal. Glass hooses and a' that, gentlemen."

"The very fact you know that—"

"So you're admitting it?" Harkins laughed.

"Right now," Russell changed the topic, "we've got you down for the murders of Julian Miller and Tom Hughes—"

"And we'll figure out your role in Bill Crichton's skydive."

"Youse are mental. And ye's are on to plums."

But you could see the panic in his eyes. John Russell didn't believe for a moment that Harkins had anything to do with Miller's and Crichton's fates. Probably not Hughes's either. Coulter was keeping his mind open, but it was a long shot. However, all three men could see how a case could be built against him.

"I really don't want to confuse you, Joe," Coulter said, leaning back in his chair again. "So let's go back to the first question. You were there last night. In Killearn. Tell us about it."

"I'd've told you from the start if you'd given me hauf a chance, instead about going on about gunrunning and killing everyone I've met. Aye, I took Hughes to Killearn. I dropped him off, round about half eleven."

"And you went into the Millers' with him."

"Naw. I didnae. He said he'd give me a ring if he wanted picked up again – we'd left Belvedere unattended. When I didn't hear from him, I just thought he'd decided to get a taxi."

"No, Joe. That's not right. You were there with him. The Rothmans."

"Och that. The aul' skinflint was forever cadging fags off me. Instead of just taking one he'd take the pack off me, take out two or three, hand them to me, and pocket the pack. It was old trick of his."

Coulter and Russell glanced at each other – that had a ring of truth to it.

"I don't believe any of that for a single minute, Mr

Harkins. If we find any traces of you inside that house, you are in very, very, deep trouble."

"What might help you at this stage, is names."

"Who did you buy the guns from, and who did you sell them on to?"

Coulter recognised the signs. Harkins sat stock-still, but his eyes darted around the little room, avoiding the two men in front of him. His breathing became a little slower, trying to contain his nerves. Whatever he was going to say, Coulter knew it would be a lie.

"I have no idea what you're talking about. You've hassled some poor bugger, just like you're hassling me, and he's given you my name to get shot of you. Well, I'm no' going to do the same." His forehead glistened slightly under the light, but he was doing a better job now of covering his anxiety. "You've got nuthin'. I've told you the truth about last night – that will check out. You know as well as me I've no reason to waste Miller. Hardly even know who he is. Hughes might have been a pain in the fucking arse but he's employed me for years. And the guns? Don't make me laugh. You've got some grass somewhere feeding you a name you want to hear. It's all shite, gentlemen. All shite."

Certainly some of it was, Coulter thought. But there was a lot of bravado in Harkins's little speech. The man had no real idea how much of it could actually be used against him. Coulter stood up, and Russell followed.

"Why don't you take a little time to think over your situation, Mr Harkins. Be our guest."

"How much time?"

"Oh, let's say ... till tomorrow afternoon?"

"Fuck off."

Coulter didn't think he'd have too much of a problem explaining the decision to Robertson. They had enough on Harkins to detain him. And the chief was as impatient as he was for something to move in this case.

"One of our staff will be with you shortly, sir. I'm sure

they'll make you comfortable." Russell smiled. "They'll tell you your rights and make sure you get a solicitor if you want one.

"Though if you would rather leave us earlier, it's easily done. A name, Joe. Who did you pass those guns on to?"

Running late this morning, she'd brought her car in, so she knocked off early and drove the now familiar route out to Belvedere. So familiar that she could check her text when it pinged on the passenger seat beside her. Louis: "So. Are you? Okay."

The trouble with text is that you can't read the tone. She hadn't answered him since this morning. Was this little nudge from across the pond a worried one, or just narky? She didn't want him to think she was being huffy, playing hard to get. The answer to his question couldn't be texted. She wasn't okay, that was for sure. What was less sure was precisely *why*. He'd have to wait until tonight. She didn't want to video chat: she was too raw, her thoughts too tangled, face-to-face wouldn't end well. She'd write a considered, nuanced email.

CD on the car was playing the Blue Nile "A Walk Across the Rooftops": "Flags caught on the fences..." She remembered there was an old packet of fags in the glove compartment, maybe one or two left in it. She tried to lean over and rummage for it, but decided that the looking was about to kill her far more quickly than the nicotine would, and gave up.

The sun stayed high enough in the sky for the schemes of the North East to look less desolate and jagged. She parked a little back from the site and walked over before calling on Cathy and Morag. Work on the new houses was slacking off as evening approached, just half a dozen or so men bricklaying, mixing, pouring concrete. The late winter sun shone low on the horizon, the colour of condensed orange juice, throwing the shadows of the half-built walls long and thin across the ground. Like the shadows of gravestones.

The earth itself, gouged and agitated under her feet, was treacly brown and so rich looking it might nourish vines and fruit trees. The only thing that grows naturally round here is breeze block and concrete.

What was it hiding – if anything? She knew for certain there was a potent cocktail of nasty substances down there. She'd read a list two pages long of what Costello had buried – you'd never guess, the soil in the evening sun looked healthy and fresh. She'd also seen the files that guaranteed that everything had been properly disposed of, decontaminated, sealed. SEPA inspectors, and lawyers for both Costello and Fulton were persuaded that everything had been done to the proper legal standards.

So where were all these cancers and ailments that Cathy and Morag had told her about coming from? Had somebody, somewhere, cut corners? Then again, maybe people round here had to lay blame *somewhere*. Glasgow's statistics were shocking – even more so in areas like this. The figures the women had quoted sounded not much worse than the norm. Some of it could be explained – deprivation, poor education, mistrust of everyone in the system, from GPs to consultants to procurators fiscal. Violence, certainly – Glasgow's murder rate was still nearly twice as high as London's for heaven's sake. Poor diet, smoking, drinking – it all fed into the general malaise of a city that was once worked to death's door. Then even the work was taken away.

The Glasgow effect. There are areas in Liverpool, Manchester that are every bit as deprived – of employment, services, access – yet life expectancy was five years longer or more. Even people like her – middle class, educated, employed, nice house, regular holidays – could expect to live five years less than their counterparts in Birmingham or Newcastle.

She'd read that one cause of heart attacks in middle-aged men and women was a sense of lack of control. Middle managers were far more likely to keel over in their mid fifties than their bosses or juniors. Responsibility without power. The feeling of being a cog in a mysterious, rusty machine. She thought about Stuart Anderson, all those spreadsheets and objectives and outcomes, appraisal meetings where the boss had all the power, including handing over a P45. So he ends up stravaiging all over town with a glaikit look on his face. Whole chunks of Glasgow were like that, blamed for eating badly, drinking and smoking, not working. An entire conurbation given the boot, and as a result losing its identity, rendered powerless. A patient of early-onset dementia, triggered by depression, fear, insecurity. It was one of the reasons she'd campaigned for independence – *any* change could only be for the good. Glasgow, the city of Civic Alzheimer's.

Maddy nearly jumped out her skin when she turned around. Cathy Maguire was standing right behind her.

"What you doing, hen? Practising mindfulness? I hear it's all the rage up the West End."

"You gave me a fright. Never heard you come up."

"Aye we're a' ghosts out here. I take it you want to ask more questions?"

"If I knew what they were. Just thought I'd come over for a chat."

"A chat. A wee cosy chat. Isn't that lovely." Cathy turned and walked down the street, away from her house. "Well you can come along to the Canal if you want."

Cathy strode on, keeping ahead of Maddy, crossing over the north edge of Belvedere, in through houses that probably predated the 1970s scheme Cathy and Morag lived in: low-rises, the cladding either hanging dangerously or completely disintegrated. Behind them lay nothing, barren land strewn with old tyres and litter and the carcass of an ancient play park. Except for the Canal – a perfectly square, squat, public house standing alone, as dead and red in its brick as Mars in the dark sky. Although there was a door, and an old brass plaque bearing the name, the place still looked as though it had its back to you. Four even walls, all of them rear ends.

It was just as box-like on the inside. Lit by bare bulbs hanging from the ceiling, there was a simple bar, sparse gantry, and five or six tables with old classroom chairs around them. At the nearest to the door sat two elderly men playing cards. They nodded to Cathy and took no interest in Maddy. At the far end sat Kenny and Morag Boyd. Cathy went to the bar and spoke to the young male bartender; Maddy joined the Boyds and sat down.

"You all right?" Morag smiled at her. She looked less worn out than the last couple of times Maddy had seen her. Kenny said hello but without looking at her. He had the one-thousand-yard stare of the battle weary soldier, eyes fixed on something no one else could see.

Above their heads old paintings and photographs were hung, on three of the four straight walls of the bar. A pictorial history of the area. First, above Morag's head, a little hamlet on the side of the hill, like something out of Walter Scott. Then the coming of the canal. There were several of those, its construction, barges sailing on it, some with passengers, others with coal and timber. Over where the men were playing cards soundlessly, the hamlet had become a village, probably not long before Glasgow had swallowed it whole. The city we have become, Maddy thought, history and progress, poking and prodding the hills and vales. Glancing back at the hamlet above Morag it looked so pretty and tranquil. But those were hard days too, life expectancy just as short, brutal and greedy lairds and landowners. It was a short and inequitable journey for most folk, then as now, from walking and digging the earth to being put under it. Cathy plonked two bottles of fizzy wine on the table, and the young barman set out four glasses.

"A celebration. To bid farewell to old Tom Hughes. May he rot in hell."

Kenny and Morag smiled and held their glasses out for

Cathy to fill them. Maddy had the car but thought she should join the toast with one glass.

"A double celebration. Eh, Morag?"

"Aye. To Jason." Morag turned to Maddy to explain. "He goes in tomorrow."

"Here's to him." Maddy raised her glass and drank.

"Dinna worry," Cathy said, her smile mocking, "we won't go on about you being more interested in the deaths o' lawyers and businessmen than a wean from the schemes."

"Cathy. I just don't know what to do. We've been through the file presented to Lord Nairne. Maybe you have a strong case for the legal limits of toxic waste and how they're disposed of and sealed. But as the law stands, everything at Belvedere was done properly."

"That site still leaks," Morag said. "It was bad enough when Costello's was here, but it's got worse since."

"There's simply no proof of that, Morag."

"They didn't look at the evidence. Not properly. Those lads from the uni were certain of that."

"What lads?"

"We were worried that SEPA weren't being shown everything. That Costello, or Petrus, and Fulton were only showing them part of the decontamination process."

"So we took," Cathy picked up from Morag, "pictures ourselves, and got students from Cally to take measurements, and photies of their own."

"Glasgow Caledonian?"

"The uni, aye," Morag said.

"Do you have these students' names or anything?"

Cathy shook her head. "They were in their last year. One was Australian—"

"Jake … Jake something."

"And the other Polish. Darius. Darius Mozos?"

"We've tried to get in touch with them. They've gone back home. Cally gave us some contact details, but they've never responded to us."

"Does the university have a record of the work they did for you?"

"No. We employed them," Morag said, "or rather, we gave them what wee bit of cash we could. It wasn't part of their course or anything. They just happened to be students interested in waste disposal. Put it on their CVs."

"What about their research? Was that in the file JCG Miller put together?"

"It was supposed to be. But we've always doubted it."

"Did you keep a copy – of their research?"

"Yes. But Miller's kept that for us, along with everything else."

"We thought it was safe," Cathy said, "but then they told us they couldn't return it to us."

"Some mumbo jumbo about legal reasons," Kenny said suddenly, until that point seemingly on a different planet from where this conversation was taking place. He took out his mobile. "I've only got a few photies of the photies." He hunched over his phone for a moment, then turned the screen to Maddy.

At the corners of the lead and concrete seal under Belvedere, black sludge and reddy-brown gunge oozed out and seeped over the surface.

"See? How could they have passed that?"

"Without even commenting on it, or asking for more tests?"

"Everything done to the proper standards? My arse." Said Cathy.

"Could you text that photograph, and anything else you've got, to me Kenny?"

In all the files she had looked at, Maddy had never seen that image.

Coulter was letting Harkins stew in his own juices for a while. DS Dalgarno, after she'd explained that Mr Gavin Hood, consultant spinal neurosurgeon, was likely to take

Bill Crichton off his coma-inducing drugs tomorrow, sat down across the desk from her boss and smiled.

"And even better news."

"What, better than being able to talk to a man who is more than likely to be severely brain-damaged?"

She put a printout on his desk. "CM International. Based in Holland, suppliers, globally, of construction materials. Including soil. This is Forensic Services' report. Fulton bought several tons of their soil and topsoil three months ago. It matches all the traces on the murder weapons and at the crime scenes. But," Amy's smile widened further, "does *not* match any of the other samples we've taken, including from the Millers' and Crichtons' gardens."

Coulter didn't appear quite as excited by the news as she was. "So. We can narrow down the search to anyone who has been near Belvedere, *including*", he mimicked Amy's enthusiasm, "the victims, everyone who works there, who lives near there and, for all we know, the victims' spouses and extended families. Not that much further forward, are we?"

Amy nodded, deflated.

"Ignore me, Amy. I'm sorry. You're right. We've been waiting for this for ages and, yes, it does narrow things down. I'm becoming a right old grump, amn't I? And maybe we'll even get something out of Bill. Always look on the bright side, eh?" Coulter watched Amy nod and get up to go, still a bit punctured.

He and Russell paid another visit to Joe Harkins. The desk sergeant said he hadn't asked formally for a solicitor. He still had his own mobile so it's possible one might turn up yet.

"He's not worried," Russell reckoned. "If he had anything to do with this he'd have been on the blower in jig time."

Coulter wasn't so sure. Guilty men, if their strategy is to look as innocent as possible, often didn't request a solicitor. Until it was too late. A big mistake, trying to look as if there's nothing to worry about.

Back in the interview room, Joe Harkins was indeed trying to look as unflustered as possible, lying back on his chair, pretending to take forty winks.

"Mr Harkins. Thought we should bring you up to date. First, your fingerprints are on the packet of cigarettes."

"I said they'd be, didn't I?"

"Unfortunately found under the body of your murdered boss."

"Also, the soil, we can now confirm, found at all the crime scenes comes from Belvedere construction site."

"Where you are security man and general gopher," Russell added in.

"What," Harkins put on a mock-shocked face, "the soil on my gear comes from the place I work? My, my, you boys are fair storming ahead here, eh." The sneer on his face wasn't quite enough to hide the man's disquiet. The long wait, left all on his own, was working. Coulter put his face closer to Harkins.

"Let me be plain. Right now, Harkins, you are the *only* suspect in the frame for a double murder and just possibly culpable homicide."

"So arrest me then."

"Oh we will. Everything in good time, Joe, eh? Unless of course, you give us a name. Who did you sell or give the guns to? 'Cause without that name, we can only assume that you kept them yourself. The case against you is looking very spick and span."

Harkins turned his face away. Coulter walked over and held the door open for John Russell. "Sleep well, Mr Harkins."

Maddy parked at her house and walked over to Epicures, arriving just as Coulter was arriving. Midweek, late evening, the café was quiet. They sat at a table and the waitress, asking their order, lit the tea light candle that sat, in its decorative little holder, between them. Although all the occupied tables had one they both squirmed a little.

"That looks truly nasty," Coulter said, peering at the picture Kenny Boyd had sent to her phone.

"Problem is," Maddy said, "without any provenance it's not much use to us."

"Meaning it could be a picture from anywhere in the world."

"Sadly."

"Do you think it is? Are the Boyds and Maguire calculating enough to try and pass off phoney pictures?"

"Or desperate enough. It's possible."

"I know it's *possible*, Maddy. But what is your opinion? Professional and personal. You know them, and you know the background."

"I don't know Kenny. He has a wall around him six foot thick and six miles high. At least whenever I'm around. His missus, Morag, she seems more saddened than anything. She's so exhausted and worried about her son I doubt she'd bother trying to pull something like that."

"And Cathy Maguire?"

"She's the leader of the gang, I'd say. Bright. Energetic. More sussed?" Maddy looked at the photo on her phone again. "But I think it's the real deal."

"We'll do what we can to try and track down these students." Maddy had told him about them when she phoned to meet him. "But it could take a long time. Too long."

They were brought their coffee by the manageress. Despite being a regular, Maddy had never really spoken to her but found the woman fascinating. Mid thirties maybe? Glam, but in an interesting way. Fifties-style bright red lipstick and Marilyn Monroe hair, her smiley down-home manner a striking counterpoint to the brash look. You felt she might at any moment break out into an Imelda May sassy rockabilly song. The woman clearly interested Alan Coulter too. Over macchiato and espresso they discussed the case, going round in circles. Until Coulter said what he was inevitably going to say. "You have to stop hanging

205

around Belvedere with the locals, Maddy. If me and my lot eventually manage to do our jobs, you are the best person to have in court."

Maddy sighed. "You telling me I'm interfering with the investigation, Inspector?"

"You know damn fine you are."

"Yet I keep bringing you vital information."

"Do you?" He nodded at her phone. "If that leads anywhere it'll take months. We don't have months Maddy. We know Harkins sold on a case of six Glocks. Two have been used, and one left to goad us."

"You think the other three are going to be used?"

"It's at least a possibility."

"Maybe the killer just couldn't get a case of three. And anyway, I'm over there and talking to Cathy and the Boyds about another matter all together."

"Petrus. And you're increasingly convinced, and trying to convince me, that your old Petrus case is connected to the murders. It's all too muddy."

"Maddy."

"What?"

"It's all too muddy Maddy. Life's too short not to enjoy a little assonance wherever you can."

Coulter rolled his eyes. "I don't know the technical ins and outs of the procurating business, but if I were Maxwell Binnie I'd be getting jumpy. A man who later throws himself, or is pushed, out a window comes to your house, asking you to lie for him. Possible suspects are giving you – personally – potentially crucial evidence. Employees of one of the dead men were in your house the night one of them was killed. Need I go on?"

No. He needn't. Maddy knew this case had slipped from her finger. And that all her work on Petrus might quite possibly be handed over to Dan McKillop, or Manda, for them to take the limelight. Why was her life always so embroiled, problematic? Was it because she was a single woman, out and about, in a city that felt, especially among the middle classes, like a village? A hamlet on the hill. She knew people, she talked out of turn. Her curiosity was as deeply embedded as her impetuousness.

Muddy Maddy.

"I have a question. When you searched the Crichtons' house, did anyone notice a medal?"

"Medal?"

"You know, one of those cheap things you get for running a race, or winning a golf competition."

"Not that I know of." Then he remembered. "There was one in Marion Miller's living room. Like that?"

She nodded. "Tell them to look out for one at Hughes's house."

"Why?"

"Just, it looked so out of place in the Millers'."

"Is that the only reason?" Coulter was immediately suspicious.

"Yeah. What else?"

He was about to counter that when a young woman, wearing a barista's apron, entered and came straight over to their table.

"Sorry for interrupting. Only Hollie happened to see you come in. From across the way?" Epicures was situated across the road from Nick's, the restaurant where Miller, Crichton and Fulton had all had a meal, the night before all hell broke loose. "They said you'd been in a week or so back asking about the night Mr Hughes was in."

"That's right, we were." Coulter angled his position fully towards her. "Sorry, you are…?"

"Kirsty. Kirsty Nolan." A pretty girl, but she didn't elicit quite the same response from the inspector as the glam waitress had. His interest was professional. "They said I should maybe tell you."

"Tell us what, Kirsty?"

"The table that night was booked for three. Mr Hughes,

and I know now from reading the papers, Mr Miller and Mr Crichton. But they were joined by a fourth man, a bit later."

Now she had the full attention of them both. "Someone they just met in passing, in the bar?"

"No. He was with them for most of the meal. Think he might have missed the starter, but it was a table for four, and he sat with them."

"Why didn't you come forward with this before?"

"I didn't know you were interested. I've been on holiday since. Not away on holiday, like, but time off the restaurant, studying. I started back last night and nobody was talking about it, then when Hollie saw you, she remembered, and remembered I'd been on that night."

"What can you tell us about this fourth man? What did he look like?"

The girl shrugged. Wanting to help but not sure what to say. "They all look the same to me, middle-aged men. Oh God, sorry," she suddenly reddened, looking away from Coulter to Maddy. "I mean, I just serve them. I don't notice much…"

Coulter had the grace to laugh. But quickly turned serious again. "Is there anything you can remember, Kirsty? How was he dressed? Was a bit older, younger maybe?"

"They all had suits on. He must have had too, I think. Otherwise I might have noticed."

"Did he speak quietly or loudly," Maddy asked.

Kirsty brightened: "Yeah, maybe he did. I mean, like the rest of them, the more they drink the louder they get. But I kinda remember him having a loud voice."

"But nothing that he said?"

She shook her head.

"How much later did he get there?"

"Maybe about three-quarters of an hour after the other three?"

"And when did he leave?"

"As soon as he finished eating? I think."

They both knew she was guessing to keep them happy. She had no real idea. "Listen, I'm really sorry. I'd have told you before if I'd known it was important."

It was important – and DS Russell should have made sure that everyone connected to Nick's knew that. His sergeant had let the ball drop again.

"Kirsty, I'm going to get an officer to come over to Nick's tonight. That okay? How long are you on for?"

"Till closing time. Yeah, sure. Of course." Like most people she didn't like the idea of having her details taken down by police. In front of colleagues and punters. As she turned to go, Maddy touched her wrist gently. "Thanks, Kirsty. That was really useful."

After she'd gone out, Maddy and Coulter turned to each other. "Any ideas?"

"Doesn't sound like Harkins."

"He'd have stuck out like a sore thumb."

"Another builder? Another lawyer?"

"You thinking Doug Mason? Nah, even Kirsty would have noticed he's younger. And better looking."

"A middle-aged, middle-class, nondescript man. Jesus."

"Whoever he is … there's quite possibly a Glock pistol being loaded for him right now."

"Or he's loading it himself, for someone else." Coulter looked miserable. This case was killing him. Half of Glasgow's policemen assigned to it, holidays cancelled, costs rocketing, the press baying for blood. Everyone was beginning to hate the hitherto popular detective inspector. His boss, his colleagues, journalists and their readers, countrywide.

He paid and left, after another sad, avuncular warning for her to watch her back at COPFS. Maddy finished her coffee scanning the café's paper – trying to find *something* that wasn't related to the killings. She and Norma Jeane exchanged a couple of smiles. As she left she thought, if she buttoned up different…

209

Despite everything, she felt serene in the night air, looking forward to her walk home. Trying not to enumerate the problems in her life. When a Cruise missile suddenly blew the night to smithereens.

"Flutterby!!"

He lurched out – of all places – Nick's, shock-white hair to the four winds, both arms rotating, fag end beaconing like a night flare. He tried to run across the road to her – well, another lurch, anorak and scarf sailing – and just about got himself run over. So he stood at the kerb, still waving, grinning like a child. A big, lumbering, tipsy, old child.

At first she couldn't move, stuck to the spot, staring at this vision. Dreamlike, her father's jacket and scarf floating in the breeze, his wild white hair, his lit cigarette... She hadn't seen the man in over a decade. Not even a photograph. He didn't look real; he looked like a phantom of her father, some deep-seated projection of him. But she found herself crossing the road, slowly, checking for cars in her peripheral vision. Until she was within a foot or two of him. Packie Shannon. In Glasgow. In her life. Now, close to him, as physical, as meaty, as *there* as it was possible to be. The sheer presence of him, the heft.

He opened his arms and took a step towards her. Then abruptly stopped, receiving some unspoken message from her. A message she didn't even know she was sending out herself.

"Maddy."

That voice, deep, baked, and smoky. He looked older. Of course he would. The old muscle looser than it was, his hair still thick and hearty but whiter now than a blizzard. She's a rabbit in the night caught in the headlight glare of an oncoming scooter.

"Dad."

He decided against the hug, and reached for her hand instead. They stood there, wobbling on the kerb, hands held lightly, looking at one another. The eyes hadn't aged. The new wrinkles around them only emphasised their small, slightly mad, vigour. Memories, thoughts, judgements writhed like eels, not only in her head but throughout her body. He wasn't a bad man. Never had been. He's a bastard, always was. He's nuts, he's fun, he's dangerous. When he's here he's here too much; when he's absent he's the hole in her psyche the cold wind wails through. She hated him – no, she just couldn't handle him; resented what he had done, leaving them. She missed him, loved him. She couldn't get away quick enough, but was paralysed.

"I knew you lived somewhere round here."

She didn't speak but he answered her question. "No, I didn't come looking for you. Just ended up here."

"How?" Her voice sounded like a child, wondering and wondrous.

"I'm in Glasgow for business." For *business*? "You never answered my message." He gave her his old mock-angry look, and she couldn't stop herself smiling.

"You'll never guess." If ever there was a Packie Shannon phrase, that was it. No, she wouldn't, ever. Never had done.

"I met this guy. Fantastic. You'd love him, Maddy. Lives around here."

"Where?"

"I dunno. Somewhere," he swept his arm majestically in a half circle, and nearly fell of the pavement, "here."

"No, I mean, where did you meet him?" That wasn't what she meant either. She meant, where would he meet anyone? Where was he living? What's his life?

"In Ireland. The Aul' Sod. You should come over. You've cousins there dying to meet you."

His mother's family was from that area, somewhere north, inland, of Dublin, she remembered. Maddy had never met her paternal grandmother, dead before she was born. After his grand tour of Italy, Packie had decided to go back to his roots, pre-Scotland.

"I run a wee bed and breakfast, and there's this guy comes

over to stay, every couple of months. The guy from round here. And d'you know what he comes over to do? Build a wall of death! How's that for crazy?"

Maddy could not at that moment imagine what a wall of death was. The phrase was familiar, but it fed into the still surreal feel of this meeting. Her father. Walls. Death.

"Man's a fecking genius. Anyway, I've been giving him a hand. I mean, there are two aul' fellas who are building the contraption with him."

Maddy knew who he was talking about. An artist with some kind of East European name. Skrynk? Skynka? She'd once seen an installation of his. In the Clyde tunnel, the one you can walk or cycle through, if you have a death wish. This guy had repainted the entire thing, and had a male voice choir singing the length of it. She'd loved it, the crazy unexpectedness of it. She'd seen the guy walking around with his dogs; the running girls at the baths all fancied him. For good reason. Trust her dad to know him personally.

"I just source some materials for them. Transport stuff around. I'm picking up some gear tomorrow to.... Ach never mind that. I'm here. With you. My baby. Flutterby."

So much in that little speech to process. Never mind what? Was it really sheer accident that he was not only in Glasgow but on her patch? Why is he here, does he have some kind of plan, a strategy? Her dad was always full of plans, not all of them crazy, some even came to fruition. His baby, his Flutterby. Did he have any notion the effect those words had on her? Being lifted up, swung around, the taste of Girvan sea spray, the smell of hot oil and vinegar. Being kissed goodnight when she thought everything was settled in the world. That justice and honesty were the foundations of life.

Trying to shut these useless thoughts down and find a reasonable reply, the door of Nick's swung open again, and out popped cousin Dante carrying two half-drunk pints.

"Patrizio!" Then he spotted Maddy and immediately

straightened up, trying to disguise his shit-faced state. "Maddalena."

So that's where he had gone – swept up in the hurricane that was her father. She could have kissed him. Cousin Dante had broken the powerful hex of the moment and allowed her an escape.

"People have been looking for you, Dante."

"Aye well, they don't normally," he said bitterly.

"Go get Maddy a drink, Danny." Trading nationalities, clans. Irish Dante, Italian Packie. Another of her dad's old hobbies. And still stealing bits of her mother's life; of the woman, and daughter, he'd left, confiscating what was important to them. "What'll you have?"

"Sorry. Can't. I have a heavy day tomorrow. Tired. I have to go."

Packie looked genuinely dismayed. "But we've only just met. First time in so many years, Maddy."

And who's fault was that? Well, actually, partly hers at least, to be honest. "Dad. You can't just turn up on the pavement late at night and expect me to drop my life."

"Yeah. Of course. Sorry. But we'll meet, yeah?"

She nodded. He took out his phone and keyed in her number. When he had finally bought her her first phone over twenty years ago he'd been dead set against them. Now he was a practised hand: the iPhone genuflection.

"How long are you in town for?"

"That depends." On what, she wondered, but didn't ask. The look in his eye suggested that it depended to some extent on her. "Two or three days."

"Okay. I'll be in touch." She wanted to tell Dante to contact Rosa, tell her he was all right. But that would mean alerting her mother to Packie's presence. If that could be avoided, the better for everyone. Why did it always seem that Maddy was the lock chamber, the mechanism that controls the flow of information, damming the truth, being forced into lying.

Packie stroked her hair lightly and fleetingly as she turned to cross back over the road. "What's your address, darling?"

She glanced round, but at Dante: "Think you'll find they don't have a late licence for alcohol in the street." Ever the enforcer.

Is there anywhere more disturbing than a hospital at night? Even WPC Alison Morrison, twenty-eight years old, Facebook open on her Sony Xperia Z3, organising next weekend's high jinks and swapping photographs of last week's, felt it. She wasn't sure if she was allowed to use it in a hospital, but she wasn't going to sit here all night without it. It's not just being surrounded by sickness and imminent death – that's all there during the day too. It's the dark outside; the window across from her is pure black, the way the subdued lighting of the room hits it. Interrupted every now and then only by the distant flickering of some plane descending into Glasgow International. But that just adds to the sense of loneliness: there are people, but they're so far away, probably asleep, dropping silently down through the sky. She remembered reading somewhere – maybe about Lockerbie? – that it took the victims, still safety-belted into their seats, several minutes to fall the five miles to the ground below. The image had stayed with her, because it terrified her.

Inspector Alan Coulter was looking out his window, too, into nothing. He hadn't gone home after seeing Maddy, though he'd thought that was where he was going. Instead, he'd ended back at the station. There was, he realised once he got there, a reason for doing it. Go see Harkins. See if the man had had enough. If he was willing to give them anything. But he decided to give it another half hour yet. There was no rush. Martha would be in bed – what difference would it make if he got home before or after midnight?

Over the river, Bill Crichton stirred in his bed. The first time he'd done that, Alison had nearly jumped out her skin. She happened to have been alone with him in the room at the time – about an hour ago. She'd gone and fetched a nurse. It was to be expected, she was told. A good sign. They were slowly decreasing the medication, and Mr Crichton was responding. Not much, Alison thought, glancing at him now. His breathing was a little different maybe. A little faster? An arm or a leg would judder a bit about every twenty minutes or so. That's why she'd been positioned back in this bloody ward. In case he said anything. Fat chance. He wasn't responding in any way to Marion Miller, sitting by his side. It was her watch right now. Quite apt, the policewoman reckoned: the wife on duty during the day, the mistress by night. She wasn't touching him. Alison got the feeling that, tonight at least, Marion was thinking something through, trying to make up her mind. The woman's brow would furrow, then she'd half nod as if the decision had been taken, but she'd glance at the patient again and the brow would furrow once more. Going over the same ground. Alison wondered if old Bill knew what was happening to him. Coming out of his coma. Like a dying man strapped to a chair tumbling slowly back to earth.

Coulter had only needed two minutes with Harkins; Harkins needed less. The man was for telling them nothing. Not yet anyway. They'd hardly spoken.

"You ready?"

"For what? Tell you what, Inspector. You tell me what you want to hear and I'll repeat it back to you."

Both men knew the investigation was taking a shot in the dark. But Coulter, wrapping his coat around him now and stepping out into the crisp, quiet night, felt that something was shifting inside Joe Harkins. Brought on by fear, yes, but only partly. Keeping him in custody, keeping the pressure up, wasn't a one-way street. It had given Harkins time to think. Throw them something. Anything. A name, or names, that'll send them off in the wrong direction. They were assuming that Joe was just a minor piece in the puzzle. What if they were wrong? What if Harkins was much more involved in these killings than they reckoned? Coulter smiled to himself – head down, resolving to walk the hour it would take him to get home – one thing's for certain: nobody's been killed since Joe's been locked up.

An incoming flight, late from Warsaw, was turning over the Clyde, dipping into Whiteinch. Both WPC Morrison and DI Coulter clocked it, vaguely. Their minds were on two men, locked up in their own ways. Left hanging. A word from either could change everything. Or nothing.

Maddy was dealing with more words than she could handle. It was eight in the evening in Queens, New York, one in the morning in Lorraine Gardens. Louis, after forty minutes of talking round in circles, looked every bit as drained as she felt. She was bringing the Glasgow night to him.

It's a bad sign when you start quoting James Joyce. "Every bond is a bond to sorrow."

"I don't think I've caught you on a good night, Maddy."

"There aren't many of those these days, Lou."

"Maybe we should do this tomorrow? Or after your father's gone. Though I'd like to have met him."

Have met him. Past tense. This wasn't an ordinary break-up conversation. The norm is that one of the parties wants to split. The power that Louis, she now conceded, quite innocently, had over her these last few days, had dissipated. They were on an equal footing. Heads and hearts both roughly in the same place. Which, ordinarily, would be a good thing. He probably just meant that he wouldn't meet Packie on this particular occasion.

But it was only a matter of time before they had to face up to realities. They lived in different countries. They both had jobs, lives, families they couldn't, even if they wanted to, give up. Had one of them been rich then there might have been a way forward. But a middle-ranking cop and a provincial procurator fiscal? They couldn't even afford to nip over for visits more than twice a year, if that. First World problems: budget flights just ain't budget enough. People in the Ukraine, Syria were being bombed, shot, forced to flee. It didn't make the pain of this situation any easier.

"You look really tired, Louis."

Between trying to tackle the problem at hand there was small talk and concern for each other. Stroking one another with words. But these felt like caresses of solace, kisses of conclusion. It was only six months ago Skype sessions were a lot bawdier, like horny teenagers with new phones for their birthdays. Funny to think that hot sex fades in long-distance relationships as swiftly as it does skin-to-skin. You'd have thought the sheer abstinence, the imagination necessary, might have lasted longer. Absence makes the libido grow stronger. It occurred to her she could drastically change the tenor of this meeting. A quick repositioning of the camera, a simple tug at a garment or two and instead of these painful negotiations the two of them would be barking and whining like beasts of the wild. Except maybe they wouldn't. Maybe it would be a truly excruciating decision. God knows she wanted to, or a part of her did, the irrational, non-verbal part that was in danger of drowning out this circular conversation. That line from *La Dolce Vita*: "We should love each other outside of time ... detached."

"Yeah, like I said, I think maybe I've got this virus."

The thing about virtual sex games – and in real-life down-and-dirty – was they were thrilling and daredevil in the heat of the act. The minute you're done? Ew.

"You'd better get some sleep."

"Look, Maddy, I will. I think – we both think, am I right? – we should stop talking. This isn't a good night for either of us." They were both on the same page. Could read each other easily. That must count for something, mustn't it? "Let's not take any big decisions under the worst possible circumstances."

They were coming to the end of this particular dirt track in their tangled road to nowhere. But how to sign off? Before, it had been a quick exchange of love yas. Often they hadn't bothered, there was no need. But if one of them said it now…? And who would go first? And what would it mean? Instead they end with a mutual, You take care. Speak soon.

Blue Nile: "Telephones that ring all night. Incommunicado…" She went to bed. Not sure if they'd tottered forward an inch, or back a mile. Work. Think of work. First World problems: two men blown to pieces, one possibly disabled for life; someone, or some*ones* out there, getting away with it, maybe not even sated yet.

Four a.m. she got up to go to the loo. She'd been dreaming about *La Dolce Vita*. But not in a good way: "Sometimes at night this darkness this silence weighs on me." And now, oh great, cramps. They'd been getting worse, and lasting longer, over the last few years. Some kind of body clock alarm? That was the last thing she wanted to think about now. There was a bus she'd almost certainly missed. Fine. She found kids boring and annoying – though, weirdly they seemed to like her. Like cats who make a beeline for the one person in the room who is allergic to them. Just what she needed – Crabbit Week, on top of everything else. God help anyone she comes into contact with over the next couple of days.

She turned on the hall light and there, at the front door, unmistakeable despite the dim light and its size, a bullet.

For once there was no problem her being at the crime scene. She wasn't there as the fiscal, she was the victim. Or next victim. Or being warned off.

She'd gone back to bed after seeing the bullet. No point in noising all these people up in the middle of the night. If whoever had posted the bullet had wanted to kill her they'd have done so there and then. She made the call at the more reasonable time of 6.30. She'd slept fine for the two hours in between.

"Do you think Miller and Hughes received a bullet through the post before they were shot?"

"If they did, we don't know about it." Coulter leaned against the cooker, sipping the tea she'd made. She'd been brewing all morning – for forensics, SOCOs, Adams, Holloway, woolly suits posted outside. Rosa would have been in seventh heaven. She'll go mad that Maddy didn't invite her round for the tea party.

They had already confirmed that the bullet was for a Glock 19, and probably from the same box as the others.

"So. Somebody's trying to tell me something."

Coulter smiled, ruefully. "That's really going to piss off my people. *We're* the ones who should be getting warned off. Not the bloody PF."

"I can think of a few who'll be wishing it had been used, instead of just posted."

Alan Coulter didn't dissent from that.

All the usual processes were set in motion: door-to-door, dusting for fingerprints – plus trying out a new process using crystals and UV light – photographs taken, questions asked. ("Why would you be in the hall at four in the morning, Miss Shannon?" "I was on my way to take a piss, Officer." "Why wait until 6.30 to phone it in?" "Nothing anyone could do." "Did you check to see if anyone was walking away?" "What, and contaminate the locus? Course not.")

They let her go before nine, insisting that she be accompanied to work by an officer. ("Constable, don't take it personally, but I'm not going to say a word to you.")

At Ballater Street everyone had heard the news.

"You okay, Maddy?" Dan, Izzy, and Manda all rushed into her office.

"Oh hunky-dory. Dan, why don't you get down to my place? You're going to get this case anyway."

"I thought I might try a different tack on this one. You

know, play it by the book. Heard of it?"

"New one to me. I really have to take you over the basics of meddling and interference, Mr McKillop. Go. Please. See what they're saying, doing."

Dan gave his best camp eye-roll, swivelled theatrically, and left.

Maddy didn't have to go and see Maxwell Binnie; Max came to her. For the first few minutes of the meeting he was all concern and helpfulness.

"This is most distressing, Maddalena. Anything we can do. If you want to speak to someone…"

"Like a priest?"

"No. Well, I don't know. Do you?" He was flummoxed, as Scots from Protestant backgrounds often are in this area. "You're a Catholic, aren't you? So…"

"Bless me, Procurator, for I have sinned."

"You could use one of our counsellors."

"I'm fine, Max, thank you."

"You know of course that you cannot take anything more to do with this terrible business."

The look of pity was still etched on his face, and his voice saddened. But the subtext was unmistakeable – she had brought this on herself. Again. *Tua culpa*.

"I was never going to get prosecuting it anyway, was I?"

"Well, we agreed that, all things being equal, it was time you landed an important case."

That's the problem: all things are never equal. Certainly not in Maddy Shannon's life.

"Maddy," he drew his seat nearer, his voice as honeyed as he could make it, which was about as close to honey as sour cream, "I'm not sure it's a good idea, given the circumstances, for you to keep working at all. You're a strong person, we all know that, but this must be traumatic. I'm given to understand that you're under a lot of pressure these days."

"You're 'given' to understand?"

His empathy expired. "Do I need to recite a list? This is just like the Kelvingrove murders all over again. You're all over this case like…"

"Like … a *rash*, sir?"

"Talking to witnesses – suspects even!"

"In pursuit of another case! Petrus has never been closed—"

"Even then – not how we do things, is it? Then there's the distinct possibility of disclosing evidence, even if unintentionally… Furtive meetings with JCG Miller employees."

"You mean lunch with Samantha Anderson and Douglas Mason? They're fellow practitioners. Glasgow's a small city. If we were to look through *your* social diary!" She immediately softened it: "For that matter, anybody's here."

"For heaven's sake, Maddy. You're a bloody lawyer. You know exactly what I mean."

He meant, live an unsullied middle-class life. Preferably in Newton Mearns, or even better outside the jurisdiction, in Dunlop, like him. Don't take buses, don't talk to ordinary smelly people. Drink fifteen-quid bottles of Pinot Noir from Waitrose, not pints in the Vicky. That was all very well – until lawyers from Killearn and the West End started getting malkied.

How did he know all this anyway – about Sam and Doug, about her talking to Cathy and Morag? Max lived a semi-hermitically sealed life. Keep the office door closed: safest form of management. But she could trace the lines of information. Police, like John Russell say, peeved at her intrusions; more peeved by her being ahead of them often enough. That makes its way to Deputy Chief Constable Crawford Robertson, known to play a round or two with Maxwell Binnie, procurator fiscal. All things being equal her aunt Fanny.

"What are we saying here? I take a holiday?"

"For instance."

"Paid?"

"Naturally."

"Over and above my annual entitlement."

"Oh I'm not sure we can…" One look at her expression changed his mind instantaneously. "Of course." He got up to go. "One week. Then we'll review the situation. Re statutory leave."

"Oh I'm sure the boys in blue will have cracked it all by then." Then she added, "And Dan McKillop will have it all neatly collated." But he closed the door before she'd finished.

Coulter wasn't there for Harkins's departure. He'd been at Maddy's when the twenty-four hours were up. DS Dalgarno had signed him out.

"Yes, I asked him again. And, not in so many words, but it was obvious what he meant, he had decided not to tell us."

"Decided?"

"He didn't incriminate himself, but he made it clear that he wasn't going to give us the name. He was looking pleased with himself. Like he'd just done a good deed."

"Maybe, in his world…"

"Can't we just do him for dealing in prohibited firearms?"

"What good would it do? No proof. And I get the impression that once Joe Harkins has made up his mind nothing on earth will change it." Coulter had just taken his jacket off. Now he was putting it back on again. "Who is he protecting?"

"Or afraid of."

"If he was acting like a Boy Scout, he presumably reckons he's doing someone a favour."

"Maybe his cockiness was in the hope of some kind of payback? Where are you going?"

"To the Day of Judgement. Lord Forbes Nairne himself. We haven't got any further on those Glasgow Cally students?"

"Sorry. Nothing either on the origin of the dump photographs."

Coulter sighed and left. Before he could get out the building PC Eddie Whatshisname shouted him back.

"Sorry sir. But someone here you might want to see."

Zack Goldie was slumped in a chair, head on the table, in an interview room. "You look like you've been through the wars, Zack. Tell me what happened."

Young Eddie had already briefed the inspector. Goldie had been lifted in the middle of the night, drunk and disorderly. Screaming abuse at danger-level decibels off Great Western Road. Zack lifted his head off the table like it weighed a ton.

"I can't handle the drink."

What was Basil Fawlty's line: "Specialist subject, the Bleedin' Obvious."

"Let me guess. This party you got flung out of … your old pal Gabriel Daniels was there, yes?"

Zack nodded, like a gorilla with a disproportionately large, and aching, head. "Stupid thing is, I'd already made my peace with him. We go the party together, buds again, then I start drinking and…" He looked at Coulter, anxiously. "I just can't stop digging myself in deeper, can I?"

Coulter looked at the notes Eddie had handed him. "Well, I'm not sure that shouting," he cleared his throat and read in a flat voice, "'I've already killed two men so I can kill you you fanny,' helps exactly."

"Did I say that?" Zack scrunched up his face and put his fists to his head.

"'I'll be back when I've got the gun … then you are a dead man … Prickface.'"

"I haven't killed anyone. I don't have any guns. You've got to believe me. I'm an arse, that's all. If you can arrest someone for being a wanker, I'd go quietly."

Coulter smiled to himself. Zack Goldie had hit on a favourite theory of his. Sane people know they are eejits; they spend their lives controlling their inner eejitness. That's why he liked Maddy Shannon so much. More

223

importantly, why he loved his wife and kids. They all, like all sane people, put up a front, but scratch the surface and they recognised, and confessed to, their hidden demons and inconsistencies. It's why he had a problem with the likes of ACC Robert Crawford, DS John Russell and their ilk – they actually believed they were completely sane. Which made them dangerously crazy in Alan's eyes.

So, although the boy exasperated him, he felt well disposed towards him for the moment. Then again... He checked Eddie's notes on times and place. Approx. 3 a.m. Great Western Road. Fifteen minutes from Maddy's house, around the time someone had posted a bullet. He would have liked to pat the boy's head and console him, tell him everything's fine. But he couldn't. Not just yet.

"You're certainly developing a fine line in self-destruction, Zack. We'll have to talk to everyone who was at that party last night" – Zack's groan was almost a wail – "and we'll need a full statement from you." He stood up. "But, son. Two things. I'll give you the name of an alcohol counsellor. But even more important than that – go home and talk to your mum and dad."

"You're joking."

"I really amn't, Zack. Yes, they'll give you haw-maw and there'll be tears and snotters. But once you've all got the crap out your systems, they're the ones who can help you. Believe me. There is no greater healing power than your mammy."

Alison Morrison had been scribbling down notes all morning, as doctors with titles and specialisms she never quite managed to catch gave their learned opinions on Bill Crichton's current condition. There was stuff about localised responses, flexion and extension of ... things. This was going to be a nightmare to write up after. But it seemed to her that the prognosis was clear as day. The man had opened his eyes for God's sake. So he was out of his coma. What state he'd be in, right enough, was a different matter.

She could have gone home long before that, or got some-one to take over. But she'd slept well enough, her feet up on a second chair. Also, she'd been sitting staring into space for about a week and this was the first time something interest-ing had happened. And clearly, nobody at the station had noticed she's done a thirteen-hour shift.

The changing of the guards had taken place round about 7 a.m. The floozy had knocked off – having slept, Alison reckoned, just as long and as deeply as she herself had – and the blushing bride had taken over. So it was Clare, the legit one, who had seen the first signs of life from her husband. The nurses and doctors were acting like it was Lazarus himself, while Clare sat looking on, only vaguely interested. The only thing she'd done was text someone. The first time Alison had seen her do that – in contrast to Marion who never stopped.

She decided that thirteen hours was quite enough and there was nothing more to see. The man was coming round – slowly. As she got up to go, Mrs Miller entered, ignored her as usual and looked directly at Clare.

"Yes?"

So that's who Crichton must have texted. Marion had been summoned. Clare took her time collecting her things and abandoning her post by her husband's bed, put on her coat, looked down at him briefly, then made for the door, stopping in front of Marion.

"You can have him. He's all yours."

Nairne had arranged to meet him at an unexpected venue, but Coulter liked the streets around the Tron Theatre. An odd assortment of tattoo parlours, old-time pubs, art shops and studios. Transmission Gallery had been made famous by a Franz Ferdinand song. Which one he had no idea, just that his daughter had played it to him, and he had this image of a big-mustachioed duke wearing a German spiked helmet singing a rock song about Glasgow.

Spirit Aid is a charity run by one of Scotland's most famous sons, the actor David Hayman. Coulter admired the guy – great at his job but spent his free time and probably his own spare cash working with kids in the developing world and in his home town. What Lord Forbes Nairne, QC, was doing there was anyone's guess. Maybe he just likes a bit of star-fucking, though Coulter wouldn't have thought Nairne was Hayman's type.

Disappointingly, the actor was nowhere to be seen. To compensate, he found Nairne sitting in the middle of a group of teenagers. The judge nodded to Coulter, making him understand he'd be with him in a minute. He was telling the kids about bagpipe music. "We've been playing these things for a thousand years, maybe mair. The skirlin's handy for dances – and getting rid o' folk."

The kids laughed. The man was comfortable with them, in an old-fashioned dominie kind of way. Coulter doubted many of them would give their schoolteachers so much silence and respect. Nairne was a man who expected a degree of deference, and he knew how to use it. He picked up a chanter and played a bit. Coulter knew nothing about bagpipes but it sounded pretty proficient to him. Nairne then gave the instrument to one of the girls sitting next to him. "Try and get a toot oot o' it, while I talk to this gentleman here."

While the kids made noises akin to a Highland cow being butchered alive, and laughed uproariously, Nairne directed Coulter to a side room, where the cacophony was only slightly muffled.

"Ach I do this from time to time. We have to keep oor traditions alive, Inspector, don't you think?"

"Why aren't they at school?" Once a policeman...

Nairne laughed. "If they weren't here they'd be oot keying your car or burgling your hoose. Davie's good wi' weans like these. Doubt if we'll find a Donald Ban MacCrimmon among them though, eh?"

Presumably a legendary piper, so no. By the squawking going on next door they were more likely to find the next world champion vuvuzela player.

Coulter showed Nairne the photograph – now printed up – of the toxic waste oozing through its lead and cement casing. Before the judge could ask the inspector made the point that there was no way – as yet – to test the picture's authenticity. He brought him up to scratch on the university students.

"But you don't recognise this photograph, sir?"

Nairne stared at it sadly. "Indeed I do not, Inspector."

"So it wasn't in the evidence you were given?"

"No."

"And if it were…?"

"And its authenticity proven, this one snap on its own would have been enough to ensure a trial."

"Yet the protestors insist it and many more like it, all of them properly dated and sourced, were included in the evidence they prepared with JCG Miller."

"Well it never reached me."

"How do we account for that?"

Nairne handed him back the photograph. "That's your department, Inspector Coulter. And I hope and pray you get to the bottom of it. For, not only would evidence like that have ensured a full trial, it would still now. Get me the provenance and I'll make damn sure this goes to court." He got up and walked to the door. "Nothing pains me more than Scots law – for which in general I have great respect – letting the people down."

The two men made their farewells and Nairne went back to his now manic kids. Coulter left thinking that, after five years of pursuing them, poor Maddy will be taken off the Petrus case, just when there's a chance of nailing it.

Detective sergeants Russell and Dalgarno were discussing the latest developments, without the hindrance of their boss being about.

"Nobody's got a proper alibi." Russell had spent the morning up at the Boyds', Cathy Maguire's, and Belvedere. "Morag and Kenny are alibiing each other. Just like they did for Tom Hughes."

"But they're accounted for for the times of Miller's murder and Crichton's fall. And when the bullet was left below his window."

"They said their wean – what's his name?"

"Jason."

"—Jason was fine in hospital overnight alone. He's getting used to it. So they went home at the back of nine, had an early night, and got up for work at 7.30 as usual. I believe them."

"What about Cathy?"

"Nobody can vouch for her ever. She was at," and here he shook his head knowingly, "the Scottish Women's Environmental group meeting at Maryhill Community Centre till ten o'clock. I checked – she was there all right, shouting the odds and rousing the rabble. She got a lift home with a sister in arms – I've checked that too. But she lives on her own, so only she knows if she never went back out the house again until noon today."

"And do you believe her?"

"The woman's a pain in the arse and her heid's full of mince, but yes. She gave me a hard time and about three different lectures, but I didn't get the idea that she was lying."

"And Joe Harkins was in here all night." Amy pinched her eyes. "We know that Harkins knows Kenny Boyd. Could he be the name he's not giving us?"

"I think the name he's not giving us is Mrs Miller or Mrs Crichton. Which one? Take your pick. They're both mental."

"But why would either of them kill Tom Hughes?"

"Money, power. For screwing up their conservatory. Miller would bash your head in for a new designer handbag. And

Crichton, she's clinically bananas, she'd stab you for looking at her funny."

"Clare Crichton was at the hospital when Maddy Shannon's bullet was posted."

"So long as you believe that Alison Morrison didn't sleep for four hours during her shift. She always looks pretty fresh to me."

"And why would Mrs Miller post a bullet through the PF's door?"

"Maybe she's got some sense after all." Russell laughed, brightening up. "You can take it from me, she'll be nowhere near this case again. In fact," he dropped his voice, conspiratorially, "she might not be near *any* case again."

Amy Dalgarno decided not to ask him why. In general she believed that old boy networks, school ties, winks and nudges at the nineteenth hole, were the domain of conspiracy theorists – but Russell made her question that conviction. "So you're ruling Kenny Boyd out?"

"I'm not ruling anybody out, Amy. Any one of these people, or a mix of them all, could be up to their necks in this. I've said all along, this is pass the pistol – a different nutjob every time."

Amy nodded acquiescing. But she remembered fine it was Coulter and she who developed that theory, not DS Russell.

Maddy took Binnie at his word. She'd sent a few emails, briefed Izzy and Manda on a dozen or so of the cases on her books – claims, suits, indictments, complaints that she'd allowed to languish since the morning Miller had been shot. Izzy was too nice to comment, and Manda in no position to, given that her backlog was worse. She just sighed when she saw Giffnock Golf Club. There were other, bigger actions, that she'd give to Dan. She'd looked for him, but he'd been in with Binnie. No doubt where the real truth was being discussed. How do you solve a problem like Maddalena?

How do you hold a moonbeam in your hand? Well, maybe not the second bit. How do you get shot of her forever, more like. Dan would defend her – but only to a point. We've all got mortgages. And institutions, careers, bring out the sleekit schemer in everyone. This particular career – plea adjusting, manipulating juries, pandering to counsel, skirting over inconvenient facts – makes you a freaking expert.

Her plan was to sneak off, unnoticed. She emailed to her home PC every file she could find connected in any way with Petrus or the Miller killings. Not that she intended to do anything, get any more involved. No, this would be me time. Go the gym, long lies, read books. She'd bought all four Elena Ferrante books and had never found time to get further than chapter one, book one. Same with the first of the Louise Welsh trilogy. She might, in a few days, look at those files, but purely as an academic exercise. If she did notice something new, or make a connection, she'd pass it on to Coulter. Other than that, stay away from work, keep out of everyone's way, Mum and Dad's – especially Dad's. Speak to Louis, and try to get clear in her own head what she wanted to happen between them.

It turned out her colleagues had other plans. By the time she was ready to go, the entire night had been planned out for her. Bite to eat at La Lanterna, then to Lauries Bar where Manda had confirmed there was a ceilidh on tonight, finish up as ever in the Vicky. It felt like a farewell celebration. Maybe it was.

Being still only the back of four, she decided to go home, shower and change. She thought she'd walk it, the day turning out bright. A furious speed-walk home helped keep the demons at bay. But, again, the world had other plans for her. Illegally parked outside the COPFS door on Ballater Street was a fat grey SUV, electric engine whispering. The passenger window slid down, and Clare Crichton leaned over from the driver's seat.

"Can I give you a lift?"

What the hell. She was off the case, on holiday. She climbed in and said flatly, "Lorraine Gardens" like it was a pre-booked taxi. Mrs Crichton said nothing as she manoeuvred out and set off towards Glasgow Bridge. Maddy reckoned it was up to Crichton to start the conversation. But the woman remained resolutely shtum. It was as if she'd forgotten that Maddy was there. Her behaviour was that of a woman alone in the private space of her car, every now and then singing to herself under her breath. Or was she talking to herself? The traffic was heavy so the journey west took a long time. Maddy stared out her window, thinking that Clare would eventually tell her what was on her mind. And if she didn't, Maddy genuinely didn't care. They whirred along the north bank of the Clyde, the hybrid engine almost soundless, seagulls wheeling over the glinting water outside. Maddy relaxed into a dreamy, sleepy state. Along the Expressway, the giant glass façade of the Transport Museum reflecting the river like a mirror. The trees on Kelvin Way still skeletal and leafless but standing in pools of crocuses, the odd early daffodil blinking sleepily. Only at University Avenue did Crichton break her silence.

"What's the best way?"

Maddy nodded to indicate straight on and put her right arm out. Clare knew what she meant.

When, finally, they were turning into her street, Clare stopped the car at the first available space. Left the engine running – Maddy wondered if it was charging – and leant over to pick up a plastic shopping bag on the back seat.

"This is for you," she said, handing it over.

"Why me?"

"Have to give it to someone."

"Mrs Crichton. We've barely ever met. Why would you think that you should give me anything?"

"Bill liked you." Maddy noticed the past tense.

"I'm not sure he still does."

"I don't care. I don't like you. Don't get me wrong. I don't

231

dislike you. I don't like or dislike anyone. I thought I liked Bill ... anyway, none of this matters." She lifted the bag up. "Maybe this doesn't either. I don't care. But I have to give it someone. And I have no intention of going anywhere near a police station."

Maddy took the bag from her, and opened it. Inside was a brown manila folder.

"Will you come in for a coffee, Clare?"

The woman thought for a moment, tapping on the steering wheel. Then made up her mind and turned the engine off.

Three quarters of an hour later, evidence markers from one to four at her doorway and in the hall, Maddy stood next to Clare Crichton in the kitchen, while DI Coulter and DS Dalgarno poured over the single sheet of paper that had been inside the folder.

"Is Bill a cyclist, Clare?" On the top quarter of the page was a little printout map.

"No."

"A runner?"

"Bill took no exercise whatsoever." Again, that past tense.

"Where did you find it, Mrs Crichton?" Coulter asked.

"You really shouldn't send male officers round to look for something, Inspector. Men can't find anything. It was under the rug in the basement."

"And you knew it was there?"

"And that you were looking for a file or something? Yes."

"Then why didn't you hand it over before?"

"Why should I?"

"Because the law demands it, ma'am. Because people are being killed. Because you have possibly just perjured yourself."

He might as well have been reading her out the football scores for all Clare Crichton reacted.

"It looks to me," Amy distracted Coulter from his furious

stare, "like a Map My Ride route. A free app, easy to download. It records your cycle or running routes. It can also calculate your distance, times, etc. Normally they're bigger than this. On a smaller scale showing the hills, miles, etc. This is very close up."

They both poured over it. White lines that could be streets, but only one or two of them. "The blue line is the recorded route," Amy said. "Looks like no distance at all. We're talking yards here, not miles." The street names were not marked.

"The blue seems to go off-road. Into ... what?"

"Green normally means fields, countryside."

"Do you have any idea where this is, Mrs Crichton?"

The woman shrugged. Coulter looked back at the map. "Just empty ground?"

"Like Belvedere?" Maddy said and Coulter nodded, thinking the same thing.

"Is it?" he asked Crichton.

"No idea."

"A couple of years old," said Dalgarno. "Before they started building on the site?"

"Clare," Coulter softened his tone – the stern cop routine was having no effect on her whatever. "Do you have *any* idea why Bill might have kept this?"

She took a moment to answer. "I saw him looking at it one day. He said it was his insurance policy."

"Insurance policy? Can you think what he might have meant?"

She shook her head. "I was more taken with the word 'my', Inspector. 'My insurance policy.' That's what he said. Not 'ours'."

"And he put it inside a folder marked Abbott. Work-related then." Coulter turned to Maddy. "If our Costello connection is right... Some kind of insurance policy for him and Julian Miller, do you think?"

"Or," Maddy suggested, "*against* Julian Miller?"

Clare nodded. "Could be. He never trusted Miller. He always dreamed, talked, about getting away from him. Said he was dangerous."

"So something he could use against him? When the time was right."

"Or when he felt he had to," Dalgarno was still trying to work it out. "To protect himself?"

"Or damn Miller."

"I'd have supported him in damning that bastard," Clare became animated for the first time since she'd picked Maddy up. "But if he was protecting anyone it wasn't me. It was him and Marion." Then she laughed, a manic note to it. "Maybe not even her. My insurance policy he said. In the end of the day, my darling husband only looked out for himself." She stepped away from them. "Didn't get him far, did it? Just screwed up all our lives."

Maddy felt she had washed her hands of the matter as she entered La Lanterna. She'd also texted her dad, promising to meet him tomorrow, now that she had time on her hands. And just to maintain the cosmic balance she'd spoken to her mum for five minutes – making no mention of Packie. Finally she'd sent Louis a Facebook message promising to spend virtual time with him too over the next few days. Sort this out one way or the other. Now she felt satisfied. Her life was in chaos, but she'd done everything she could reasonably be expected to do to keep things from crashing completely.

The meal was civilised. Dan had begun by reassuring her that everything was okay with Binnie. Take a week or so, and with luck the police will make some headway with the inquiry. Soon everything would be back to normal.

"I've always been a bit allergic to normal," Maddy said.

"Tell us about it!" Manda topped up all their glasses.

"Now I want nothing more. Nine to five, telly in the evening. Might even take up golf at the weekends."

"Oh I'd pay good money to see that," said Dan.

"Can't be as ridiculous as you in your cycling gear. But you're right. No, I'll start running regularly."

"So tonight you can eat and drink and be merry." Ironic, coming from Izzy who looked as if she ate only a spinach leaf a day and was known to do two hours of Bikram yoga before work. She seemed to be enjoying the wine as much as any of them tonight.

The only thing that was bothering Maddy was Clare Crichton. When she'd gone off to shower, Coulter was still grilling the woman. Why had she suddenly decided to hand over the map? Clare had just shrugged again. Despite her play of indifference Maddy had detected something resolved, settled about her. By the time Maddy had got dressed, all three of them had left. Probably Coulter had shouted to tell her, but she'd been in the shower, or drying her hair. Had Coulter noticed Clare's state of mind?

As they were leaving the restaurant she gave him a call.

"You suggesting she might do something stupid?" she could hear the digging going on around him.

"That's a terrible euphemism – 'something stupid'. Sounds like putting your top on the wrong way round, or leaving a tap running. Not topping yourself. I don't know."

"It occurred to me too. And I did the only thing I could think of. I've kept her in for further questioning. Which will give us tonight, tops."

"Unless you arrest her for perjury."

"We may have to. Though it's the last thing she needs. Even if we do, we can't keep her locked up until she's tried. I've instructed the station to try and convince her into seeing a counsellor, or bringing her family down from Inverness."

Maddy needn't have worried. He was a good and wise man, Alan Coulter. Even with a woman who had unnecessarily held up his investigation, cost him a fortune, and who quite possibly could have saved a man from being shot, had she come forward earlier.

"Get your dancing shoes on," Dan called back to her. "Heel to the floor, do-si-do, and wheech your partner round and round…"

As she followed her friends to the ceilidh bar, about three miles north four burly young officers had their jackets off, were sweating already despite the cold evening, and covered in mud. It was guesswork really, where Coulter and Dalgarno had got them digging. The sergeant had done some work on the image at the station while Coulter had been getting the team together and keeping Crichton in for questioning. She had managed, by comparing it to similar cycling and running maps, and increasing the scale of Bill's, to get some notion of scale. She couldn't be sure but it looked like footsteps rather than yards. Looking at the distance between the starting point of the blue line and the road behind it, it was almost certainly at the main entrance and about fifteen steps north, close to the site periphery. The surveyor who operated the theodolite for Fulton's was useful. She had a better eye for maps and she confirmed that the land around there would never be built on, but be the end of a garden. If Bill Crichton had ever wanted to dig back up whatever he had buried it would make sense not to have it under tons of concrete and brick.

But having no idea what they were looking for – even if it was the missing file, what was it encased in? Finding a thin folder in anything up to twenty square feet of muddy surface area was the proverbial needle in a haystack. The officers drafted in for digging were far from enthusiastic, clearly unconvinced that it was worth getting wet, mucky and knackered for.

"We don't have an option, son," Coulter said when one of them grumbled a little too loudly. "Even if we have to stay here all night."

Joe Harkins had been watching them from inside his cabin since they arrived. As the evening got darker, Coulter sent Amy to see if the watchman had any torches. Harkins turned out to be more amenable than they'd expected. No doubt he didn't want to piss off the polis more than he had already. Between him and Grace, the theodolite woman, they managed to find, and rig up to the power supply, two floodlights. The only place they could put them was on the ground, a few feet back from the hole in the mud, so that two intense beams of light shot across the surface of the dark mud, making the whole scene look like a horror B-movie.

As the men shovelled gloops of sludge, shimmering in the floodlights, Amy, Coulter, and Grace the surveyor discussed in which directions they should widen the hole.

"Question is," Harkins said, "how deep should they dig?"

Coulter nodded, trying not to reveal his surprise at Harkins's apparent goodwill. "What are we assuming here? If Crichton made the map, and there *is* something buried here, did he bury it himself?"

"If he did," Harkins said, "it'll be about two inches down. Big heid, skinny as a famished rat. He's like a walkin' toffee apple."

Coulter smiled, and thought how much easier this would be if the toffee apple in question would wake up and talk.

Back in the city centre, Dan McKillop was swinging Maddy round with a degree of elegance, but when he should have only have been twirling her, thus throwing out of kilter the entire Gay Gordons. Which, of course, is what makes it fun. A roomful of genuinely practised and graceful dancers is dull; a frenzy of semi-bladdered amateurs who haven't clue what they're doing is a good night out.

She'd had about four glasses of wine with the meal, a gin and tonic on arriving at Lauries, but now – to be sensible – was drinking pints. The euphoria that blots out all problems in life was in full flux. About a dozen colleagues from Ballater Street had joined them and, as happens in Glasgow, some of them had recruited acquaintances along the way, and complete strangers joined in because Maddy's group was having the best time. The band, playing furious acid croft – dizzying jigs and reels fortified with electronica, guitar riffs, disco beats – sounded simultaneously like heaven and hell to her ears. Life should always be like this: wild, unthinking, surrounded by laughter and shrieking. Where yesterday and tomorrow don't exist. There was just the smallest part of her aware that it was all an illusion. That Miller and Hughes were still dead, Crichton dying, and the person responsible still had three unused guns. Possibly he was out there at this very moment, taking aim, maybe in this very room, or a block or two away. A swig of St Mungo's beer, another spin with a guy she faintly recognised but couldn't quite place, and all that was swept away, scattered out across the dance floor and diffused into the night and the music.

A dance ended and another began but she headed for the table – for a rest, a sip, a seventy-five-second time out. Samantha Anderson was at the table when she found it.

"Up on your feet, Sam. Dance the night away." No slurring. She was still of sound mind and understanding.

"Not tonight, Maddy. I'm having to go soon. I just wanted to tell you…"

Maddy was in no mood to sit, let alone get into middle-class sisterhood with Sam Anderson. So she crouched down in front of her.

"Stuart is taking early retirement. He's been to the doctor." Sam had to shout over the full blast of the turbo ceilidh band. "Depression."

"Oh shit, Sam. I'm sorry."

"No. It's fine. He's been much better. Now that he knows."

"Yeah. Good. How about you?"

"I'm glad too. To know what it is. You know?"

Maddy did. But she didn't want to think about it. Not tonight. Not now. The gloom and self-hating and existential dread were for tomorrow, when the old black dog would

238

most surely come and slobber over her hung-over soul. She stroked Sam's face, which she recognised was a little drunken, and squeezed her hand. "Stay strong."

"I just wanted to let you know."

"I'll call you, Sam. Promise."

Sam smiled and got up to go. "And, Maddy, enjoy your break. We're all behind you. You're a terrific lawyer."

Maddy watched her negotiate her way round the flailing dancers towards the door, and felt guilty. Guilty for not wanting to talk to her tonight, for not helping in any way. It was nice of Sam to say what she did, though probably none of it was true. She also felt guilty about still not being able to remember Stuart's face. A choice of two things to do now – either sneak quietly out and meet that slavering Dobermann halfway home, or push the self-flagellation back for a couple more hours with beer and noise and a blundering Strip the Willow.

There was no chance that Coulter was going to let his diggers home early, even though, by now, the task seemed pointless. The map was too vague a guide, too blunt, and anyway whatever it was they were looking for might have disintegrated long ago. Or it could have moved in the mud – Crichton was no engineer: he'd have no idea that objects, if not buried deep enough and secured, could swim for yards in any direction in this soft, wet, clay. But it was Coulter's only hope and even if he had to replace his digging team with fresh officers, or start shovelling himself, he was going to take it to the limit.

It was Joe Harkins, of all people, who caught the first glimpse.

"That a stone?"

"Aye," said one of the mocket officers. And just to prove it he tried to yank it aside. Bigger than he'd thought, it stayed put. The ray of light from one of the lamps revealed sides and a corner too angular for anything natural. Coulter jumped into the swampy hole, now about twelve foot square and four foot deep. When he pulled at the sodden grey shape, it resisted for a moment, then slurped out suddenly, throwing the detective inspector into the mud. His team all stifled a laugh, Harkins even sharing a quick, amused glance with DS Dalgarno. Coulter didn't care. He'd found the treasure.

Maddy jigged down the line, spun around, and regained her feet just in time to hook up with her next partner.

"Step we gaily on we go," shouted Doug Mason over the roaring music.

"When did you get here!?"

She had to wait until they'd circled the next pair of dancers to get the answer.

"It's all over town…" Circle. Spin. Step. "…Maddy Shannon's having a party."

She was pleased to see him. She was pleased to see everyone, anyone, tonight. At the top of the line they did their little twosome steps, Doug grabbing her tight. Just over his shoulder she caught Dan's face – one eyebrow raised in that mocking censorious stare of his. She was never quite sure just how light-hearted and consenting that look really was. What the hell. The ceilidh was in full swing, the band on fire, and Maddy Shannon was out to grab all the life she could.

The moon had come out, casting a silver complexion over Belvedere, making the soggy site and surrounding scheme look almost romantic. Coulter hadn't intended to open the Tupperware box there and then. Best to get it back to forensics as untouched as possible. He'd simply picked at one corner to see how it had been sealed and if it would be a problem to open, and the lid had sprung off.

Lying at the top of the deep, heavy box was a clear plastic document wallet. And inside that, an A4 sheet of three printed photographs. One of them was the image Kenny

Boyd had on his phone, toxic-red sludge seeping over the sides of a rickety concrete casing. The other two were even worse. Rusty canisters, punctured, floating in grey stagnant water, at least one of them once yellow and still faintly bearing the skull-and-crossbones hazard sign. The other of a film of green fungus, taken at such at angle that you could see the buildings above them. The same houses that Coulter could see from where he was standing, at the far side of the site.

Harkins and Dalgarno edged in closer to see them too. The watchman took a breath and Coulter turned to him, thinking he was about to say something. Either he hadn't been, or he changed his mind. He turned his back and walked away.

Draw a line from where the box had been found at Belvedere, to Lauries Bar at the Trongate where Maddy and her colleagues were dancing the world into oblivion, and it would pass straight over the Royal Infirmary.

A constable had been placed outside Bill Crichton's ward and he was bored to the point of dropping off until suddenly there was commotion all around him. The woman, who the young officer had been told was the patient's bit on the side, had been sitting quietly with him, either squeezing his hand or reading a magazine every time he had looked in on them. But now doctors and nurses were flashing past him, the woman was crying and gulping for breath, and there was an insistent bleeping coming from one of the machines in the room.

"What's happening?" he asked everyone who passed him until one of them – a young doctor – finally answered. "It's all gone fucking pear-shaped in there."

A Glasgow night: dancing and dying and digging for tainted treasure.

IV

Some believe that the Big Bang is an argument for the existence of God.

I wouldn't know.

Everything I do is driven by reason. And there is a reason for everything I've done. Premeditated. It has to be. To carry out my work I've needed tools, times, planning. How did I do it, they will ask later. By hard work and dedication.

There is information everywhere. You don't need to contact another living human being. It's online, on television, in libraries, magazines in waiting rooms, on your phone. Snippets of knowledge, scraps of data, advice. Hints of wisdom. There are some people who know everything there is to know about one particular thing. Like which kings came to power when. Or the law, or how to change spark plugs. How the world began, and how it might end. How a gun works. What kind of people use them, and die by them.

Planning and dedication are the only guides I have had.

And isn't it strange when you, and only you, can see the map clearly, if just for a while. It gives you a certain freedom. Being the only one who knows exactly what is happening.

And what will happen next.

This really, honestly, does have to stop.

She woke at five in the morning, after only about two hours of on-off sleeping. Anxiety that she was going to be late for work, then realising it was still the middle of the night and, anyway, she was on leave. Then forgetting all that, and going round the full circle again. Now she was fully awake, or thought she was, and lay piecing together the dreaded Night Before.

She hadn't drunk that much, she decided. If she had she'd be suffering more. Either that or the hangover hadn't kicked in yet. No. She hadn't even finished the beer she'd been bought. A few sips between jigs and reels. So, after the wine – and, oh yes, that G&T – she'd only had about half a pint. Over a period of six hours or more. With a meal. And two hours of non-stop dancing. That wasn't too bad, was it?

She sprang straight up in her bed. Doug Mason! She'd danced with him for ages, then they'd got a taxi together…

It was still dark, so she tentatively stretched her hand across the bed. Please, God, let there be no one there…

There wasn't. She was alone.

So where had Doug got to?

They'd taken the taxi back to here… She'd poured him a brandy – but herself a coffee. They'd chatted for a bit. Or rather they'd bellyached and felt sorry for themselves. Both their jobs shaky. Louis. Doug never finding the right woman. People getting killed. The usual late-night grumbling.

And then he'd made a grab at her. She laughed now in her bed. He hadn't meant it to be a grab. She would recognise a serious grab and she'd have lamped him. He'd meant it to be a silky smooth embrace, but his motor skills had failed him again. She'd burst out laughing then, too. But there had been a moment of contact between them – and it had had the same effect on them both. It wasn't right. It wasn't wrong, but it didn't feel good. Even in that second or two of contact it was clear – to Doug as much as to

Maddy – this wasn't meant to be. They'd smiled, backed off from one another, and tried to make conversation for a few more minutes. Just to reboot the relationship, establish the social norm again, eradicate that brief fumble between them.

So where was he now? She'd gone to her bed after giving him a duvet for the couch. Presumably he was still there.

So, all in all, nothing to be ashamed of, nothing to regret. Except she did. She felt terrible. What Dan calls the Four O'Clock Jury, ripping yourself to pieces mentally, deploring every decision you've ever taken. The only cure for that was to get out of bed. Lie there and the Dark Night of the Soul never ends.

She showered and threw on a pair of joggers and an old shirt she kept for loafing around the house, crept into the kitchen, and made a pot of coffee. Moving around, doing things, kept the doldrums at bay. Like swimming, the minute you stop splashing, you sink like a stone. She'd intended to leave Doug – if indeed he was still on her couch – sleeping for a while yet. She quite fancied a walk. It had been a long time since she'd seen the sun come up. She considered Skyping Louis, but decided that the Morning After the Night Before wasn't the best time to be seen on screen. Nor the best time to talk, given her state of mind. Anyway, it was about two in the morning over there. This was a new experience for Maddy Shannon: not having anything specific to do that day. Not rushing somewhere, catching up, spinning plates.

Doug Mason decided the matter. She must have made more noise than she'd thought. It was only the back of six when she heard the toilet flush, the bathroom door open, and his feet padding towards the kitchen.

"Good morning."

"Haven't we done this before?"

"Déjà vu all over again."

"Coffee? Or are you planning on going straight home to die?"

"How many times can a man die? In under a month."

"Don't know about men, Doug, but if other women are like me, several times a day."

The poor man did look under the weather, which in this city is serious. He leant against the doorjamb, in only his boxers and shirt, the latter as crumpled as a discarded chip poke.

"How about you go and make yourself decent, and I'll bring you in coffee and paracetamol?"

He nodded. It was about all he could do. He turned and she watched him shuffle back across the hall. Nice legs, though, have to say.

She percolated another pot of coffee, super strong – his taste buds would be shot, what mattered was the caffeine – found some co-codamol, and poured out two big glasses of water.

When she took it through to him, he hadn't managed to do anything but slump back down on the couch.

"Douglas, Douglas. What are we going to do with you?"

Alan Coulter had got no sleep whatsoever. Hadn't even been home. He'd decided to leave the box more or less *in situ* and called forensics to send someone right away. While they were waiting it occurred to him that there could be more buried around the same place. The officers couldn't believe their ears, and took up their shovels again with a sigh.

Coulter had met Terry Walls, the forensics specialist, before.

"Certainly not going to get any DNA. How long's it been buried?"

"We don't know. But we think, anything up to four years. What I'm worried about though is getting whatever's in there out without damaging it."

Bernie pulled on latex gloves and shone a paramedic's torch on to the still mud-smeared container. Through the cloudy plastic they could make out the shapes of the contents. "Looks like piles of papers... Inside plastic wallets. Not the best way to seal anything, but we might be lucky."

"Can we take it back to the lab and start working on it now?"

Walls glanced at his watch.

"Sorry. But this is urgent."

The inspector told the seriously weary digging team that they could knock off. "Thanks lads. I know that was a bastard, but you've done good work here tonight."

He called into the station to get a new team to cordon the area off – they might just want another look around in the light of day. Then he waited alone, having sent Amy Dalgarno home to get some shut-eye too.

Cockcrow watch it was called, wasn't it? He remembered it from Sunday school. The depth of the long, silent night. Therefore keep watch at cockcrow for you do not know the hour when the Lord shall arrive. Something like that. The darkness seemed to push the buildings around Belvedere back so that he could just about make out their ghostly forms behind the piss-coloured street lighting. There was birdsong somewhere though he couldn't see any trees. What kind of birds nest in concrete and breeze block?

Harkins brought him out a cup of tea.

"What is it you're not telling us, man?"

The watchman stood beside him, sipping his tea, but said nothing.

"Five years. That's what you'd get for trading firearms. That what's worrying you? Out in three?"

Harkins shook his head. "Mair than that." He smiled slyly at Coulter. "Way I heard it, they guns were *police* guns. You're hardly occupying the high ground. Inspector."

"And how would you know that, Harkins? You're right – you'd be in for much longer if we add perjury, obstructing police officers in execution of their duty..."

"Which you could say I'm already guilty of."

"What if I don't?"

"What if, if I had anything to tell you, which I don't, you keep my name out of it?"

"I'll see what I can do."

Harkins went back to staring and sipping his tea. "I don't believe you."

"More people could die, Harkins."

Harkins gave an almost imperceptible shrug. Coulter knew what he was thinking. Miller and Crichton might as well come from another planet. It was like hearing about some exotic animal dying somewhere: nothing to do with him. And as for Tom Hughes, Harkins didn't hate him enough to kill him himself, but nor did he like him enough to care if someone else did.

The forensics lab was further east in the Scottish Crime Campus at Gartcosh. Coulter drove through the dead, stagnant streets, just the faintest hint of dawn somewhere directly ahead.

He'd hardly found where Terry Walls was working before the call came through from the hospital. Crichton had suffered a traumatic seizure. He might survive it, and since the episode an hour or so ago, he was more settled. But he might not.

"Can the man speak?"

John Russell was already at the hospital. "No idea. If Marion Miller would stop greeting and screaming we might find out."

Maddy lay on the floor, her head propped up against the couch Doug was still sprawled over. Out the window day looked as if it couldn't be bothered breaking.

"Go. Get a shower."

"Okay."

They'd had the same fascinating conversation three times now.

"I didn't even drink that much last night," Doug moaned.

"Yeah right." They'd had that deep discussion already too.

Then she heard the key in the door. Shit. This was early even for her mother.

"What the hell? It's not even seven yet."

"Ugh?" Doug had heard nothing.

"Does she know I'm on leave? How can she? She'll have some mad plan for me." She called out: "Mamma?"

She got up quickly from the floor. Rosa would make a meal of this. A semi-naked man and Maddy in joggers and half-unbuttoned shirt.

The door opened, and the bunch of flowers entered first. And Maddy knew at once.

"Hey. Surprise!"

Louis came in a bit ruffled from his flight, but beaming. For about a second, before his eyes darted from Maddy to Doug – who suddenly had the motor skills to sit up straight – and back to Maddy again. The smile morphed to a moment of puzzlement, and then dismay.

"Caught you at a bad time?"

They wouldn't let DI Coulter into Bill Crichton's room. He was standing, looking through the window, with WPC Morrison who had relieved the night-duty officer, John Russell and the still sniffling Marion Miller. Crichton's condition had been described in that age-old meaningless phrase, "critical but stable".

"Usually means they're gubbed," DS Russell had said. In Miller's hearing, earning him a frown from his boss and Alison Morrison. Marion Miller seemed to have agreed, however, just closing her eyes, resigned.

The consultant, Gavin Hood, came out now. "Mrs Miller, you can step inside. Inspector, sorry, but I'd rather see how Mr Crichton gets on with Mrs Miller first."

"Can he speak at all?"

"He has managed a word or two." He turned to Marion. "Including your name."

Marion rushed in, a glimmer of hope in her eyes. Before she closed the door, Coulter stepped behind her, touched her arm. "Marion. If he speaks to you at all, ask him something from us."

The woman looked in no mood to do any such thing.

"A name. Who was with him in the restaurant that night. Apart from your husband and Tom Hughes." She stepped away, but he kept his light touch on her arm. "Whatever happens now, if Bill can help us in any way, it'll be so much better for him. And for you. Will you do that?"

As she closed the door behind her he couldn't tell if she would or not.

"You know she's not next of kin," Russell said to Hood.

"I'm aware of that, Sergeant. But the next of kin hasn't been near him for two days, and that lady has kept a constant vigil."

They watched from outside as the nurses cleared a space for Miller and put the chair next to his bed again. She bent her head down close to Bill's. She wiped his forehead and tidied his hair. Her lips were moving, talking to him. His lips seemed to move too, but whether he was just struggling for breath or actually uttering a word or two, Coulter couldn't decide.

"Is there any chance of recovery?" Coulter asked. When there was no reply he turned and saw that Hood had gone. Looking back into the room, there was air of finality, of surrender, about both Bill and Marion. He'd seen, sensed, that before. Several times in professional situations such as this. But also with his father, who had gone in for a small operation but had taken a heart attack just after. The twenty-six-year-old Alan Coulter had had just under an hour to watch his dad give up the ghost.

That terminal loneliness, it infects everyone close to the immediate victim. That day by his father's side he wasn't with his family. They were all there, circling the bed, his mother, brother and sister, but each of them were alone.

If there was a connection at all it was with the dying man, solitudes intersecting. Right now, he wasn't standing there with long-term colleagues, but with strangers.

He felt the need to make contact with somebody. Not Martha. Not because he didn't want to but because it would damage her. He hadn't called her at times like these since way before she had taken ill. It wasn't fair. Bad enough living with a policeman, no need to take the worst of it home. Too early to call the kids, and anyway, they were "home" too and should be quarantined from this part of his life. There was only one person he knew would be awake, and who would know how to talk to him.

"Hey. It's early, sorry. Listen, Maddy, I know you're supposed to be getting away from all this. But I know you," he tried to keep his tone light. "Chances are Crichton is going to die. And without giving us anything." He was aware of her being unusually monosyllabic. He'd probably woken her up after all. Except she sounded as if she was moving around, busily. "It's not supposed to work out this way, is it? They're supposed to give you the one thing you need before they go. That's how it was going to be, in my head."

"I'm on my way over now." Was all she said.

"No, wait, Maddy, I was only calling because…" But she had hung up.

Coulter sighed. DS Russell was going to love Shannon turning up. Not even in any official capacity. Oh God, the rumours…

Marion looked round at them through the window. Coulter, putting away his phone, raised his eyebrows in hope. Marion Miller just shook her head and, turning back to Crichton, she took his hand and wept.

"Where the hell are you going?!"

"I'm sorry, I'm sorry. I've got to get out of here."

He had believed them. He'd even laughed. But Maddy knew that a seed of doubt had been planted. What would

she have thought, had it been the other way round? She'd
have done what Louis was doing now, trying to look cool
about the whole thing, assuring everyone it was fine. But
inside her head, that image would always be there. Till her
dying day.

To make matters worse, ten minutes after Louis had
appeared, in the midst of her convoluted explanation –
it didn't even sound true to her own ears – her dad had
started to call her. She'd dingied him three times already.
Then she got a text saying he was leaving tonight and
he'd – dearly – like to see her. Please say yes, Flutterby. Just
for half an hour… She'd almost missed Alan's call, thinking
it was Packie again.

"Wouldn't it have been more likely for *me* to storm off?"
Louis said, more exasperated than angry.

"I'm not storming off. It's work."

"I thought you just told me you were on holiday."

Doug had gone off to shower. Once he'd made his plea
of innocence, crossing his legs as if that somehow made his
trouserless state more socially acceptable, he'd grabbed his
clothes and slunk off.

"Well I am. But this case…"

"I've a feeling you shouldn't be going wherever it is at
all."

"And you'd be right. But I can't stand this, Louis. I can't
stand *myself*. Here. With you, like this. And though I
shouldn't, I need to know what's going on *there*."

"Give me your car keys. I'll be your driver."

The journey was absurd. They tried to make the conversation that should have taken place an hour ago had
circumstances been something approaching normal. How
are you? That's great you came over. So how come you're
on leave? How's your viral thingy? Things okay at work?

They each answered the questions in turn, but neither
of their minds were on it. Louis, presumably, was still trying
to work through the shock of this morning, his lovely little

251

plan turning to shit. He had to concentrate, too, on the driving – he hadn't much experience of Glasgow roads. Once or twice he almost turned into oncoming traffic. It occurred to Maddy that that might be the best thing for her right now. That'll teach you.

Her mind was everywhere at once. Was she pleased he had just popped over the Atlantic Ocean? Was that a romantic surprise, or interference? What the hell was she going to do about Dad? Should she tell her mother or not. But most of all she thought about Crichton. Work. What did people do without it? Work you could think about with some degree of logic.

Just as they were driving into the Royal Infirmary, she caught sight of Morag Boyd, standing outside the reception area, having a smoke.

"Louis. Let me off here. I need to speak to that woman."

"Where will I find you?"

"Just stay in the café, will you? I'll come get you. Once I know what's what."

He nodded, having no choice. Maddy got out just as Morag was finishing her fag.

"Morag."

The woman was about to go back in. But she nodded, changed direction, and walked over to Maddy.

"You here for Jason?"

"Today's his big day. They've had to put it back a day or two – he needs to be at his strongest."

"And is he?"

"He's a brave wee lad," she smiled. "He's more worried about *us*."

They went inside together, and stopped before going their separate ways.

"Kenny up there with him now?"

"We're taking turns for ciggies. We'd both given up, then... Cathy's up there too."

"Give them both my regards, will you?"

"Aye. Sure. Thanks."

Maddy finally found that William Crichton was in a room off ward 52. Coulter was waiting for her at the lift. Five minutes after the man had been officially declared dead.

"Without saying a word." Coulter looked glum.

"Because he couldn't?"

"Oh probably. But… Did Marion even ask him? I can see why she wouldn't. Their last words … if there were any." He put his hands in his pockets. Maddy knew him well enough to know it was a sign of stress. "I can't tell you quite why, Maddy, but I get the feeling that they did talk. Well, exchange some words. And he decided not to tell."

"Protecting his reputation? His legacy."

"It's what we all do, I suppose," he sighed. "It's certainly what everyone's doing in this bloody mess. Him. Harkins. The Mrs Crichton and Miller…"

Where they were standing, she could see DS Russell and a policewoman along the corridor. She took Alan's arm and led him round the corner where there was a little waiting area with seats.

"The fourth man. I keep trying to put a name, a face, to him."

"Aren't we all."

"The medal I got. Like the one in the Miller house. The bullet put through my letter box. It's all connected to Belvedere and Petrus and Costello."

"Yeah, well, I worry about finding a story that *seems* to link everything, but—"

"Who else was involved, or even might look like they were involved, in all of that? Start with me."

"You're not a middle-aged man, and you're alibied up to the hilt for that night."

"Forbes Nairne."

"He might be the next victim."

"Even if he'd been deceived himself, it must *look* like he was party to the cover-up."

253

"Talking of which. We found the Abbott file. Or box. Forensics are looking into it now. Looks like Kenny Boyd's photograph is the real thing. I think you might have your proof for Petrus and the rest of them dumping toxic waste."

She gave a bitter laugh. "After all this time. When it's too late. For me anyway. But more, for the poor buggers who suffered as a result." She looked down, and remembered that she was dressed in old joggers and even older, crumpled, shirt. She must look like a madwoman. "What about Maxwell Binnie?"

"Your boss?"

"He's *the* PF. He's the one whose name gets in the papers. Or Crawford Robertson?"

"My boss?"

"Local bigwig in the police. Neither of them have been exactly helpful throughout this entire investigation. And didn't you say that these Glocks originated in the police stockpile?"

Coulter had been trying hard not to think about that. "*Stolen* from the police stockpile. Are we talking fourth man in the restaurant here, Maddy, or next victim?"

"Either. Both?"

"In that case you might as well add my name to the list."

"Or Detective Sergeant John Russell."

Coulter almost laughed. "What the hell's he got to do with it? You're just saying that because you don't like him."

"I freaking hate the guy."

They heard voices approaching. Russell and WPC Morrison stopped at the lift without noticing Maddy and Coulter, who sat stiff and silent, like schoolchildren, until the lift door had closed.

Along at Crichton's room they looked in on the recently deceased William Crichton. They'd left him alone with Marion for a while. Maddy tried to remember the man she had vaguely known before all this began. The man who she'd thought was pleasant, quiet, decent. But all she could bring to mind was the night he'd come to her house. The excuses. The special pleading. The arrogance and angst of a minor-league bully.

Marion Miller was standing stock-still, her back to Bill, staring out the window. Morning had finally come forth, and with more confidence than it had indicated. There was even a chance that it might turn out to be that most elusive of things, a bright early spring day in the West of Scotland.

Seemingly out of nowhere – she was wearing gel-soled trainers – Clare Crichton appeared. She walked straight past them and into her husband's room. Maddy felt Coulter tense, bracing himself in his policeman's way for trouble to erupt between the women. Clare did not give her husband a glance, but went straight over to Marion. Miller couldn't have heard her either, when she turned they saw the double surprise on her face. That someone had come in. And that that someone was her lover's wife.

The women said nothing. Marion's eyes burning, waiting to see what she was going to have to deal with, getting ready to hit back. But Clare simply took her hand, and held it. Marion looked down at their clasped hands as though they belonged to other people.

"It's okay," Clare Crichton said, and put her arm on Marion's shoulder

It took Marion a moment to react. When she did it wasn't so much a look of surprise on her face, as relief, then tearful gratitude. Clare slowly and gently led her over towards the door. Again, without a backward glance at Bill.

Coulter had to move back to let them pass. "Where are you going?"

Clare stopped, and looked at him. "What were you expecting, inspector? The virago? A she-devil? Is that what you were hoping for?" She looked at Maddy, with distaste. "This woman needs looking after. So do I." She led Marion, who followed compliantly, in a dwam, along the corridor.

"You've been following us both for weeks, so don't worry, I'm not going to do anything terrible. I never have."

They watched the two of them go. Anyone passing would have mistaken them for recently bereaved sisters.

"Do you trust her?" Coulter asked.

Maddy thought for a moment. "Yes. Yes I do."

Coulter, however, was on his phone, making sure there was a detail on them.

Maddy remembered about Louis. "Louis' here. You want a coffee?"

"Louis Casci? Here?"

She just smiled. But before they got to the café, Coulter's phone buzzed several times. He'd been turning it off – this being a hospital – and the messages had been stacking up. He was reading them and walking, until one of them stopped him in his tracks. It came with an attachment that took up all his attention.

"What is it?"

He didn't hear her. She stepped back and looked at his phone. Photographs of documents, some of them soaked, eroded, the print smeared. Then more images, some of them enlarged and possibly digitally enhanced. Close-ups of dates, signatures.

"October 2010. That'd be, what, eighteen months before construction started at Belvedere?"

"Five months before JCG Miller's case file was compiled."

"And what's that signature there?"

Coulter didn't wait for an answer but closed the attachment down and made a call. "Terry? I think I can see what your photographs are suggesting. But you tell me."

Maddy looked on as Coulter mumbled "yes", and "I see", and "can you be sure" for what seemed like twenty minutes but was probably less than one. When he finished the call she spoke before he did:

"Forbes Nairne had seen and signed off a different set of evidence, before the one he threw out?"

"And both were sent to him by Julian Miller."

"With all the photographs proving the site hadn't been properly sealed?"

"Maddy. Don't jump to conclusions. Only Terry Walls, this forensics guy, and now you and I have seen these. We need specialists to look at them in greater detail. We need confirmation of times and dates."

"Jesus." Maddy looked shocked. "Forbes Nairne was the fourth man? In cahoots with Miller and Hughes?"

"Slow down. Bloody hell, you say you hate John Russell but you're just like him. It's a crucial step forward, and hopefully it'll take us closer to understand what's been happening here, but—"

"In which case, he's undoubtedly on the killer's list."

Coulter unlocked his phone again. "I'll get a detail on him now."

Maddy felt this urge to move, to take some kind of action, but she had no idea what. Alan was right – they really didn't know anything for sure yet. More, it just didn't sound right to her, that Nairne would be party to something not only so malicious, but premeditated, planned out, over months, years probably. She didn't know the man well, but she trusted her judgement on people. Forbes Nairne was haughty, vain, but so were many powerful men. She always felt those were the kinds of traits she herself was lacking to be really successful. But Nairne *wicked*? He was nearing the end of a long illustrious career. Not everyone had always agreed with his rulings, his interpretation of Scots law, but few would imagine that he had ever been purposefully dishonest. Unless it was a late-career moment of madness, a crazy pension plan. Or maybe that impeccable career has been littered with wrongdoing and misconduct that he'd managed to cleverly conceal. Even if that were true, she still felt this urge to protect him.

A mere depute PF didn't have contact details for such grandees, she had no idea where he was, and anyway

Coulter was organising proper protection for him. There was nothing to suggest the judge was in any immediate danger. Whoever was doing all this killing couldn't know that the investigation now had a vital clue and, if they wanted to finish their business, they might have to speed the process up.

Then again, it seemed to Maddy that the killer hadn't shown any signs to date of giving a monkey's what the police knew or didn't know.

The need to move, be active, reminded her that Louis was waiting for her downstairs. The man who had flown across the Atlantic, at some genuine personal and actual cost, she had left sitting in a hospital canteen, without even giving him any sterling to buy a coffee.

With Coulter on his phone and Maddy lost in thought they ended up downstairs in a different part of the hospital. In order to find the café they had to go outside and walk round to the entrance of the older part of the buildings. There, at the door, presumably having another cigarette, was Morag, and standing next to her Cathy Maguire and a man Maddy at first thought was Kenny. Approaching them, both she and Coulter recognised the third figure to be Joe Harkins.

"Have they taken Jason in, Morag?" Maddy asked.

The woman just nodded.

There was something in the positioning of the group, Cathy and Harkins standing closer to each other than either was to Morag, that made Maddy think those two were more than just friends and neighbours.

"Kenny's still up there." Morag looked over at the busy road beyond the gate. "I can't wait any longer. Got to get back to work." Her tone was lonely and sad, like the sound of the collared dove Maddy woke to some mornings.

"Me too," said Cathy, grounding a fag end grimly under her toe. "You taking the car?"

Morag shook her head. Maddy could see that every time

she spoke the woman was in danger of breaking into tears. "Leaving it for Kenny. He's going to stay here for a while. Not that there's anything…" she stopped before her voice gave way. "You carry on, Cathy. Catch ye later."

Cathy Maguire took her at her word and marched off without another glance at any of them. It was on the tip of Maddy's tongue to ask her for a cigarette – the craving came over her, sudden and sharp – but now she watched her dash away, head down, checking her watch twice. Must be late for work.

Morag turned to Joe Harkins. "I'll be back as soon as I can."

Joe put his hand on her shoulder and nodded. "He'll be fine, Morag. He's a brave boy."

"Aye," she said. "No point in you staying here any longer either, Joe. They won't let you back in upstairs."

"I'll hang aboot, see if Kenny wants a pint."

"Wouldn't bother. I think he'll want his own space, Joe. If we can't be wi' Jason, we'd both rather be on our own."

"Aye. Right. Okay."

Morag put her hands in her coat pockets and walked off towards the busy road beyond the gates.

Harkins didn't budge. He looked over at Coulter who was exchanging texts and emails on his phone with, Maddy thought, almost teenage dexterity. She knew Alan was aware of Harkins's gaze but was refusing to acknowledge it. The watchman looked at her, then back at the inspector, still studiously ignoring him. The two or three steps it took to plant himself right in front of Coulter seemed to Maddy to be in slow motion. Coulter finally looked up at him in a kind of decelerated motion too.

"Go on." Coulter said.

Another pause, before Harkins spoke one word, blankly, clinically: "Kenny."

Coulter nodded. In that second or two there was an entire exchange between the two men. The name one had wanted and the other had known and withheld. Time wasted, a man possibly needlessly killed. And, why now? Why wait until this moment? The answer to that was in Harkins finally breaking the stand-off between them. When he looked away, and up, towards the sky and the wards that towered over them ("tall building reaching up in vain", Blue Nile), Maddy thought she saw the shine of tears in his eye.

Coulter about-turned and ran up the steps, disappearing into the hospital. Maddy watched Harkins's shoulders slump. He shrugged at her, and ambled off into the city morning. He didn't look like a man who was running away, though he knew that, whatever happened now, the police would soon be knocking on his door.

Maddy's instinct was to follow Alan. But she managed to resist it. She wasn't sure, anyway, that she wanted to witness what was probably about to happen. Coulter would be at this very moment racing up to the surgical ward and calling for backup. Harkins had sold the guns to Kenny Boyd. At the very least Kenny was about as prime a suspect as you could get. For two murders and a possible culpable homicide. He had been on everyone's list for weeks. The problem was – and surely still is, she thought – that his alibis all checked out. For both murders, Crichton's fall, even the bullet being left outside her own door. They'd all been vouched for – Kenny and Morag and Cathy.

You're on leave, Maddy. It'll take its own course. Nothing good could come of her interfering again now. Louis' waiting.

Except he wasn't. He was nowhere to be seen in the café. And his mobile was turned off. She asked if there was another tea shop and was told, yes, one had been recently opened in the new part of the hospital complex. To get to that she'd have to go outside into the street again and retrace her steps back to the new building. Before setting off she checked that no one had seen an American sitting on his own, or maybe asking for her.

"Naebody's been asking for you, hen, but aye there was a big American fella. Copper, is he?"

Extraordinary that even doubtlessly law-abiding café staff in Glasgow can pinpoint a policeman. Including one from another country. The canteen lady had no idea where Louis had gone. Heading back out Maddy tried him on her phone again. This time she got him. "Sorry, I was held up."

"No worries. Want me to take you home yet?"

"And here was me hoping for a fancy lunch."

"The way you're dressed?"

She kept forgetting. She was not her mother's daughter. Rosa, wrapping and selling chips, had changed her apron every hour; when Packie had left her, turning their lives inside out, Rosa di Rio put her best dress on under the aprons and took more, not less, care of her make-up. When push came to shove you dressed up, not down. Maddy realised that her baggy joggers and unironed shirt were emblems of how middle class she had become.

"Okay let's go home first."

Like Morag, it now dawned on her. In her good dress for the day her son was being taken in for a potentially life-threatening operation. Kenny too, now that she thought about it. He had a suit on. She'd never seen the man so formally dressed before. As she walked over to the car park to meet Louis she felt the need again for nicotine. But cadging a fag off a worried mum would have been crass. Harkins, too, had been tussling with bigger demons.

They were all smokers. Kenny and Morag's alibi for the morning of Miller's murder had been that they were *here*, vouched for by nurses and doctors. But how long would it take to walk or drive from the Royal to Merchant's Tower, fire a bullet, and come back? It was a complicated building the hospital and only certain areas where you could smoke. Nobody would think twice if you went off for a ciggie and didn't come back for half an hour. Even three quarters – enough time, particularly early morning and mid-evening when the traffic was light, to go west, to Maddy's and Crichton's houses and drop off a bullet? Maybe.

Louis arrived at the car at the same time as she did.

"You okay?"

"Yeah. Sure. How was your coffee?"

She didn't hear his reply. No cigarette break could cover the fifteen-mile drive to Killearn, kill Tom Hughes, and drive back again.

"Hullo?" Louis said. "I really have got you on a bad day."

"I'm sorry, Louis." Then she spoke her thoughts out loud, knowing that the policeman in Louis would at least realise that she was calculating something even if he couldn't know exactly what. "The one time they all alibied each other was for the night of Hughes's murder."

"Go on." Louis opened up the car for them.

"I think some people in the Canal – that's the local bar – said they saw them. But that could be easily arranged."

Louis manoeuvred out of the car park and into the street, allowing her space to think.

As they passed Glasgow Cathedral she saw Coulter and Russell, with Kenny Boyd between them being marched through cars parked off-road. Maddy sat bolt upright. Louis stopped the car.

"Go on."

She hesitated a second, leaned over and pecked his cheek, and got out. "Thank you."

When she got to them Kenny was opening the boot of an old Renault Clio. All three men glanced at her as she approached but, whatever was happening here, it was more pressing than her presence. Even to DS John Russell. Kenny was trying to find his keys, going through his pockets, his hands shaking.

"Do we really have to do this now? My boy's going under the knife for Christ's sake!"

"Just open the boot, Mr Boyd," Coulter said.

"It's no' like I'm going anywhere! I've told you they're here. Youse could wait a bit."

"No, we really can't."

Kenny found his keys, opened the boot, which was strewn with his working materials – overalls, tool case, paint-brushes, rags. He pushed it all aside and unhooked the lid of the spare wheel winch compartment. Nestled snugly in there, the spare wheel below removed, was a black dark plastic box. Kenny grabbed the handle.

"Hang on," Russell said. He took out his mobile and filmed the proceedings. "Okay."

When the case had been lifted out, Coulter told Kenny to stand aside. Russell made sure he was still within camera shot. The inspector took latex gloves from his pocket.

"I was only trying to make a wee bit money on the side. Dae'in a favour for Joe. I needed the dosh. Wi' having to be at the hospital so often I wasn't working as much..." Nobody was listening to him. All eyes were on the box. Gloved up, Coulter figured out the system of clips and latches. "Is it locked?"

"No. I don't know. Maybe. He didn't give me a key. I'm only haudin' on to them."

DS Dalgarno arrived from the hospital as Coulter opened the unlocked box – inside was a tray, with the empty cavities in the shape of three Glock 19s.

"Where are they, Kenny? Where are the guns?"

Kenny Boyd stared dumbfounded at the case. "I ... they were there when he gave them to me. I think. He said... I don't know!"

Russell got on his radio, still filming with his left hand. "We need officers here *now*! Cathedral Square."

Dalgarno put her hand on Boyd's shoulder. "Kenneth Boyd I'm arresting you for possession of prohibited weapons—"

"Not now! Jason. I've got to be *here*. For my son."

Coulter was staring at the box of guns. There were only three after all. One for Miller, one for Hughes, and one left outside Crichton's house. He was looking straight down on the case; Maddy a step behind him could see the side of it, deeper than it looked, lodged into the winch compartment. She reached over, and lifted the tray out. Underneath was another identical tray.

"Please. Take me back to Jason. For the love of God. I've no' done nothing."

Coulter's and Maddy's eyes met. The case had contained six guns, as they had expected. But in the second tray, only two were left. One unaccounted for.

Louis had parked illegally, engine still running, on Castle Street.

"Oh sweet Jesus." Kenny had understood at the same moment as Maddy. "Oh Morag," he stared at the missing guns. "What have you done?!"

"Maddy. Where you going?" Coulter called after her as she walked towards Louis and the car. She didn't turn round and she didn't answer. Where was the missing gun? Getting in the car she said to Louis: "The High Court. Straight on. I'll tell you where to turn."

As he joined the traffic, Coulter was running after her. "Come back!"

"Wind down the window," she said to Louis. When he did, she called out: "If I find her, bring Kenny!"

Coulter threw his hands up in the air and she could see the expletive on his lips, floating off into the traffic.

Louis slid the window closed again. "Wherever it is you're going – I gather you shouldn't be?"

She didn't answer, but Louis drove as fast as he could anyway, almost jumping a red light at Duke Street.

"You've got your killer, yes?" Louis was trying to work it out. "And something could happen now?" Maddy nodded. "Why not let the police deal with it Maddy? Coulter knows what he's doing."

"There'll be sirens, guns, flashing lights, uniforms … she needs someone she can speak to."

Louis sighed and nodded and kept jockeying through the lunchtime traffic. Coming up to the Trongate he just missed a light at London Road. He had no choice but to stop. Maddy waited for a moment, then opened the door.

"The High Court. I'll be quicker running." She closed the door before he could answer, and although a hundred conflicting thoughts ran through her head as she sprinted off down Saltmarket there was enough space to realise that this would most certainly go down as Louis Casci's worst holiday ever.

She was correctly attired after all. Trainers, trackies, light shirt, small shoulder bag she howked across one shoulder. Cars blew their horns as she dodged between them. On a day as warm as you could expect of a Glasgow spring she must look like some spontaneous jogger; as if she'd been in her house and had looked at herself and thought, If I don't run right now I'll get even fatter.

She silenced that part of her mind that told her this was a pointless mission, a stupid one, maybe even a dangerous one. She had no idea where exactly to look for Morag and/or Nairne, or what she would do if she found either of them. She just kept moving, heading towards the river – an almost convincing blue under the crisp February sun. Running, it seemed, was easier when it wasn't the reason in itself but a means to an end; she didn't notice the strain, only the need to get to her destination quickly.

Coulter wasn't of a mind to do Maddy's bidding. Right now he was more exasperated than even Russell could be over the crazy fiscal. Except she was right. Or might be. Boyd was leaning against the car, head in his hands, weeping. He didn't look like a man who had killed anyone; he *did* look like a man who had realised for the first time that his wife might have. Somewhere in the distance they heard the first siren.

"Any news on Nairne?" he asked Dalgarno.

She shook her head. "Left Edinburgh early this morning. He has a hearing in the High Court but not till this afternoon."

"And Morag Boyd?" They had already put a description out for all cars and beat officers. Late thirties; mid-length dark hair; approx. 150 pounds; heavy army-green anorak with hood; black skirt, tights and shoes. Russell checked his phone and radio, and shook his head. Coulter thought for a moment, then took Kenny Boyd by the arm.

"Come with me."

"You're not doing as *she* said?" Russell was aghast. "The response cars will be here any minute."

Coulter marched Boyd back to the hospital where he'd left his own car.

"I can't back you up on this one, Alan," Russell shouted. *On this one?* Coulter wondered again if his sergeant was far closer to, and more in tune with, their superior officers than he was.

The only destination Maddy could think of was the little room that Forbes Nairne had more or less made his own. Would Morag know that? Unlikely. But she must link him in her mind with the High Court, so where else would she go? Maddy slowed down as she approached the Doric entrance – running would only attract attention. Again her garb turned out useful – she looked like a witness, or a relation. The policeman inside noticed her, but let her pass without comment. Possibly because he recognised her. That mad bat of a fiscal.

Heading through the parts of the building open to the public she made her way to the new wing at the back and up to the restaurant area. She tried to think like Morag might. Looking left and right, scouring the place. The one or two rooms that were designed for meetings between hearings were down a corridor to her left. The one at the end was the one Nairne used.

There was no one in there. But a jacket was draped over the back of the chair she'd seen Nairne sit in before. And, just as she was closing the door, she saw a glove, a single, light, disposable gardening glove, lying on the floor.

Rushing back up the corridor, trying desperately to figure out where to go next, she passed the gents and just as she did she heard a voice inside.

Coulter hadn't wanted to use his portable siren but he was getting hopelessly snarled up on High Street. He kept Boyd in his peripheral vision and the car doors locked – but if the man decided he was bailing there'd be little Coulter could do. When the radio had told them that a woman corresponding to the description issued had been sighted walking past the Briggait, Boyd's head had slumped. Maddy's hunch might prove to be right. Then again, that description could apply to thousands of women in the city centre right now.

They could both hear police cars wailing, closing in from every direction. Coulter got on the radio. "Tell everyone to shut down their sirens!" Despite the irony of his own screeching, to get him through the next couple of blocks. He'd turn it off before it could be heard from the High Court building. Last thing they needed was to cause a panic. His instruction hadn't been effective anyway, there seemed to be more, not fewer, sirens blaring, and all of them getting closer.

Maddy was standing at the door. Nairne at the far end of a series of urinals, his flies still undone and his face drained of blood. Between them, her back to the wash-hand basins, Morag Boyd held the Glock 19 shoulder high, only one hand gloved now, the barrel pointed at the judge's chest.

She had positioned herself in the centre of the room so that she could turn her head to see the door but keep the gun trained on her prey. When Maddy had entered both had looked round at her.

"Maddy." Was all that Nairne could say. The tremble in his voice saying more than words could have. He quickly turned back to look at Morag and the gun, his hands paralysed in the act of zipping himself up. Morag had looked at

Maddy as though expecting her but not interested in her. Now she was speaking to Nairne, both hands holding the gun, dead still, like a trained assassin.

"I had an uncle once. A docker, till he got made redundant. Nothing, I mean nothing, he didn't know about plants." Nairne nodded, trying to keep up the pretence of a casual conversation, but clearly not understanding, or even possibly hearing, a word. "Linnaeus? Uncle Frank knew all about him. Darwin and the Beagle."

He stared at her, bewildered, as though she were speaking some unknown language.

"Morag," Maddy said quietly. Perhaps too quietly; the woman kept on talking to Nairne.

"He'd just have been another workie to you." She flicked a look towards Maddy, including her in the statement. "You think we're all nonentities. Naebodies. Stupid."

Nairne unwound a little, beginning to understand where this was going. "I assure you madam—"

"No. You lot always do the talking. Lawyers and doctors and employers and planners. Not this time. Not here." She slipped back the magazine on the gun. From outside, a police siren could be faintly heard.

"Please, don't." The judge had recovered enough composure to zip himself up – either to give himself the dignity to negotiate, or to die.

"You can't even remember my name, can you? Just one of 'them'. The ordinary, useless, joes you make your laws for, make your money from, and complain about."

"Morag," Maddy took a step nearer which didn't disconcert her in the least. "Put the gun down. I'll make sure he hears you out."

"I don't care, really, if he hears me out or not," she replied keeping her eye on Nairne. "I'll tell him over his dead body." She changed her stance, putting one foot behind the other, readying herself for the impact of the shot.

"When does this stop, Morag?" She took another step.

"Am I next?"

Morag glanced at her, her expression inscrutable. So, yes, Maddy thought, quite possibly.

There were several sirens now, all of them getting closer. "Why should you remember my name?" Morag said to the judge. "Or my son's? We're just ghosts to you. It's Jason, by the way. Jason Ramsay Boyd. Eleven years old. A great wee footballer. Or was. Won more medals than you could count. Being scouted by the big teams. Until he took sick."

Maddy understood now who had sent her, and Julian Miller, the medals. "Morag. It's Jason you have to think of now."

"But to you," she kept her eyes fixed on Nairne, "he's just another ned. You're so sure we're all incapable, dependant on you, that none of you could imagine it was *me*, the woman from the scheme, who planned and carried out all this. But you see, actually, I do know stuff."

"Jason needs you, Morag."

"Listen to her." Nairne had finally found his voice, his confidence creeping back.

"We all do. If we look stupid it's because we have to. It's because you make us *feel* stupid."

"He needs you now. Today, Morag. Please, put the gun down."

"She's right, Mrs Boyd. If I've done something to offend you, believe me, it was never my intention."

"You know what? I'm not sure whether or not you were in on the deal with Hughes and Miller, or whether you're just shite at your job. Either way, you ought to be punished. And nobody's going to do that. Except me."

Maddy was managing to get closer to her because, she calculated, Morag wanted her to. Wanted this to stop. She'd done enough killing. They could hear the police cars arriving at the building. If she'd been going to shoot she'd have done it by now. For the moment, though, she kept the gun squarely pointed at Nairne's heart.

"Do you believe in the afterlife, Nairne? What's going to happen when this bullet hits you? Heaven? Or nothing. Hell maybe?"

"Mrs Boyd. Let us help you. You and your son."

"He's right, Morag.."

For the first time Morag turned her head to look directly at Maddy. "You think I do anything else?" she allowed Maddy to step right up next to her. "But, see, I'm a terrible mum."

"That's not true."

"Oh it is. I couldn't protect him." There were shouts somewhere outside the room, down in the entrance hall. "Didn't have the power or the money. Couldn't take him away from the poison, the damp. Couldn't fight back." She looked back at Nairne.

"I'm so sorry." Nairne looked genuinely appalled. For the first time not merely consumed by simple fear. Footsteps were running around downstairs. Lots of shouting, but clear amongst them, Kenny's voice: "Morag!"

Maddy put her hand on Morag's holding the gun. The woman seemed not to react, allowing the touch. Except at that precise moment Maddy's phone rang. Morag's eyes flared, she stiffened, and her finger impulsively tightened on the trigger.

"No!" Maddy was struck momentarily with terror. "It's just my Dad,"she heard herself say. Morag stared at her for what seemed an eternity, the phone still ringing. When it stopped she relaxed a little. She turned and looked at the Judge, who remained as still and blank as he possibly could. Maddy's hand was still on Morag's and she pressed gently down, till the gun was no longer pointing at him.

Nairne's response surprised them both. A man whose life only a second ago hung in the balance recovered in a blink of the eye. He stepped away from the urinal, throwing his shoulders back, a full foot or more taller than both the women.

"Who the fuck do you think you are? Giving *me* a lecture? Daring to threaten me? Do you understand who I *am?*"

"Forbes," Maddy said. Perhaps the man hadn't quite recovered after all. His eyes were gleaming, pupils dilated, his hairline damp with sweat. But his voice was full of confidence and power.

"Believe me, you do indeed know nothing. Without people like me people like you would be lost. You'd kill yourselves and each other with your primitive passions, your imbecility. How could *you* take the law into your own hands?!" His voice was cracking with anger and disdain. "*I am* the fucking Law. *You* can't see the bigger picture because you don't even know there *is* a bigger picture."

"What are you saying?" Maddy stared at him.

"If one or two of your savage little offspring die even earlier than expected, it's of little consequence"

It wasn't Kenny Boyd who burst through the toilet door first, but Louis Casci. They could hear Coulter and Kenny and other officers kick open all the doors along the corridor. Maddy prayed that Louis wouldn't try and play the hero. Morag not only still had the gun in her hand, but was resisting Maddy's pressure. If he tried now to intervene... Maddy was relieved when he showed no sign of moving, but stood rooted to the spot, his eyes flicking between her and Morag.

The door flew open again. This time Coulter, his hand gripping Kenny's arm. Maddy's heart missed a beat – this could change the dynamic drastically. She could feel the blood pulsing in Morag's wrist.

Morag pushed back against Maddy's grip again. "Kenny. You weren't supposed to see this. I'm sorry, love."

"Morag, Morag," the man was drowning in sorrow and fear. "It would have been all right."

Nairne stepped towards Louis and the inspector. "Arrest this bloody woman."

"Nairne." Maddy called him back. "What were you saying

a moment ago? Jason's cancer is part of 'a bigger picture'?"

Nairne smiled mirthlessly at her. "*Lord* Nairne. You're no' as clever as ye like to think you are, Shannon." With the police in the room his recovery seemed finally complete. "The Law demands *interpretation*. Beyond your pay scale, my dear. To keep things running smoothly."

"Kenny," Morag said sorrowfully, "it's never going to be all right." Then she pushed hard against Maddy's grip, raised the gun, and shot Forbes Nairne through the head.

You will never know me, Jason.

Even if all this hadn't happened. If I had been a normal mum in normal circumstances, you still wouldn't have known me. I just hope and pray that you will get to know yourself better than any of us knew ourselves.

You will never read these words, yet here I am talking to you. That's how little I understand anything, really.

Your Da's a good man, son, and you, if you get better, I know will be a good boy. If you don't get better, maybe there is something more than all this, and we will be together, in some way we can't imagine.

But you will survive. It will be hard for you, when you hear what I have done. Please believe me – I thought it all through. I read, and thought, and thought again. Never let them tell you we cannot think for ourselves.

Jason, somebody, sometime, has to do *something*.
Mum.

Louis' reactions were the fastest. Maddy's hands had sprung away from Morag's and the gun and the force of the shot had shoved her back, so she didn't see the movement. Louis sprang from six yards back, at the door. "Maddy!"

He managed to get to Morag before she fired again. She pointed the gun for a split second at Maddy, but then turned it to her own head. Louis managed to barely touch it, just enough to flick it a little, so that the bullet grazed along the side of her head. There was a moment of complete stillness, before blood began to trickle from Morag's head, and she fell to the floor, weeping, her head crowned in blood. Kenny at her side, a dolorous Glasgow pietà.

V

Morag Boyd had been rushed to hospital where her injury was confirmed to be relatively minor. Despite Russell's protestations, Coulter had agreed that Kenny Boyd should be allowed to return to the hospital in time for Jason coming out of surgery.

The rest of the afternoon Maddy and Louis had spent making statements. Captain Casci of NYPD had to be fingerprinted, which he endured stoically. He was rather less stoic about being told he could not leave the United Kingdom until he received official permission. "Yeah. We'll see about that."

Before they left Police Scotland HQ in the early evening, the news came through that Jason had survived the operation, that the tumour in his head had been fully removed and that, once he had undergone radiotherapy and chemo, the doctors felt his chances were reasonable. Cathy Maguire had already drawn up papers with Mr and Mrs Boyd to act *in loco parentis* for Jason, should the need arrive. Kenny's crime was serious – possession of unlawful weapons – but it was his first offence, so there was some hope, given the family situation, that the court might go easy on him. Then again, the entire family might be judged to be dysfunctional and a danger to an afflicted ten-year-old. The Boyds and Ms Maguire had challenging battles facing them.

Maddy had been told, too, that Clare Crichton had taken Marion Miller back to Killearn to collect some clothes, and then had driven her to her own house in Cleveden. They were last seen shopping for dinner together, for all the world like two close sisters.

As Louis drove her along Dumbarton Road, the bars filling up early, in celebration of an unexpected golden evening, jackets slung over shoulders, voices louder and jauntier than they'd been in months, Maddy said: "Straight on."

"What? We not going back to your place?"

"One last favour?"

She saw Packie Shannon outside the main entrance to the airport pick up his bags sadly, certain now that she wouldn't show. He looked old. She'd never considered him old before, or had contemplated him even ageing. "Dad!" He turned and the childish, gleeful grin took decades off him. A gust of wind blew his bright white rowdy hair about. (What's that Moustaki song again? *Cheveux au quatre vents…. l'air de r*revêr*.*) Her dad seemed to be perpetually caught in a blustery storm.

"You left it late," he said without any hint of reproach. Almost pride – like father like daughter. "I've got approximately ninety seconds."

"Sorry. Busy day." Now there was an understatement. He dropped his bag and hugged her so comprehensively and tightly that she felt she was six again, utterly surrounded and defined by him. "You know you nearly got me killed?"

"Yeah?" He seemed rather pleased at the idea, "How's that?"

"Last time you phoned. I was… Never mind. It's a long story."

"Tell me sometime. I just wanted to tell you before she did – I tried to see your mother."

"*What?* You contacted her? How? She knows you're here?" Always so many questions in her father's wake.

"Dante gave me her number. Keep an eye on him by the way – he's going through some kind of late-life crisis." Geez, but the brass neck; the man had never scored high on self-awareness. "But she wouldn't speak to me."

"You expected her to?"

"I wanted to tell her – and you – something."

Louis arrived, having parked the car. "Hi."

What a moment to turn up. Tell her what? He was dying? He was getting married again – to a 25 year old? He was becoming a Bhuddist monk? Anything was possible.

Louis gave up waiting. "Louis Casci. Pleased to meet you?"

"Packie. How about ye?" the older man studied the younger one briefly but intensely then smiled broadly. And for the first time ever Maddy realised that, physically, the two men were of roughly the same build and height. Fuck.

"This your fella?"

"What? Tell us *what*, dad?"

Packie checked his watch and picked up his bag. "I'm coming back to Glasgow. Maybe in a couple of months." He stepped towards the doors, which opened. "I want to start again. I want us to start again. Me, you, your mum."

She opened her mouth but no words came out. There *were* no words in response to such a wild, absurd, misconceived, conceited, ridiculous statement. Packie Shannon threw the arm that held his bag round her shoulder and kissed her cheek. Still standing open-mouthed yet still not managing to breathe she watched her dad shake Louis' hand like he was an old pal, and with a final wink to them both, disappear inside the airport.

"Dad! You're a fucking idiot!" She couldn't decide whether she wanted him to hear or not.

They reached Lorraine Gardens. "Lover boy will be gone by now, yes?" said Louis as they walked to the door.

"Bloody hope so."

"I have to say," Louis smiled, "he is younger and better looking than me."

"Yep. He is."

A moment of doubt, then Louis bust out into a raucous cheery guffaw. Just like he used to. And they began to feel like their old selves again.

The moment they were inside they were at it. Maddy

knew it was partially the months of celibacy, but more it was the need to escape. From the murderous glare of a woman so exploited and misused by "professional" people like her; from the haphazard emotions and antics of her father; from every decision she had made on the last twenty-four hours. Twenty-four years. Perhaps Louis, too, was at some similarly tense juncture in his life for he tore at her as savagely as she assailed him. Or rather, his body.

It was all over with in minutes. They lay there panting, clothes torn and shed, like extras from *Les Miserables*, sweat pouring from them, and laughing like weans who'd got away with some transgression.

"So," she said when she got her breath back, "you've come all the way from far Americay. Least I can do is buy you dinner."

"You want to go out to dinner? Tonight? After ... everything?"

"God yes. What else would we do? Sit at home and greet?"

"I thought that woman was going to kill you."

"I think it might have been a toss-up in her head too." Maddy got up and rummaged in the drawer of the coffee table, until she found the old ten-pack with two cigarettes left in it. "All's well that ends well, eh?"

Louis shook his head. "You are a genuine nutjob, Shannon. You do know that?"

"Deed I do. Want one?"

"Nope. I'm a vaper now."

"Oh fuck off."

She phoned her mum, taking far too much immature delight in speaking while she was still semi-naked to Rosa di Rio. She didn't have long to enjoy it – mamma, it transpired, was on her way out to meet some of her Western Baths friends. Maybe that's why their daughter turned out to be a nutjob – her old dears were always on the move. Back in Girvan, working twenty-four seven in the chippie; these days in age-denial.

"You know that Dad was here?"

"Has he gone now?" Rosa didn't seem the least perturbed. "He tried to speak to me on the phone. Well, you can imagine what I said to him, *cara*." She sounded almost cheery about it. Surely – *surely* – her dad's mad plan was as mad as it appeared to Maddy? She decided not to raise the issue right now. "Your father *è un idiota*, Maddalena."

An hour later she and Louis were walking in the setting sun towards Finnieston.

Sitting in the Ox and Finch, having ordered food and chinked their first glass of champagne, the day delivered one last surprise. Dan McKillop phoned her mobile. They spoke briefly, and Maddy not only put her phone away, but turned it off. Let the rest of the night be just her's and Louis'.

"Seems I'm not sacked," she told him.

"Your institutions are more forgiving than ours. I'd have booted you out years ago."

"Thanks, pal. But I'm being sidelined. Dan's next in line for the big job. I'm out. Instead, they want to transfer me to the SFIU."

"That some kind of psychiatric unit?"

"Thank you again. I so do look forward to your visits, Captain. The Scottish Procurator Fiscal's Fatalities Investigation Unit."

"Sounds like they've got the measure of you, my dear."

"There's even a case for me, starting next week. A woman, unidentified, found dead in the street, probably having fallen from a window. Well, I've got some recent experience of that at least. In her bag, twenty thousand pounds in notes that look like forgeries."

Louis held his glass up for another toast. "Congratulations on your new job. How long have I got before it takes over your life?"

"Oh certainly not until tomorrow morning," she smiled. "So we'd better use the time profitably."

She was lying, of course. Work never stopped. Not inside Maddy Shannon's head. As far as the police were concerned the Miller case had been solved. Two dodgy lawyers, a judge, and a construction boss had met their messy ends. One killer, just the way the system liked it. Maddy couldn't help but think that that system had failed Morag Boyd badly. There could be no possibility of a plea of self-defence – she had killed, at least three times, and in cold blood. But to Maddy's way of thinking it was indeed a form of self-defence, some kind of deeper justice she'd have to ponder sometime soon. As the waiter served her her squid and chorizo she decided that the four victims – five, including Morag – were not the real, at least not the final, culprits in all this. Petrus, and their subsidiaries had got off scot-free. JCG Miller had – quite literally – buried evidence, with the collusion of Forbes Nairne, to protect Fulton's negligence and corner-cutting. Sealing the toxic waste would only have been partially down to the local construction company. The big international conglomerate were – clearly – above, or beyond the law.

Not in Maddy's eyes. Petrus, she knew, was not out of her life yet.

"Penny for them," Louis said, raising his glass, smiling benignly.

"I'm trying to decide how I'll interfere with you later on." And she would decide that. In a minute.

They tucked into their meals as Trendy new Finnieston came to a boil outside their window, on the first night of a Glasgow spring. Enjoy it while you can, guys, it'll probably be pishing down this time tomorrow. Brightly lit bars built into crumbling old tenements. Posh folks out in shiny shoes and summer jackets, tough girls baring their midriffs, defiant. "Chimney tops and trumpets / The golden lights, the loving prayers…" The end of just another day, growing darker and brighter – like some fairy godmother was blackleading the sky, down on her spectral knees polishing

ACKNOWLEGEMENTS

Moira: It'll all be worth it. Soon. Honest. No, really.

Emma and Daniel: Your entire student lives have been skint. And this is why. Enjoy.

PJR: Okay, I forgive you for buggering off halfway through (kinda). You more than made up for it throughout the rest of my life. Miss you every day, bro.

Allan C, Dana, and VV: Thanks for your continued faith. So long's I don't bring you all down with me.

Mark M: Don't get me wrong, but I think about you – and Aliyyah – every time I go to the lavvy.

Mo Leven, Paul C, J David, D Hayman Sr, Mick M, and everyone else who read, advised, listened to my fretting, held my hand or bought me a pint. Cheers.

Louise W, Denise M, Ian R, Russel, Sandra, Linn A, and the entire Tartan Noir community – don't tell the readers but you're all rather cuddly and nice and generous.

Fergal D: You got the first line this time, bud. Same percentage deal as before though.

Eric C: Who saw the Maddy twinkle in my eye, so long ago.

Glasgow: "Sometimes loving and hating this city / amount to more or less the same thing."